MURDER AT CASTLE TRAPRAIN

JACKIE BALDWIN

Storm
PUBLISHING

To request permissions, contact the publisher at rights@stormpublishing.co

Ebook ISBN: 978-1-80508-234-7
Paperback ISBN: 978-1-80508-236-1

Cover design: Eileen Carey
Cover images: Arcangel, Shutterstock

Published by Storm Publishing.
For further information, visit:
www.stormpublishing.co

ALSO BY JACKIE BALDWIN

Murder by the Seaside

Dead Man's Prayer

Perfect Dead

Avenge the Dead

To Jenny and Adam

ONE

Grace sat outside the Espy café with Harvey at her feet looking out over the sea at Portobello Beach. *Life doesn't get much better than this,* she thought, taking another sip of her coffee and turning her face towards the early morning sun in contentment. It was unseasonably warm for the fourth of September. She gave Harvey the piece of sausage she had saved from her roll and he scoffed it happily. Reflecting on the intensity of the last few months, she could scarce believe the direction her life had taken. Thinking of her young grandson, Jack, her mouth twitched into an involuntary smile. After losing her son to suicide nearly three years ago she would never have dreamt that she would receive such a precious gift.

Glancing at her watch, she drained her cup and stood up.

'Right, boy, time to earn a crust,' she informed Harvey.

Walking along the Esplanade, she admired the silver paint on the blue sign fashioned from a piece of driftwood she had found on an outgoing tide. Already, her former career in the police was starting to feel like it had happened to someone else.

As she blew in the door along with some sand carried on the light breeze, she greeted her staff with a smile. Jean was hard at work typing up reports and gave her a distracted wave. Hannah was doing employment checks for a large company. They had landed a few new contracts as a result of the positive publicity from their last big case. Brodie, her former husband, had stuck his neck out and seen to it that they were credited for assisting the police in the media. She poured a coffee for each of them and grabbed her mail before going through to her own office at the back with Harvey.

A few minutes later Jean poked her head round the door. 'I've got a Sacha Komorov on the phone. He wants to discuss a potential case with us but is adamant he can't come into the office. It's apparently a pressing but delicate matter.'

'Isn't he that Russian oligarch that owns Traprain Castle?'

'The very one,' said Jean.

'Tell him I can come out to the castle at eleven,' Grace said, her curiosity well and truly piqued. She used the remaining time to do a little research. Komorov had grown up in the working-class city of Ivanov, four hours from Moscow. His father seemed to have been a minor official with a whiff of corruption sticking to him. His mother died when he was fourteen and his brother only two. Not much was known about how he had acquired his vast wealth but he was believed to have started off as a member of a violent street gang then progressed from there into the Russian Mafia. He became involved in the construction of hospitals and the provision of medical supplies, building a legitimate façade, but he was also believed to be deeply involved in corruption and funnelling monies to Vladimir Putin's regime. Clearly, he was someone who did not court publicity. There was very little known about him after he had moved to Scotland from Russia and purchased Traprain Castle. His wife, Katya, had been a renowned prima ballerina with the Bolshoi Ballet until she suffered a career-ending injury.

Closing down her computer, she moved through to the reception area where both young Hannah and Jean had their own desks. Harvey padded through with her and lay down beside Jean, his biggest fan. Grace poured them both another coffee from the pot and took one for herself, sitting down in one of the comfortable seats in the small waiting area.

Jean sat back in her chair. Her face was red and she fanned herself with a piece of paper. As a lady of a certain age, Jean was prone to hot flushes at times. Grace reached behind her to open the window behind the vertical blinds and the cool sea air entered the room.

'That's better,' said Jean. 'It doesn't feel like autumn's around the corner.'

'Do you think this Russian guy will be our next big case?' asked Hannah, eyes bright with excitement.

'Let's hope so,' replied Grace with a grin. 'But right now, you know as much as I do. It could be something or nothing. I thought you guys both wanted a quiet life after all of that?' she teased.

Her staff looked at each other, remembering the many traumas of their last full-on investigation. Since then, as word had spread about the agency, the work had come in but nothing of that magnitude had reared its head. Instead, it had been all hands on deck to clear all the credit checks, employee background reports and cheating spouse cases that had replenished their depleted coffers. Grace had taken advantage of the lull to train her staff up in surveillance techniques and police procedure so they didn't find themselves compromised.

'My fingers have developed calluses from all the typing,' said Jean, holding out her hands in mock horror.

'My rear end may have to be surgically removed from this chair,' said Hannah dramatically.

Grace had worried that the last case might have put them off as there had been some hair-raising moments so she was pleased to hear that they were raring to go. 'Don't knock the bread and butter.' She smiled. 'It doesn't exactly thrill me either but at least our bank balance is looking a lot healthier. I reckon it's time we got ourselves a juicy new case. Hopefully, Sacha Komorov will be the one to provide it. I imagine he doesn't do anything by halves.'

They weren't the only ones feeling frustrated. Grace had been a high-flying detective in a Major Investigation Team before her son died.

Grabbing her keys, Grace threw on a light jacket and picked up her satchel.

'Are you guys still on for tonight?' she asked Jean and Hannah.

'Looking forward to it.' Jean smiled.

Hannah nodded but her face was closed off. Grace's mother had been extremely excited to learn that her deceased grandchild, Connor, had fathered a child, but she had a tendency to voice her opinions rather too strongly. Grace had known that her mother and Hannah would clash as Morag was an appalling snob and Hannah herself carried a large chip on her shoulder, which made her prickly and defensive at times. Instead of having dinner at her mother's house, it had been decided that it would be more relaxing for Hannah and little Jack if her sister, Cally, and her husband, Tom, hosted dinner at their house.

A short while later she was driving out along the A1, leaving the hustle and bustle of the city in her wake as the air grew fresher and the concrete gave way to rolling green fields. The arable crops would soon be harvested. There would be a glut of vegetables in the local shops and farmer's markets throughout East Lothian. She had to resist the impulse to yell 'Tractor!' every time she saw one as Jack was going through a farming phase. As it was such a glorious day, she decided to take the coastal route, aiming her car at the bright blue ribbon of sea and rolling down her window.

After about thirty minutes she came to a high stone wall with two huge and intricately wrought black iron gates. There was glass atop the walls but whether designed to keep people in or out she couldn't say. The overall impression was of forbidding grandeur. At her approach the gates swung open noiselessly and closed behind her as she drove up the impressive driveway. She followed the curve of the road until the turreted castle was laid out before her in all its restored splendour. Parking her car in one of the designated spots, she briefly wondered whether she should use the tradesman's entrance before steeling herself to walk up the grand steps at the front.

She rang the bell, hearing it echo throughout the property. The studded wooden door swung back to reveal a stern unsmiling woman in a severe tailored suit. Her pallor coupled with jet black hair was so striking that Grace's thoughts flew immediately to *The Addams Family*.

'Grace McKenna for Mr Komorov,' she said, venturing a smile, which was not returned. She wouldn't like to perform stand-up comedy in front of *this* woman.

'He's expecting you,' the woman said, her voice heavily accented.

She followed the stiff shoulders through a generously proportioned, wood-panelled entranceway. A fire burned in the handsome stone-carved fireplace and the scent of lilies from a huge crystal vase on a round walnut table mingled with the smell of burning wood. This then opened into an octagonal inner hall, which was filled with natural light spilling from a domed glass atrium from which she could glimpse a crenelated tower and spiral chimneys. A few exquisite paintings adorned the blue walls. Trying not to gawp in wonder at her opulent surroundings, Grace was shown into a stunning library where she was left to her own devices.

The room was large with comfortable leather couches and another stunning fireplace. The fire in here had not yet been lit.

To the rear of the room was a magnificent leather-topped mahogany desk with an assortment of papers scattered over it. The carpet was pale green, warmed by a rich pattern, and the walls were painted in the soothing colour palate of sage and cream. Grace drifted over to the floor-to-ceiling bookshelves and, recognising one of the books she had studied at school, she pulled it off the shelf.

'Careful with that!' snapped a deep voice behind her, causing her to jump and spin round. 'It's a first edition.'

Feeling at a disadvantage, she passed it to him unopened and he carefully returned it to its rightful place before turning to greet her with a small smile that didn't reach his cold blue eyes. Tall, with a narrow silver streak running through his thick head of black hair, he towered over her.

'Shall we?' he said, gesturing towards two burgundy leather wing-backed chairs on either side of the fireplace. 'The reason I asked you here is that a valuable object of mine, the jewel of my collection, has been stolen. I want you to investigate and identify the traitor in my household. It requires the utmost discretion.'

He looked pale and strained, a nervous tic twitching at the corner of his mouth.

'Have you reported it missing to the police and your insurance company?' Grace asked.

'I have reported it to the insurance company. The claim is pending.'

'And the police?'

'Let's just say that coming from Russia I have certain trust issues when it comes to authority.'

'You do know that I used to work in the police?'

'Yes, I have researched you thoroughly,' he said, still unsmiling. 'I have also researched DS Brodie McKenna, with whom you continue to associate.'

Grace bit back a retort as her face flamed in annoyance. This was taking due diligence to a whole new level.

'And?' she said, her voice cool.

'I am satisfied as to competence and integrity.'

'It can be useful to consult with DS McKenna as he can at times access information that I am not privy to. May I discuss the case with him informally, as I see fit?'

'Very well, as long as the contact remains solely between you both and does not leak out into the wider police domain.'

'Why don't you tell me what has been stolen?'

'What do you know about Fabergé eggs?' he asked.

'Some of them are exquisite and incredibly valuable,' Grace said. 'I visited Russia with my father a few years ago. He was a massive fan of Russian literature. We saw many fine examples at the Fabergé Museum in St Petersburg.' It had been their last trip together before he died.

'Then you'll be aware that Fabergé was commissioned by the Tsar of Russia to create a gift for his wife in the form of a jewel-encrusted egg with a fabulous surprise inside. Fifty were created but seven remain unaccounted for since the Revolution.'

Grace felt a flutter of excitement.

'Wait, you're telling me that the stolen item is one of these missing eggs?' She swallowed hard.

'Yes. It was the Hen with Sapphire Pendant. Although there were no photos of it in existence, I have had it authenticated by two experts and restored to its former glory. I have a photo of it before it was stolen.' He picked up an iPad and, once he had located the image, passed it across to her.

The photo showed a gold and rose diamond casing studded with sapphires. The second image showed the egg split open to reveal a tiny golden hen covered in rose diamonds bending over a nest of gold straw studded with diamonds as if it had just picked up the blue sapphire egg in its beak.

'That is absolutely stunning. How much is it worth?' asked Grace.

'Impossible to say without exposing it for sale but to me it is priceless. It's not only about beauty and craftsmanship, it's about history. To own something that is so unique. A fragment of Russia's bloody history. You cannot put a value on that.'

'Under what circumstances did you acquire it?'

There was a momentary hesitation behind his eyes.

'If this is going to have any chance of working, you're going to have to be completely honest with me,' Grace said. 'I can't get you results on half of the story. Like I said, I'm not the police.'

'The missing Imperial Eggs have become an obsession of mine,' he said. 'Private collectors at this international level are an elite group. We are competitors in a global treasure hunt for the most exquisite and rare pieces. I have connections all over the world. Many collectors could not afford to acquire such a piece themselves but will refer it to a private collector like myself for a handsome commission.'

'Is that what happened?'

'It was discovered in a small antique shop in Antwerp by a local dealer who did not realise the scope of the find. I believe he paid £300 for it. It was then offered by auction to a small number of elite collectors. My bid was accepted and I then had to get it here under the tightest possible security using multiple decoys. It was quite the operation.'

'Why have I not seen anything about this in the press?' wondered Grace.

He gave her a patronising look. 'We have no desire for celebrity, quite the reverse. Most private collectors are guarded about the jewels of their collection. To be otherwise is to invite the robbers to your door. It also exposes one to other, shall we say, societal pressures.'

'I can imagine,' said Grace drily.

'I like to keep my private life private,' he said with an assessing look.

Some of us don't have that luxury, she thought, remembering all the column inches devoted to her son's apparent suicide and then her unfair dismissal from the police.

'Were any of the rival collectors from the UK?' she asked.

Komorov's lip curled and his face darkened.

'Twenty-three. One of them was Harris Hamilton. He owns the neighbouring estate of Balhousie and is a thorn in my flesh. I couldn't let him get his crude hands on such an important Russian piece.'

'Is it possible that if he was thwarted at auction he decided to steal it from you?'

'I wouldn't put it past him,' he said, his lips thinned with anger.

'I'm going to need a list of all those present together with contact details,' said Grace. 'Were there any signs of forced entry?'

'None.'

An inside job? No wonder he was bent out of shape. 'Can you show me exactly where it was taken from?' she asked, standing up.

'Of course,' he said, standing up. 'Follow me.'

TWO

They walked further down the wood-panelled hall and took a right turn at the end. Komorov paused beside a bookcase and reached behind it. There was a muted click and the bookcase slid to one side, revealing a small lift with a blue carpet. Removing a card from his inside pocket, he inserted it and the door slid open.

'Shall we?' he said, gesturing for her to enter. Grace felt a little uncomfortable squeezed into such a tight space with someone she hardly knew. Neither of them apparently much good at small talk, they stuttered into silence as the lift made its smooth descent down four floors to the basement.

As they exited the lift, soft wall lighting came on to reveal the way ahead. The air was cool and she could hear the muted hum of a generator. A door slid open as they approached and Grace could see bold splotches of modern art on the white walls, all immaculately lit and displayed to great effect.

There were eight rooms or galleries, all featuring different kinds of art hanging on the walls. The last room they entered was different and displayed an eclectic series of treasures. They all appeared to be connected to an alarm system. In the centre of the room was an empty display case.

'How could this happen? Did the alarm not sound?' asked Grace.

'The alarm circuit was rerouted via a generator and the circuit feeding the Fabergé egg was effectively bypassed.'

'Is the only access down here via that lift or is there another point of entry? I mean, what if there was a fire for example?'

'There are two sets of alarmed steel doors to conform to regulations. Neither of them were disturbed.'

'So, you think that someone within your home or who visited it managed to get your lift card, came down here and made off with the Imperial Egg?'

'It's the only explanation that makes any sense, although it pains me to admit it,' he said.

'Do you know when the theft took place?'

'I can't be completely sure, but the last time I saw it was on Friday evening. I brought my dinner guests down to see it the following evening and it was gone. It was humiliating,' he said, his face tightening with anger. 'All of our guests and staff submitted to a search before they left that night but nothing was found.'

That must have been awkward, thought Grace.

'What about CCTV?' she asked, having noticed the small cameras following their every move.

'Their feeds were disrupted for the time period. I didn't notice at first because they were stuck on a repeating loop so everything looked normal.'

'I doubt very much that this was a one-man job,' said Grace. 'There's also a degree of technical competence, which suggests this was a well-planned and intricate operation, albeit with some inside help.'

'That's the part I'm struggling with,' he said. 'I'm furious, though sadly not surprised, that someone with access to my home would betray me in this way. And to steal the most precious item in my collection, something that I have been striving to obtain for so many years. There were so many other items that they could have stolen and moved on relatively easily. The Imperial Egg, however, is unusual and will attract a huge amount of attention. Now that it has been restored, everyone will recognise its worth. It will be too hot to handle and therefore seems an odd choice.'

Grace had no answers for him. Yet.

Having retraced their steps, Grace returned to the library and sat opposite him as directed. In their absence a silver tray had been placed on the coffee table between them with tea and freshly baked scones. Grace felt her tummy rumble and helped herself to one. They were still warm and melted in her mouth. She closed her eyes and nearly moaned in pleasure. Opening them once more, she felt her cheeks redden as she saw his amused look.

'Sorry, these are divine and it feels like a long time since breakfast.'

'I like to see people enjoy their food,' he said with a small smile.

After demolishing her scone, which she washed down with a dainty cup of tea, Grace whipped out her notebook, all business again.

'I need to have a complete list of everyone in your household and access to their personnel files. There can be no exceptions,' she said, as he opened his mouth to protest. 'I also require close-up photographs of all members of staff and members of your household, including yourself.' She pointed her phone at him and captured him glaring at her. 'I also need the schematics for the security system and detailed plans of the house. Any vehicles that belong to the household must be detailed as well as those visiting the house on a routine basis.

'The lift and gallery I will need to dust for prints though

given the professionalism of the robbery, I'm guessing that there will be nothing untoward. I'll need prints from everyone who has been allowed down there for exclusion purposes.'

Komorov looked unhappy. 'Is all this strictly necessary?'

'Yes,' Grace replied firmly. 'I'm afraid it is. I give you my word that they will all be destroyed on the conclusion of my investigation.'

'Very well,' he sighed.

'Who is in charge of your security? Do you have someone on the premises?'

'Yes. Viktor Levitsky has been with me for many years. He has a cottage in the grounds.'

Epic fail for him then, thought Grace. 'I'm going to need to speak to him,' she said.

Komorov hesitated. 'He's Russian and not likely to be very forthcoming, I'm afraid.'

Grace looked at him. Surely, if he was the boss, it was up to him to secure Viktor Levitsky's cooperation?

'When you have a job vacancy, how does it get filled?' asked Grace. 'Do you use an employment agency?'

'I leave all that to my housekeeper, Irina Petrova. She too has been with me for a long time. I'll get everything that you asked for collated and couriered to your office. I don't have the building plans for the castle, however. The architect drew them up for the renovations but went out of business a year later without forwarding them to me.'

'As the likelihood is high that this was, in at least some respects, an inside job, I suggest embedding Hannah, the youngest member of my team in your household. She could work part-time as a maid or in some domestic capacity as people are more likely to speak to her if they don't know she is working for me.'

'Not a problem.'

'I would prefer that absolutely no one in the household

knows anything about Hannah, not even your wife. She could perhaps be told that Hannah is the daughter of someone you owe a favour to and needs to gain some work experience.'

'Is all this cloak and dagger stuff really necessary? I consider my wife completely above reproach,' he said, a glimmer of steel in his eyes.

'Yes, it is,' she said, meeting his gaze with an answering glare. 'If I can't run the investigation in a proper manner, then we are both wasting our time.' She rose to her feet, hoping her bluff would pay off.

'Fine, we'll do it your way,' he snapped, jumping to his feet. 'But it's ridiculous including her as a suspect. It was going to be hers all along in any event. As the Tsar of Russia presented the very first egg to his wife on Easter Sunday, so I was going to formally gift it to Katya on her birthday, which was on Saturday.'

'Did she know that?'

'No, it was to be a surprise,' he muttered.

'I see,' Grace said. There was no mistaking the fervour of his love for his wife in his eyes. 'It's not that I suspect your wife of being involved so much as to ensure she doesn't give the game away to anyone else by treating Hannah differently from other members of staff. They have to regard her as one of them.'

As she pulled open the door into the hall, she saw the tail end of a red chiffon scarf vanish round a corner and the sound of hurrying heels clacking on the chequered tiles. She glanced at Komorov, who had an amused, some might say besotted, smile on his face.

'My wife, Katya,' he said. 'She is always in perpetual motion. I can never get her to sit down and relax.'

Grace smiled awkwardly back at him. She had a feeling that the woman had been listening at the door. If so, just how much had she been able to hear?

THREE

Grace rushed along the Esplanade to the office, her mind spinning with the new case. Komorov could have gone with a bigger agency but had clearly decided to take a leap of faith based on her investigative experience in the police and also, perhaps, because he perceived her to be a bit of a maverick having previously taken the police to an employment tribunal and won. It was a massive undertaking for such a small agency and she hoped they were up to it. She'd bought cakes from a local artisan bakery to celebrate.

As she pushed open the door, Harvey rushed up to her as though she'd been gone a day instead of a couple of hours. He was bouncing around like a puppy although he was now six years old. She dumped her stuff on the table and bent down to pet him.

Turning to Hannah and Jean, she gave them a big thumbs up.

'We got the case!'

'So, what's he like then, this Russian bloke?' asked Hannah as she helped Grace carry things through to her office in the back.

Grace thought before she replied. 'He's very tall and stern looking. I remember from when I visited Russia years ago that they don't smile to grease the wheels of social interaction like we do here, not even in shops when they're trying to sell you stuff. It was a bit disconcerting. They seem very dour at first.'

'So, what's the case about?' asked Jean eagerly, as they both sat opposite her at the desk. Grace dispensed a treat to Harvey, who gobbled it down then adopted his usual position lying at her feet.

'Have you ever heard of the missing Imperial Fabergé eggs?' asked Grace, leaning forward.

Hannah frowned and shook her head.

'I thought you said it was exciting?' said Jean. 'Don't tell me it's about some boring old ornament?'

Grace burst out laughing. 'If by boring you mean a gift commissioned by the Tsar of Russia for his doomed wife. A beautiful jewelled egg that opens up to reveal a surprise inside.'

'The rich man's Kinder Egg,' Hannah muttered.

Grace rolled her eyes at her youngest employee. 'Our client is a private collector of immense wealth and reach. Treasure hunters have been searching high and low for the seven remaining Imperial Eggs that went missing during the Bolshevik Revolution. Each one is worth millions.'

Hannah sat up straighter at that.

'Was it insured?' asked Jean.

'Yes, the insurance must have been through the roof,' said Grace.

'What about the police?' asked Jean.

'He doesn't want them informed,' said Grace, shaking her head at her client's folly. 'I guess having spent most of his life in Russia he has an innate distrust of what he sees as the apparatus of the state. I suspect the insurance company will force the issue at some point.'

'But how does he expect us to crack the case?' said Jean. 'If it was stolen to order by some international gang, they're probably no longer even in the country.'

'He thinks it was, at least partially, an inside job,' Grace replied. 'That gives us a finite pool of suspects to investigate. Moving something that hot takes time. It's not as easy as you would think. Of course, if at any point I feel the scope of the investigation exceeds our resources then I'll have to point him in another direction. However, should we succeed, it will be quite the feather in our cap. Hannah, how do you feel about doing a bit of undercover work?'

'Like a Russian spy?' Hannah said, her imagination going into overdrive.

'No, like a domestic in the household.'

'I'm still up for it,' she said gamely, though she'd clearly dropped back to earth with a thump.

'You start tomorrow at 9.45 and finish at 4pm each day so you can pick up Jack from nursery. Tell them about your work for Brian at the golf club. The official story is that Sacha's doing a favour for a business associate as you need some work experience to get onto a hotel management course. Nobody in the household, apart from Sacha Komorov himself, will know that you are part of the investigating team.'

'Not even his wife?' asked Jean.

'No, I made him promise,' Grace said.

'I was doing some research when you were out,' said Jean. 'Such a shame what happened to her. She used to fly through the air like she had wings. I would love to have seen her dance at the height of her career.'

'I didn't know that you were a ballet fan, Jean,' said Grace.

'I had ballet lessons as a child,' Jean said, looking a little embarrassed. 'I would have loved to take it further but a growth spurt put paid to that idea. Still, when I'm there watching the dancers glide across the stage, I always like to imagine what it would be like to be one of them.'

'I would rather pull out my own fingernails than sit through a ballet,' said Hannah with her usual candour.

'I saw a photo of Katya Komorov online just after the fall,' said Grace.

'Her partner, Sergei Nanov, dropped her,' said Jean 'There were suspicions of foul play in some quarters, but it was all hushed up. Shortly afterwards he left the company, but he's never been seen again. Supposedly he ended up in the Volga River, either by his own hand or somebody else's.'

'Russians sound very dramatic,' said Hannah.

'They've always struck me as quite contradictory,' said Grace. 'On the one hand there's this tradition of passion and drama and on the other hand there's this great stoicism as well.'

The tinkling bell and Harvey's enthusiastic reaction told Grace that Brodie had arrived.

'Our client doesn't want the police formally involved in this case but Komorov has given me permission to consult directly with Brodie on an informal basis, thankfully. Best not to tell him much beyond the bare bones for now, though.'

A brief tap on the door and her ex-husband's face appeared round it.

'Can't tell me what?' He grinned. 'Plotting to overthrow the government?' Harvey pounced on him in delight and he made the obligatory fuss, producing a meaty treat from his pocket.

Hannah looked like she was going to burst with the effort of not regaling him about their latest case.

Brodie handed over a Thomas the Tank Engine backpack to her. 'Jack left this behind when Jules and I were babysitting. I thought he might need it.'

Jules and I. Those words pierced Grace like a sword. Even though their divorce had been granted several weeks ago, she still found it hard to accept that hippy-dippy, sandal-wearing, lentil-munching Julie was in Brodie's life to stay. The fact that she was the daughter of her old nemesis and Brodie's boss,

Superintendent Blair, didn't help either. Even her job seemed airy fairy. She was an art therapist. None of this showed in the warm smile Grace nailed to her face.

'Thanks,' said Hannah. 'He had a great time with you both.'

'So, a mysterious new case, huh?' he teased, looking at them all one by one to see if he could get one of them to break. They all regarded him with lips firmly sealed.

'Fine,' he sighed. 'I'll get out of your hair. Let me know if I can help in any way.'

'I'll walk you out,' said Grace.

It was a glorious day so they walked across to perch on the low wall separating the paved Esplanade from the wide expanse of golden sand at Portobello Beach. The sea was a deep cobalt blue today and the sun caused the water droplets thrown up by the waves to sparkle. They sat close together, their bodies touching and she felt the bitter sweetness of it. If Connor hadn't drowned, would they still be together?

'What was that for?' he asked. Looking at her sideways, his eyes crinkled with concern. She must have sighed aloud.

'Nothing,' she said brightly. 'Just contemplating the vast amount of work in front of me. I always find the start of a new investigation a bit daunting.'

'You and me both. Since we wrapped up that latest murder investigation a week ago I've been waiting for the phone call to plunge the team into chaos again.'

'Be careful what you wish for.' She laughed. 'The client has given me permission to consult with you as I see fit. He'd looked into us both, apparently, before hiring me. He must have seen the coverage in the media of our last case back in May.'

'Go on then, spill,' said Brodie, his warm brown eyes alight with curiosity.

'The client is Sacha Komorov and he has had one of the rarest Fabergé eggs in the world stolen from his collection. It's effectively priceless.'

Brodie whistled. 'I've heard of him before. Word is he was peripherally involved in the Russian Mafia but has been squeaky clean since he landed here. Organised crime sniffed around him for a couple of years, I think, but seemed satisfied he was content to live on his vast fortune. I take it he doesn't want to involve the police?'

'Apparently not, so keep it to yourself for now. If the situation changes, you'll be the first to know.'

'Do you ever miss it?' Brodie asked. 'There was a time when you were so wedded to the police, I couldn't imagine you ever doing anything else.'

'It wasn't exactly my choice to leave, but I've no regrets,' she said. 'Mind you, I miss having access to all the resources you have at your fingertips. The red tape and office politics? Not so much.'

'Give me a shout if you need any help,' said Brodie, peeling himself off the wall. 'I'll do what I can.'

'Likewise, Brodie,' Grace said jumping off the wall and heading back inside to make a plan of action. It was good to know that despite their recent divorce they still had each other's backs.

FOUR

The courier arrived from Komorov as promised, leaving a whiff of leather and oil behind him as he dropped two sizable boxes to the floor and stuck a clipboard under Jean's nose for signature.

'Not one for the social niceties then,' she muttered to his departing back.

'Looks like I'll be burning the midnight oil tonight,' said Grace as the three of them lugged the boxes over to her desk.

'I can come over and help later if you like, once I've put Jack to bed,' Hannah said. 'My sister, Katie, won't mind watching him.'

'I'm happy to help once we're back from the meal at your sister's,' said Jean. 'We shouldn't be later than 8.30?'

'Honestly, it's fine. You'll have your work cut out organising all the paperwork into files tomorrow once I've taken a preliminary look at the contents of the boxes to ensure that everything that I asked for is there.'

Jean smiled and nodded. She'd been so excited about the dinner invite to her sister's house. Grace felt bad for her. Her ex-husband, Derek, had been controlling and kept Jean totally buttoned down. Although she was now free of the stress of living with him, she seemed lonely and hadn't yet developed much of a social life. Not that she was one to talk.

Once her staff had gone home to get changed, Grace took Harvey for a stroll through Figgate Park. Now when she saw little boys swarming over the climbing equipment, her lips curved in an involuntary smile as she looked forward to seeing Connor's son grow. Before, it had only reinforced her own sadness for the child she had lost.

Harvey pranced along on his lead, keen to spot either other dogs or, better still, an elderly person with treats in their pocket.

Once back at the flat she gave Harvey his supper and quickly showered and changed. She'd arranged to pick the others up and arrived with a full car and Harvey in the boot just before six. Jack was chatting nineteen to the dozen to a delighted Jean but Hannah was pale and tense. Grace hoped that her mother wouldn't put her back up again. She could be a bit full on and opinionated, and Hannah clearly hadn't warmed to her on the few previous occasions that they'd met.

Cally lived in a large high-ceilinged flat in Warrender Park Road near the Meadows. It was an area overrun by students but her sister liked it and had no desire to move. As soon as Grace rang the bell, her sister threw it open and pounced, enfolding them all in hugs.

'Come in, come in! I'm so happy to see you all! Hello, Jack,' she said, sending a beaming smile his way. 'Hamish,' she yelled, 'Jack's here.'

Hamish, her eighteen-year-old son, wandered out from the lounge followed by Cally's other kids, Emily and Archer.

Grace turned to Hannah to introduce them. She was standing staring at Hamish with a stricken look on her face, her eyes drinking him in. Dammit, she should have warned her about the strong resemblance between Connor and his cousin, Hamish. He'd been away travelling before starting university this term when Hannah had met the rest of the family.

Hamish looked puzzled at first but, being a sensitive lad, soon realised what was wrong.

'Hey, Hannah, mind if I pinch Jack? I've got all the little ones in the family room doing stuff until dinner.'

Hannah nodded mutely and he stuck his hand out to Jack, who happily followed him and the other kids, who were all asking him questions at once.

'Drink?' Cally asked Hannah.

'Yes, please. A Coke, if you have it.'

'And for me, thanks,' said Grace. 'I'm driving.'

'White wine for me, please,' chimed in Jean.

'Take a seat in the lounge,' said Cally. 'Mum and Brian are in there already. Tom's in the kitchen.'

As soon as Hannah and Jean walked into the lounge, her mother turned to Hannah. 'Aren't you going to bring my grandchild in to see me?' she said imperiously.

Grace could see Hannah withdrawing and jumped in immediately. She knew it was the proprietary way she had said it, like she had some kind of ownership over Jack, that had done it.

'Mum, you'll have plenty of time to see him later. He's only just got settled with the other kids.'

'People are so touchy these days,' said her mother in a stage whisper to Brian.

'I do love your outfit,' said Jean, changing the subject to distract her. 'May I ask where you got it?'

Her mother preened in pleasure and they started chatting about clothes shopping.

'Excuse me,' said Hannah quietly. 'I'd best check on Jack.' Grace watched her departing back with a sinking feeling. She'd so wanted Hannah to get along with her family, but her mother had already managed to put her foot in it.

'Dinner's ready!' called out her sister half an hour later and they all moved through into the large kitchen.

Hamish, Hannah and the kids all came through as well. Hannah was looking more relaxed and was laughing at a whispered aside from Hamish. They managed to ensure Jack and Hannah were seated at the opposite end of the table from her mother. She wasn't unkind but she could definitely be a bit much for someone as reticent and unsure of herself in company as Hannah, who had grown up in difficult circumstances and wasn't used to formal dining. Jean was a wonderful guest and helped in any way that she could by supplying small talk to paper over any awkward moments.

Looking at Hannah and Hamish chatting away to one another gave Grace an exquisite pain that she would never voice. He looked so like Connor, and for a moment she could almost delude herself that he had never gone. *Snap out of it, Grace*, she admonished herself.

Afterwards, she managed to catch her sister on her own for a few minutes.

'I bet you could do with lying down in a darkened room right now.' Grace grinned.

'You got that right,' Cally said. 'Jean's lovely. She's had Mum eating out of her hand all night. A real treasure!'

'I think Mum was a bit much for Hannah again,' said Grace.

'She just can't help herself,' sighed Cally. 'Jack's adorable. What a lovely little boy. He's such a credit to his mum. As for Hannah, she still looks like she could do with some mothering herself. I like her, I really do, Grace. It must have been so hard for her when Connor died. I can't even imagine having to deal with something that huge at such a young age.'

'She still hasn't opened up about it and I don't want to pressure her.'

'You're right. I'm sure she'll tell you when she's good and ready.'

'We'd best head off now, Cally. Thanks for tonight. I don't

know when we'll manage to do this again. We've just taken on a new case.'

Hannah, Jean and Jack were waiting at the bottom of the stairs having already said their goodbyes. Cally hugged them all.

'I hope this becomes a regular occurrence. Don't let my crazy sister work you all into the ground.'

Hamish was leaning against the door into the lounge. He lifted his hand in farewell but his smile was intended for Hannah.

Hannah's phone pinged. She looked at it then looked across at Hamish and gave him a small smile.

This was an unforeseen complication, Grace thought, as she settled them all in the car and drove off with a farewell beep of her horn.

FIVE

After she had dropped the others off, Grace lugged one of the boxes up from the office to her flat and settled down in front of the wood-burning stove with a small glass of wine. Harvey staggered over and flopped on her feet. Her mind flitted back to how well Hamish and Hannah had seemed to get along this evening. She had always known, hoped even, that Hannah might meet someone else who made her happy; she hadn't factored in that it might be Hamish. They were so alike in terms of looks he could have passed for Connor's brother, but they differed in personality, she reminded herself. Connor had been an intense boy. He was either incredibly happy or plunged into the depths of despair. He rarely seemed to inhabit the middle ground. A typical creative personality. Hamish, on the other hand, was more measured and sensitive to the needs of others. Perhaps growing up with younger siblings had helped. Perhaps she was overthinking things. They'd only just met, after all, and he was on the verge of starting at medical school in Edinburgh. It was likely that friendship was the only thing on the cards for them both.

To distract herself she plunged into the box and took out the

list of employees who could have obtained access to the basement gallery at the castle. The employee who had been with
them the longest was Irina Petrova, the housekeeper who had
let her in. She had travelled with the newly married couple
from Russia five years ago and had worked for Komorov for
years before he met his beautiful wife. As trusted housekeeper
she had the entire run of the place. She would also be aware of
the significance and value of the missing Imperial Egg, given
her Russian heritage. Could she have been tempted to betray
her employer for money, love or even patriotism?

Another person with access to the treasures was their curator, Oliver Compton-Ross. That name just reeked of privilege,
she thought, as she dug around in his file. He seemed to be paid
extremely well to manage the collection and jet all around the
world in pursuit of additional pieces that he then pitched to his
boss as potential acquisitions. *Nice work if you can get it*,
thought Grace. Someone like him would definitely have the
contacts and ability to move on such a valuable piece to another
private collector with obscene amounts of money in his purse.
Looking at his photo, she saw a handsome young man with the
kind of fresh-faced good looks and expensive clothing that came
as standard with a top private-school education.

Sacha Komorov had also mentioned a rival collector from
the adjacent Balhousie estate, Harris Hamilton, who had been
at the castle for dinner the night the Imperial Egg was found to
be missing. Why was that name familiar? Wasn't he in the news
a few months ago? Grace did a quick Google search and discovered an old article showing Hamilton running for a position on
the local council. He'd apparently had to resign due to a run-in
with Green activists, which had gone viral.

Feeling her eyes grow heavy, she searched for information
on Komorov's wife, Katya. Looking at the photograph, which
showed her expressive dark eyes and heart-shaped face, she
could see why Komorov had been entranced by her. Clicking on

a clip of her dancing she could also see why she had made it to the lofty heights of prima ballerina with the Bolshoi Ballet. After a bit more digging, she found a recording of her ill-fated last performance and winced as she saw her leap into her partner's arms to be borne high above his head, her back arched, as he spun her around. All of a sudden, she inexplicably dropped to the ground, collapsed at his feet like a puppet who'd had its strings cut. The curtain abruptly came down and the audience noise rose to a clamour. Looking at the date, she could see that it was just six months before Komorov brought her to the UK as his wife. A new beginning? Marry in haste, repent at leisure? Could the Imperial Egg be her passport to a new life or even a way to reclaim her life in Russia?

There was no shortage of suspects and she hadn't even begun to scrape the surface. Harvey got to his feet and nudged her with his nose then stared at the door.

'Is it walk time?' she asked, which elicited an enthusiastic response that almost sent her glass flying. Laughing at his antics, she grabbed her coat and they walked downstairs onto the Esplanade. The sun was sinking below the horizon and there was a slight bite to the air as they walked onto the beach. It was almost deserted at this time of night and she inhaled deeply, allowing the salty tang of the sea to work its way into her soul and ease out the kinks of the day. Although she'd come to Portobello originally for the wrong reasons, she now felt that she was staying for the right ones. The sea had a calming effect on her and it pleased her to feel the essence of her son around her as she strode his last connection with this world. Looking across from the water's edge to the Espy Bar and Restaurant, she could see everyone having a great time but had no desire to be part of it. She had the agency and she had Harvey. For now, she was at peace. It was enough.

SIX

Grace was up bright and early to walk Harvey before giving him his breakfast and depositing him in the office with Jean, who doted on him. She then jumped in her car and headed out into East Lothian, feeling the air freshen as she drew closer to her destination. There was a distinct nip in the air this morning and the leaves on the trees were already beginning to turn golden. Had a member of Komorov's household betrayed him? He'd given her carte blanche to question everyone in his household, assuring her that no one was off limits. If she didn't track down the thief soon the Imperial Egg might be lost once more, hidden in the private collection of someone who wished to keep such a treasure for himself. That was exactly what Komorov had done, though at least initially his acquisition had been motivated by romance. That was some grand gesture, she thought with amusement. When she'd been with Brodie, a grand gesture had amounted to flowers from the garage with a bottle of wine or a box of Maltesers thrown in. She'd still felt like the luckiest woman in the world, though. Dragging her mind back to the task in hand, she drove through the gates of the estate. Hannah was driving to the castle separately in her company car so that no one would suspect that they were working together.

Everyone who worked for Komorov had to sign a non-disclosure agreement so it hadn't yet got out about the theft of the Imperial Egg. It could only be a matter of time, though, and then the press would descend in their hordes. This time she parked in the car park and let herself in the staff entrance using the seven-figure keypad code she had been issued with yesterday. Apparently, a new code was issued every Monday morning to staff members. Walking along the corridor, she stuck her head into the kitchen where she spied Irina Petrova, the housekeeper, sitting at the table having a cup of tea from a bone china cup and saucer, which Grace guessed wasn't one of Tesco's finest, unlike her own.

'Is now a good time?' she asked.

The woman's back stiffened and her fingers tightened around the tea cup but she bade Grace sit down beside her at the vast distressed pine table. The kitchen was a mixture of the traditional and ultra-modern with gleaming surfaces and gadgets galore. The early morning sun shone in the window directly onto the housekeeper's curiously inexpressive face. What turmoil thrashed beneath that controlled exterior? wondered Grace, as she sat down and accepted the cup of tea offered.

'I'm sure that Mr Komorov has explained why I'm here,' she began.

'Yes, you are investigating the stolen treasure,' Irina replied, her voice deep and heavily accented. 'Like secret police?'

'Er, not exactly,' said Grace. 'More like private police, I suppose you could say. I'm here to work out what everyone here knows to try and establish how the egg could have been removed with a view to getting it back.'

'The egg is gone forever. It will never be found.'

'How can you know that?'

'It is probably on its way back to Mother Russia where it belongs.'

'How would you feel about that?' asked Grace, watching her closely.

'How do I feel?' She barked a laugh, looking genuinely amused. 'I have no feelings about it. Egg was here. Egg is gone. The world keeps turning. Feelings are for rich people, not for the likes of me.'

'I understand that you are authorised to go in the gallery once a week for cleaning. Mr Komorov must think very highly of you to trust you with access to his treasures.'

'He is a good employer. We are together for long time.'

'What about his wife, Katya?' asked Grace. 'Is she a good employer, too?'

Irina shrugged. 'She is okay. Could be worse.'

'When was the last time you went down to the gallery before the egg was stolen?'

'It was the day before. I go down every Friday afternoon to hoover and polish.'

'Did you notice the egg that time? Was it something that drew your eye?'

'It was not there the week before so, yes, I did notice it. But, until I heard it had been stolen, I did not know how special it was. It belongs in the Motherland.'

'Russia?'

'Of course. It's stained with the blood of the Tsars. It's more than a trinket. It is history.'

'You say you would polish down there. Did that include the display cases?'

'Yes, of course, otherwise they don't look nice. They can't clean themselves,' Irina said, frowning.

'What about the items themselves? Who takes care of them?'

'The curator does that. Mr Oliver Compton-Ross is down

there a lot doing this and that. He rolls his eyes when I polish or hoover. He thinks I do not see but I see everything. He thinks he is the big man. But I know he is small here.' She pointed to her heart with a look of distaste.

'Clearly nothing much gets past you,' Grace said.

Irina Petrova gracefully inclined her head.

'So, who else has been down there since the egg was acquired?'

'Mrs Komorov went down the day before it was stolen.'

'Wasn't the egg supposed to be a surprise for her on her birthday?'

'I think someone whispered in her ear.'

'Did her husband know she had seen it?'

'No. I think not. There is a lot he does not know.'

'Such as?'

The housekeeper's lips tightened until they resembled a steel trap.

'Anyone else?'

'Only Nikolai Komorov. He is Mr Komorov's brother and lives here in the castle. Black sheep.' She pursed her lips and shook her head.

Grace thanked her and started to get up.

'Wait, there is one more,' said Irina Petrova. 'Viktor Levitsky is in charge of security. Mr Komorov asked him to do some work down there last week.'

'So, if an employee has to go down to the gallery for necessary purposes, how is that organised?'

'I keep a swipe card for the lift under lock and key in my office safe. It must be signed out and signed back in by me. I keep a log book.'

'Can I see it?'

Irina Petrova glanced at her watch, sighed then stood up almost violently, repressed anger radiating from every pore. 'Follow me.'

Ramrod straight, she marched out of the kitchen and along the corridor, which twisted this way and that until the walls became narrower. Although no expense had been spared aesthetically in the main part of the house, the servants' area was strictly utilitarian with industrial green vinyl on the floors and white walls. There were no pictures or adornments of any kind.

They arrived in front of a door with a sign saying *House-keeper* with the word *PRIVATE* below. Irina Petrova hesitated then turned towards Grace. 'Wait here, please.'

'I'd like to see exactly where the swipe card is stored,' said Grace firmly.

Anger flared briefly in the woman's eyes but she capitulated and opened the door wide. 'Very well.'

Inside was a large study-sitting room where no expense had been spared. There was a handsome oak desk that was clearly well used and the rugs on the sanded floors looked expensive. The room was filled with expensive-looking trinkets and there were two fashionably upholstered wing-backed chairs beside a wood-burning stove with an antique mantelpiece. A selection of signed watercolours adorned the walls and there was a silver tray of drinks with an array of crystal glasses on a side table next to a kettle and coffeemaker. Clearly, she had a liking for the finer things in life.

Some of what she was thinking must have shown in her face as Irina Petrova's chin lifted in defiance. Swiftly, she moved to a concealed wall safe and inserted a key from a chain around her neck. She removed a well-thumbed hardback notebook and handed it over. 'Please return this to me directly as soon as you are finished with it,' she said.

'Can you check that the swipe card is still there?' Grace asked.

Irena sighed but took out a padded envelope and looked inside. She tipped out the white swipe card with a metallic strip along the back and showed it to Grace before locking it back in the safe.

'As soon as Mr Komorov realised the egg had been stolen, he came to find me and we checked together that the card was still there.'

'Could someone have cloned the card?' asked Grace.

'Mr Komorov's card was still there too. It is possible, I suppose, though I don't see how. The key remains around my neck at all times.'

Grace thanked her and took her leave. She still had to dust the area around the missing display case for prints though she doubted it would be of much benefit.

SEVEN

Later that same morning, Hannah sat bolt upright in a chair in front of Irina Petrova's desk. It felt a lot like being sent to the headmistress at school. Her new uniform of a black pinafore and crisp white blouse only enhanced that impression.

'This is most irregular,' the housekeeper scolded. 'Mr Komorov has never thrust anyone into my household like this before.'

'I intend to do my very best, Miss Petrova,' Hannah murmured demurely.

'See that you do, or you will be out on your ear. Polly is being trained up as Mrs Komorov's new maid so you will shadow her for your first week before assuming her workload.'

There was a light tap on the door.

'That will be her now,' said Irina Petrova. 'Enter!' she yelled.

Polly Gray was dressed in the same demure manner as Hannah but had a glint of mischief in her eyes that made Hannah sure they would get along.

'Right then, off you both go,' said the housekeeper, clapping her hands together and shooing them out of her office like they were wayward hens.

'This place is unreal,' said Hannah as they made their way up the staff staircase to the top of the castle to work their way down. 'I feel like I've landed up inside a period drama.'

'They pay really well,' said Polly, 'but they expect their pound of flesh for it. How come you get to knock off at four, you lucky cow?'

'I need to pick up my son from nursery,' she said.

'*You* have a child!' Polly hissed, round-eyed. 'But you're younger than me. I can't even imagine what that would be like. Are you still with the father?'

'He died,' said Hannah shortly.

'God, that's awful. I'm so sorry,' said Polly, giving her an impromptu hug.

'What about you?' asked Hannah, a bit out of breath as they climbed the last set of stairs. 'Do you think you'll stay long?'

'I'm saving to go travelling,' said Polly. 'The pay's good and they're not too bad to work for most of the time. Another year and I'm out of here. Thailand, here I come!'

Hannah felt momentarily jealous but then gave herself a mental slap. What did she have to complain about? She had a little boy that she loved to bits, and Grace and Brodie had made sure she felt part of their family. Working in the agency was pretty cool, too.

'That sounds amazing,' she said with a warm smile.

They stopped in front of a door embellished with gold leaf.

'This is Katya Komorov's room,' she whispered. 'Whatever you do, don't get on the wrong side of her. She can be a bit of a bitch. Don't miss a single surface when you're dusting. She does spot checks with a white cotton glove.'

'Blimey,' said Hannah. 'I'll watch my step.'

Polly tapped on the door.

'Enter,' an imperious voice sounded within.

'Good morning, madam,' said Polly. 'This is Hannah. She'll be stepping into my role once I move up.'

Hannah felt quite star-struck and had to fight the urge to curtsey as she came face to face with the most beautiful woman she had ever seen in real life. She was incredibly slender and waif-like but there was nothing weak about her. She clearly packed some muscle and Hannah could see the outline of her well delineated six-pack beneath her flimsy top. Her face was all sharp angles but her eyes, big dark pools, drew the most attention. She was so small and delicate that Hannah felt like a big clumsy oaf in comparison. There was an awkward pause during which Hannah realised she had been staring.

'Good morning, madam,' she said, dropping her gaze.

'As long as you are meticulous in carrying out your duties, we will not have a problem,' Katya said. 'I also require my employees to exercise the utmost discretion. Do you understand?'

'Yes, madam,' said Hannah. Unlike Irina Petrova, Katya spoke English almost flawlessly with just a mere hint of an accent.

'If I catch you gossiping about me to anyone, anyone at all, you will be dismissed without notice. Is that clear?'

'Yes, madam,' said Hannah, feeling she had stumbled into a world where employment law did not exist.

Suddenly, Katya was all smiles as though the sun had come out and chased away the clouds.

'Now, I will leave you both to get on. Polly, I will see you later at 3pm to discuss some upcoming requirements in relation to your new role.' With that, she swept out in a cloud of expensive perfume.

Hannah turned to Polly and raised her eyebrows comically and was surprised when Polly put her finger to her lips and ushered them into the luxurious ensuite bathroom, turning on the taps.

'I forgot to warn you, sometimes Katya leaves a voice recorder switched on when she leaves the room. She has multiple devices, not just one, so it is safest to assume that she is always listening in.'

'That's crazy,' whispered Hannah.

'This whole house is a bit nuts.' Polly shrugged. 'Keep your head down and you'll be fine. Don't forget to say some stuff when we're in there so she won't know that we know.'

Moving back into the luxurious bedroom – bigger than the floor space of her whole house – Hannah set to work under Polly's direction. As they were changing the sheets, Hannah pointed to a display cabinet which contained close to twenty Fabergé eggs of different sizes and style.

'Those are gorgeous,' she said, pointing to them. 'I learned about them in school when we were studying the Russian Revolution. I have a cheap souvenir one that one of my school friends brought me back from St Petersburg.'

Polly glanced over and shrugged.

'They don't really do anything for me,' she said. 'Bit old-fashioned.'

Understatement of the century, thought Hannah, choking back a laugh. Polly was a bit of a birdbrain but she liked her.

As they were walking along the hall to the next room, something struck Hannah.

'I've just realised there was no stuff belonging to Mr Komorov in there. Don't they share a room?'

'No, Mr Komorov has the suite next door.'

'Isn't that a bit weird?' asked Hannah. 'Aren't they meant to be madly in love?'

'He's madly in love with her at any rate,' laughed Polly. 'Her, not so much. I heard it was her who insisted they each have their own space. Anyway, it's common to do that if you're loaded,' she added airily, in the manner of one who knows these things.

Polly tapped on a door further along the corridor, then, in the absence of a reply, used one of the keys on the chain attached to her belt to let them both in. The contrast in décor was striking. Sacha Komorov's space was very masculine in muted tones of blue and grey with minimal embellishments. Even the mattress was hard and unyielding as though he was someone who disliked giving in to such notions of comfort. He did, however, have some fabulous art on the walls, which somehow lifted the whole room with its rich swirls of colour and shapes.

'Don't worry, we can speak freely in here.' Polly grinned.

'I hear that they have a secret gallery in the house, too,' said Hannah. 'Do we have to clean that as well?'

'No, the housekeeper, Irina Petrova, sees to that personally. Rumour has it that it's filled to bursting with treasure. I've never even been in there.'

'Maybe Mr Komorov should open it up to the public for an exhibition or something,' said Hannah. 'It seems a shame that they're the only ones that get to see it if it's as special as you say.'

'A few others have got to go down as well. Nikolai, the boss's brother, Oliver Compton-Ross...'

'Crikey, that's a mouthful.' Hannah grinned. 'Who's he when he's at home?'

'He's the posh git who's responsible for the boss's collection.'

'Harsh!' said Hannah.

'I have my reasons,' said Polly, straightening the bed up. 'My advice, steer clear.'

EIGHT

Grace had been told that she might find Katya in her dance studio. As she rounded the corner on the floor beneath the kitchen, she came to an abrupt halt. Further along the corridor a handsome man was watching intently through the window on the door as Katya danced. At first glance she thought it was Komorov himself as he was the same height and build but this man was younger and... infinitely more charming, she thought, as his face lit up with a smile and he beckoned her towards him. He was still wearing what was obviously last night's dinner suit and was lean and trim. She approached and looked through the clear panel, too, and her breath caught in her throat as she saw Katya dancing, the exquisite strains of *Swan Lake* leaking out from under the door.

'She's extraordinary, no?' he said, his voice husky.

Grace stole a sideways glance up at him and saw unmistakeable passion mixed with the admiration for her dancing.

'I thought she couldn't dance anymore,' she said.

'Her ankle won't stand up to the rigours of dancing at a professional level but she has worked incredibly hard to be able to dance now for pleasure.'

They both watched the ethereal dancer as she gracefully pirouetted, her arms and face alive with emotion as she lost herself in the ballet.

'Nikolai Komorov,' he said, sticking out his hand for her to shake.

'Grace McKenna, private detective,' she said. Was it her imagination or did a fleeting sense of alarm flick across his face?

'Should I be worried?' he asked with a quizzical expression.

'Only you know that,' she said with what she hoped was an enigmatic smile. 'Are you free to have a chat now? I was after Katya but I don't want to interrupt her.'

'What's this about?' he asked after he had taken her up to the library, his dark eyes watchful.

'Your brother has hired me to look into the theft of an item from his private collection. I presume you are aware of what precisely was stolen?'

'Yes, of course, the Imperial Egg,' he said.

'You don't seem particularly upset?'

'Why would I be? It didn't belong to me,' he said, which Grace felt revealed a lot about his relationship with his brother.

'Did you see it before it was removed?'

'Yes,' he said, a note of bitterness creeping into his voice. 'My brother summoned me immediately to worship at its feet.'

Grace's surprise must have shown on her face as he immediately flashed her a charming smile.

'Don't get me wrong, it was an amazing coup to find and secure such an important link to our heritage.'

'What do you do for a living?' asked Grace.

'I'm a junior partner at Rossiter and Roebottom.'

'The auction house?'

'Yes. I have a degree in fine art. My brother insisted I go to university yet he has managed to amass all this, despite leaving school at fourteen.'

'A different time,' said Grace. 'Is there a large age gap between you?'

'Yes, he is twelve years older than me but he seems even older than his years.'

And you seem younger, thought Grace, not impressed by him. He was coming across as a spoilt indulged playboy. She wondered if his position in the auction house had come about through hard work or his brother's influence.

'Do you meet many collectors of his stature in your line of work?' she asked.

A flicker of annoyance flashed across his face. 'No. I meet wealthy people but people like my brother are a whole different level. They don't go through the usual channels.'

'You live here too, Nikolai?'

'I do. I enjoy the commute. It helps to clear the city out of my lungs. I suppose I should move out but Traprain Castle is a hard act to follow.'

'Do you have any theories as to who might have stolen the Imperial Egg?'

'Me? Of course not.' He frowned, folding his arms in a defensive posture.

'I take it you were here that night?'

'So?'

'Can you take me through your movements from the moment you arrived, please?'

'Is this really necessary? I find this interrogation... intrusive.'

Grace was getting more and more exasperated with him but sensed that she'd get further if she played to his clearly enormous ego.

'I'm sorry, I know that you probably have loads more important stuff to do,' she said. 'However, I really do need your help in piecing everyone's movements together.'

'Very well,' he sighed. 'I knocked off work at 3.15 and drove out here. I knew that my brother had some guests for dinner and intended to wow them all by a trip down to the gallery to show off the Imperial Egg as the grand finale. It was Katya's birthday and all he had planned was a stuffy dinner and a bit of show and tell.' He shook his head disparagingly then smirked. 'You should have seen his face when he saw the empty display case. I thought he was going to have a stroke.'

'You rather sound like you enjoyed his discomfort?' said Grace, staring at him curiously.

'Of course not! At first, I assumed maybe someone had pranked him or it had been moved elsewhere for a good reason so it was just amusing seeing him so perplexed. But when I realised it had been stolen, I felt bad for him. We all did.'

'Who were the dinner guests?'

'Sacha and Katya, obviously. Oliver Compton-Ross and Harris and Hilary Hamilton.'

'Harris and Hilary Hamilton?'

'Inviting them was pure badness on my brother's part.' Nikolai grinned. 'Harris owns Balhousie, the neighbouring estate. He's an avid collector and very competitive with Sacha. He'd go to almost any length to get one over on him.'

'So, take me through your movements and who you encountered from when you arrived until Sacha discovered the theft, including the staff.'

'The staff?' he said, raising an eyebrow. 'You surely don't think they had anything to do with it, do you? Surely none of them would have the wit and intelligence to pull off something like this?'

'You sound as though you almost admire the thief.'

A slight smirk twisted his mouth but was gone so quickly she couldn't be sure.

'I arrived at around four and popped my head into the library to check the arrangements with Sacha, then I carried on up to my room to shower and change before drinks at six. On my way upstairs I saw Oliver and Katya chatting outside her room. He's so infatuated with her it's embarrassing.'

'Does Sacha know?'

'How could he not? Mind you, I don't fancy the chances of anyone trying to steal the jewel in his crown.'

'Not the Imperial Egg?'

'Not even close,' he laughed, a hard edge creeping into his voice. 'The castle is the gilded cage in which she is displayed.'

There was an awkward silence. Nikolai cleared his throat and continued.

'I met everyone downstairs at six. The servants? Let's see, Irina was gliding around. I did notice her having a tense exchange with someone at the entrance to the servants' quarters when I went out for a smoke.'

'Who?'

'Hang on.' He frowned in concentration. 'Yes, it was Viktor Levitsky, head of security. Much use he turned out to be.'

'Do you know what it was about?'

'Frankly, I neither know nor care.' Abruptly, he stood up, towering over her. He glanced at his watch. 'I'm sorry, I really do have somewhere to be.'

Grace stifled her annoyance. He was infuriating. 'May I have your card in case I have any further questions?' she asked, springing to her feet. He'd hardly told her anything at all but she couldn't detain him against his will. Longingly, she thought of her old police powers.

He hesitated but handed it over reluctantly.

'Thank you,' she said, smiling sweetly as he strode off, shoulders hunched in annoyance.

If she had to guess she would say that Nikolai had had it easy compared to his brother, with Sacha smoothing his way in life for years. But was the undercurrent of jealousy she could sense simmering beneath the surface corrosive enough to have pushed him into stealing the Imperial Egg?

NINE

Grace's next target was Viktor Levitsky, head of security. In fact, she was a bit annoyed that she was having to trail all over looking for him and that he hadn't replied to her email to set up a meeting. If she had been in his shoes, she'd have been falling over backwards to make herself available. After all, his security measures had clearly not been up to scratch or the egg wouldn't now be missing. He had a small office near to Sacha's study but clearly didn't spend much time there. She'd popped her head in more than once already. It was sparse and functional and had probably been a store cupboard before he'd taken it over. Turning away from there again, she spied him walking up the front steps. She slipped into an alcove, suspecting he would turn on his heel and walk the other way if he saw her loitering. He was a handsome man, tall like the two brothers, with jet black hair and dark eyes. His expression was severe and unsmiling. As he entered the hallway, she saw his eyes flick this way and that, then, apparently satisfied, he quickly entered his office and closed the door.

'Gotcha,' murmured Grace. She slid out from the alcove,

and walked to the door. Knocking first, she turned the handle and walked straight in.

Sitting behind his desk, Viktor banged his laptop shut and glared at her.

'Grace McKenna, private investigator,' she said with a smile, walking forward with her hand outstretched in greeting.

'I know who you are,' he said, squeezing her hand until the bones cracked. Grace didn't react to his attempt to seek dominance.

She sat without waiting to be invited. The air crackled with hostility. What was this guy's problem? She fumed. 'I would like to nail down the timeline for the theft with you,' she said. 'When did the Imperial Egg arrive at the castle?'

'Around lunchtime on Friday the first of September. Mr Komorov wanted it in place as a surprise for Katya's birthday dinner the next night.'

'Who set up the security alarms once the egg was in place?' she asked.

'The alarm company we have always used, AMR Systems based in Edinburgh.'

Grace nodded. She had heard of them before and they had a solid reputation. 'So, they came out and set everything up on the Friday? Who was present when that was being done?'

'Myself, Sacha and the curator were down in the gallery with their chief engineer. They installed the additional alarm and tested it in my presence.'

'Has the security system ever glitched before?' asked Grace.

Viktor shook his head emphatically. 'Never. They know what they are doing.' He sighed and ran his fingers through his hair. 'Or at least, I thought they did.'

'Look, I know that you're probably not happy about me being brought in to investigate but I hope I can rely on your cooperation?'

'Of course,' he said, the hot angry look he gave her somewhat belying his words.

TEN

Grace walked into the office just before five that afternoon to sounds of hilarity coming from her room at the back. Pushing open the door, she was greeted by a scene of happy mayhem. Harvey rushed over, tail wagging to give her a cursory greeting, then dashed back to sit at Jack's side in case he dropped any of his snack. The toddler was sitting at the table beside Brodie and an assorted muddle of books and crayons. Grace had forgotten that Brodie had a day off and was taking Jack back to his house for tea tonight. Jean and Hannah were nursing mugs of hot chocolate from the machine that Grace had bought for them all after their last fat cheque. She walked straight over to her little grandson and gave him a kiss and cuddle. He dropped half a custard cream and Harvey hoovered it up, then averted his eyes, hoping she hadn't noticed. Jack's resemblance to her dead son was becoming more and more pronounced, which gave her both joy and anguish.

'How was nursery, Jack?' she asked, squatting down to his level.

'I made a rocket,' he said proudly, jumping off his seat and running over to Hannah, who pulled it off the shelf with a flourish.

'That's awesome, Jack,' she said. 'A rocket to the moon?'

'No, Mars,' he said, giving her a withering look, as he returned to his juice.

'Of course.' She laughed.

'How's the new case going?' asked Brodie. 'I think they're crazy not reporting it to the police,' he said. 'No offence.'

'None taken. It worries me, too.'

'Let me know if there's anything I can do to help.'

'Will do, thanks,' she replied. Looking at the warm solidity of him as he sat there, the pain of losing him to Julie twisted her gut in such a way she could hardly move. How could she have been so stupid as to let him go?

'I think the whole thing's really romantic,' sighed Hannah. 'I remember studying Russian literature and history at school. Sacha Komorov is dark, brooding and intense. To track down a missing Imperial Egg for Katya and give it to her as a token of his love? Just, wow!'

'Except he didn't,' said Brodie, bringing them all back down to earth. 'It was nicked. Best to stick to a box of chocolates and a bunch of Tesco's finest.' He grinned. 'Never fails!'

Hannah threw a cushion at him.

'No wonder Grace gave you the heave,' she said then clapped her hand over her mouth, horrified. 'Oops, sorry, I didn't mean...'

'It's fine, Hannah,' said Brodie, as he shot Grace a rueful look.

'Anyway,' said Jean, rushing to fill the awkward silence. 'What progress have you made?'

'It's very much looking like an inside job,' said Grace. 'The gallery can only be accessed by a lift from the ground floor. Sacha Komorov has a swipe card and so does the housekeeper, Irina Petrova. She keeps it in the safe in her locked room and the key to the safe is on a chain round her neck, which she never removes.'

'What if armed robbers burst in? Does he have a panic room?' asked Brodie.

'I don't know, he didn't say,' said Grace. 'I think that he barely trusts me at the moment. I get the feeling that he's waiting for me to prove myself somehow. Jean, can you try and get hold of the building plans for the castle? I gather that when he bought it ten years ago he did a lot of renovations before moving over here permanently with Katya five years later. He must have had to get planning permission so East Lothian Council should have a record of them somewhere. The architect's firm he used went out of business.'

'Will do,' said Jean, scribbling in her notebook.

'I'd also like you to get as much background on our client's wife and brother as you can find.'

'You think the wife or brother could be implicated?'

'I don't know. They have a shared cultural history, as does Irina Petrova. Russia can cast a long shadow. It's possible the origins of this crime stem from their past. Look into her as well. How did you get on, Hannah?'

'Katya Komorov is a strange one. She has a motion-activated voice recorder in her room, would you believe? Paranoid or what?'

'Maybe she has cause?' suggested Jean.

'They have separate suites, which seems a bit weird. Polly told me that a lot of really rich people do that. Hers is like an Aladdin's cave filled with treasure including lots of Fabergé eggs. I counted nearly twenty. His is very minimalist apart from the art on the walls. Katya might be tiny but she's pretty fierce. I wouldn't like to get on the wrong side of her, that's for sure. I'm shadowing Polly for the rest of this week but I'll be able to have a better nose around once I'm working on my own.'

'I suspect she was listening at the door when I was meeting with Komorov,' said Grace. 'Hopefully, she didn't hear much.'

'How long has Polly worked there?' asked Jean.

'About two years, I think. She's only planning to work there for another year then she's off travelling,' said Hannah, looking wistful.

'Nikolai mentioned a rival collector, Harris Hamilton, who owns Balhousie, the adjacent estate. He and his wife, Hilary, were at dinner there the night it was discovered that the egg had been stolen,' said Grace. 'Sacha also has a curator for the collection, Oliver Compton-Ross. He had full access to the gallery as a matter of course. He definitely needs digging into. Someone like him would have the contacts to get the Imperial Egg into the hands of a private collector.'

'Komorov is clearly betting on the egg being too hot to handle in the immediate aftermath of the theft,' said Brodie.

'Vivid mental image there.' Hannah smirked, causing the others to roll their eyes at her.

'Can you have a poke at your confidential informants?' Grace asked Brodie.

He shook his head regretfully. 'Sorry, Grace, no can do. Unless a formal complaint is made there's nothing in the way of active policing I can do.'

Grace knew he was right but it was still frustrating. She was starting to feel she had bitten off way more than she could chew with her tiny team.

ELEVEN

The next morning Grace was inserting her key into the door leading up to her flat when Harvey started barking and growling. She glanced behind her but there was nothing there. He was probably just spooked by the wind.

'There's nobody there,' she soothed, but he was having none of it. Opening the door wide, she felt a sudden tap on her shoulder. Instantly, she swung round in a defensive stance, dropping the lead.

'Quick, let me in,' said a woman in a voice she recognised. Grace looked at the blonde woman wearing a trench coat nipped in at the waist with a hat and sunglasses.

'Katya!' she exclaimed, scarcely able to believe her eyes as she recognised her from the photos that Komorov had sent across. She flung the door wide and the woman rushed in with a nervous backwards glance. Harvey looked at Grace like he thought she had lost her mind and growled low in his throat to indicate he wasn't happy with what was going on.

They went upstairs and Grace let Katya into the flat and bade her take a seat while she made them a tray of coffee. Harvey sat and stared at the woman with a look that said *no funny business.* Ever since she'd been attacked in the office during their last case, he'd been less trusting of strangers.

'I do not like dogs,' Katya said, sending Harvey a look that would have felled a lesser dog.

'I didn't recognise you at first,' Grace said, gesturing at the blonde wig. 'How did you find me?'

Katya removed her glasses and Grace was struck again by how beautiful she was.

'Your business card was in Sacha's pocket. He told me he had hired you to find the Imperial Egg. I need your help,' she said. 'Can I rely on your discretion?'

This was unexpected, to say the least. 'Well, that depends,' said Grace. 'You know that Sacha has instructed me to find out who stole the Imperial Egg?'

'Yes, of course,' Katya said. 'It has nothing to do with that.'

'Why me?'

'You already have access to my life so Sacha will not question your presence at the castle. I don't know who I can trust. You are an outsider. It is better that way.'

So far, so not flattering, thought Grace. 'Okay, tell me what the problem is. I'm happy to listen but, if I think it could involve a conflict of interest between you and Sacha, I'll not be able to proceed any further. Agreed?'

'Agreed,' muttered Katya, looking daggers at her.

Prima donna as well as prima ballerina, thought Grace, already regretting her decision to hear her out.

'I have a stalker. He creeps closer and closer. One day soon I think he will slit my throat,' she said with full dramatic flair. 'I want this stalker stopped. I prefer to have him killed but it is not easy here.'

'No,' said Grace faintly. 'It's, er, not easy to have someone killed at all. This stalker, how long have you been aware of him?'

'A long time. Since I was in Bolshoi Ballet.'

'But didn't you leave there five years ago?'

'Yes. He stopped but now it has started again. For three months he has been creeping closer. He wants to wrap me in his cloak of darkness.' She shuddered.

Grace stared at her, perplexed. Was this woman for real or was she immersed in some elaborate fantasy?

'How do you know your stalker is male?' she asked.

'I have had a few stalkers,' Katya said matter-of-factly. 'When you look like this and are also a fabulous dancer it is expected. I do not expect you to understand.' She made a sweeping hand gesture that Grace felt summed up her essence and found it wanting. 'So far, stalkers only men,' she added with a tiny gleam of excitement flickering in her eyes that Grace found both intriguing yet repelling.

'Have you told Sacha?'

'No. He would charge after him like a bull. Most likely, he would kill him and go to jail. That would not suit me. I handle things my way.'

She was tiny with a fragile ethereal beauty but Grace could feel the steel that scaffolded her diminutive frame. This explained the voice recorder Hannah had mentioned. She must be terrified underneath all her bluster. 'Okay, so what made you aware of the stalker three months ago?'

'This,' she said, reaching into a designer bag and extracting a Fabergé egg. She thumped it down on the coffee table.

Observing Grace's thunderstruck expression, she gave a tight smile. 'Relax, it is cheap souvenir only.' Katya leaned forward and pulled a small lever whereupon the egg split open to reveal a hangman's noose with a tiny ballerina in a tutu swinging from it by the neck.

'Surprise!' she said, with an ironic tilt of her head.

'How do you know that it's the same stalker that you had in Russia? Why would he follow you here?' Grace asked.

'I received a Fabergé egg like that once before, just before my accident. It came with a beautiful good luck card. The egg contained a ballerina with a smashed leg. At the time, I thought it had merely broken in transit. Afterwards, I started to wonder. How could the leg have been smashed when the hard outer shell was undamaged? And now this happens. Is it not obvious?'

Katya sat back in her seat, crossed her legs and glared at her with an unmistakeable challenge in her green eyes.

TWELVE

'Katya, this is serious. I really think that you need to involve the police.'

'No! No police!' Katya jumped to her feet. 'If you won't help me, I'll find someone who will. Someone who is not frightened like a little mouse.'

Grace looked at her. She could feel she was grinding her teeth in frustration but this impossible woman could be in real danger. She would no doubt find someone less scrupulous to take her money but not only might they have inferior investigative skills, they might also get under her feet when investigating the robbery. Sighing, she waved to Katya to sit back down.

'Why did you wait so long to do anything about it?' asked Grace.

'At first, I did not realise. I thought it was only a secret admirer. It wasn't until I saw this,' she said, pointing at the creepy ballerina on the table, 'that I knew he was back.'

Donning a pair of surgical gloves, Grace examined the egg minutely without touching it then dusted it for prints. She found two full and a partial. She then turned to her new client.

'Now you,' she said.

'No, I don't want to.'

'I need yours for elimination purposes,' Grace snapped, her patience wearing thin. 'I've been fingerprinting everyone at the castle for that reason. I simply hadn't got to you yet. Reluctantly, her client extended her long slender fingers. Once that had been done, she turned to Katya once more. 'Tell me exactly when you noticed the new Fabergé egg.'

'It was Sunday the third of September, the day after my birthday when the Imperial Egg was stolen. I had been dancing in the studio and came up to my room to shower and change. It was at the very front of my shelf.'

'Do you dance at the same time every day?'

'Yes, I am disciplined so I have training routine.'

'Were there any visitors to the house at that precise time?'

'Yes. Harris Hamilton and his wife, Hilary, were there for lunch. Also, Sacha's curator, Oliver Compton-Ross, and Sacha's brother, Nikolai. The Hamiltons and Oliver had stayed the night in the guest bedrooms on the second floor.'

'Have any of them exhibited inappropriate behaviour towards you before?'

Katya rolled her eyes and gave a small smirk. 'All of them apart from Hilary. That woman has a face like a horse and sounds like a donkey. Hee-haw. She does not like me.'

Go figure, thought Grace. 'How widely known is the fact that you love Fabergé eggs?'

'I say it in many interviews. I have wealthy patrons in Russia. They know they can please me by buying an egg. I build up a nest egg, that way.' She cracked a wide smile and her whole face lit up.

'Does your husband not get jealous of all your admirers?'

A cloud passed across Katya's face. 'No, sometimes I wish that he would.'

'Were there any changes to the domestic staff around then?'

'No, I don't think so, but then I don't really notice them as long as they perform their functions.'

Hardly employer of the year, thought Grace.

'There has been more,' Katya announced, rooting about in her bag. She produced a bundle of letters, tied with ribbon.

The letters looked as though they were handwritten on creamy watermarked paper in a flowing cursive script but they were actually printed. They were undoubtedly love letters, becoming gradually more intimate in tone. Each one contained an exquisitely fashioned charm of a dancing ballerina.

'This is why I was not alarmed at first,' said Katya. 'It seemed harmless.'

'Have you noticed anything missing from your room?' asked Grace.

'Yes, items of a personal nature: a practice leotard, under-wear, a pair of shoes, even a dress. I assumed they went missing in the laundry room. It's a big household. But you think...?'

'Possibly,' said Grace. 'Have there been any other gifts like the Fabergé egg? Anything that could be construed as at all threatening?'

'There was a bottle of champagne left chilling in my room last Friday. It tasted peculiar so I spat it out and didn't drink it. It came with a note.' She drew it out and handed it to Grace.

Your wings may be clipped but your spirit can still soar.
Enjoy the champagne. There will always be more.

'It's ambiguous at best,' said Grace, noticing that it was in the same font as the love letters. 'I'm assuming that you didn't keep the bottle so we can't know if it was poisoned or merely corked. Were there any guests that day?'

'Nobody that I can think of. I don't pay attention all the time. Sacha is a busy man and has people dropping in and out.'

'Well, from now on I need you to be vigilant and keep notes

of anything at all that strikes you as odd. Another reason you would be better to tell Sacha is that he could arrange a bodyguard.'

'No, my mind is made up. He will put Viktor on my heels like a snapping dog. I could not bear it.'

'Do you share a bedroom with Sacha at night?' asked Grace.

'Why is that any of your concern?' Katya snapped.

'Because if you don't it might be advisable to change that for your own safety.'

An expression of distaste flitted across Katya's face. 'Very well.'

Grace went to a locked drawer and removed some pepper spray and a personal alarm.

'Keep these on you at all times. Here is my personal number. Call me at any time if there is any more contact. And be on your guard at all times.'

THIRTEEN

Grace dropped in to the office and caught Jean up on her surprise visitor.

'It makes you wonder whether the Imperial Egg could have been stolen by the same person who left that creepy egg for Katya, doesn't it?' Jean ventured.

Grace stood and thought about it. 'Whilst I certainly can't rule it out at this stage, I would be a little surprised if that proves to be the case.'

'They're both Fabergé eggs,' said Jean.

'Granted but one is a modified cheap knock-off and the other is a priceless piece of craftmanship and history.'

'I thought that you said you don't believe in coincidence?' said Jean.

'I don't generally, but, given that the creepy egg came a week after the Imperial Egg was stolen, maybe the stalker used that first theft as a diversion or piggy-backed on it somehow. Maybe he wanted Katya to think that he had masterminded the theft to make him seem more powerful in her eyes,' said Grace.

'I suppose you could make a case for the opposite as well,' said Jean. 'Maybe the person who stole the Imperial Egg knew

Katya had had problems with stalkers and planted the fake egg to divert suspicion away from himself.'

'Or herself,' said Grace. 'We're assuming both the robbery and the stalking were committed by men but that's not necessarily the case.'

'True,' said Jean. 'According to Hannah, Katya can be rude and abrupt. I imagine she has the potential to make enemies of either sex.'

Grace glanced at her watch. 'Can you phone Hannah and catch her up before she starts work? She's probably heading there now after dropping Jack off at nursery.'

'Will do,' said Jean, looking up from her notebook. 'Anything else?'

'Have a dig around into the lives of Oliver, Sacha, Nikolai and Viktor Levitsky. See if you can speak to any friends or former partners to check if any of them have exhibited any red flag behaviours with previous partners or objects of affection. Their past behaviour may afford us some clues. There might be something in the society pages. See what you can find out about Viktor Levitsky and his relationship with Irina. Look at his past employment history, any previous criminal records etc. I'm going to drop Harvey off for the day with Brodie before I head out to the castle.'

Twenty minutes later she drew up in front of Brodie's neat house in a modern housing estate on the outskirts of Edinburgh. Opening the boot, she let Harvey out and he trotted straight up to the front door and gave a loud woof to announce his presence.

The door was flung wide before she had a chance to ring the bell and Brodie appeared in jeans and a T-shirt, immediately dropping down to make a fuss of the dog. Julie appeared behind him, sporting a short summer dress and wedges that made Grace feel frumpy in her suit and sensible shoes.

'Time for a coffee?' asked Brodie. Did Grace imagine it or did Julie's face tighten a fraction?

'Thanks, that would be lovely,' she said, walking in. 'How are you, Julie?' she asked just as Jack came tanking in and wrapped himself round Grace's legs.

'Hello, sweetie,' she said, ruffling his hair and squeezing his squishy little body in a hug. 'I thought you were at nursery today?'

'I thought as we were both off today, I'd offer to have him,' said Brodie. 'I phoned Hannah last night and she was quite happy as he's still full of the cold. Jules is so good with him.'

'I can see that.' Grace forced a quick smile in Julie's direction. Was Julie getting broody for her own child? wondered Grace with a sinking feeling in the pit of her stomach.

There was an awkward pause.

'Actually, Brodie, there's some stuff I wanted to run by you in relation to our new case.' She hoped he would take the hint. She took client confidentiality seriously anyway, but the fact that Julie's father was her old nemesis, Superintendent Blair, made her especially reluctant to talk about work in front of her.

'Why don't you bring your coffee through to the den?' he said. 'It will save little ears hearing anything they shouldn't. Is that okay with you, love?' He addressed Julie, the casual endearment painfully registered by Grace.

'Of course,' said Julie. 'I was just about to set up some painting in the kitchen anyway.'

'He'll love that,' said Grace, feeling she had to offer something back to this woman who had committed no offence apart from being gratingly perky and loving the same man she did.

Once they were both squashed into the single bedroom that doubled as a study, Grace quickly brought Brodie up to speed on the bombshell revelations from Katya. Brodie let out a low whistle and looked worried. 'I don't like it, Grace. I don't like it at all. You need to convince them to call in the police.'

'I've tried but Katya won't budge.' Grace sighed. 'I'm particularly worried about *this*,' she said as she took out the egg in its clear plastic evidence bag. She pressed the lever through the plastic to show Brodie what was inside.

'If that's not a death threat then I don't know what is,' he said, shaking his head. 'I hate the idea of you working out there with just Hannah for back-up.'

'If I get this analysed for prints by a private lab, is there any way you could run the prints through the system?'

'Not without an active case to pin it against,' he said, scratching his head.

She had expected his reply but it was still frustrating. So many investigating tools she had taken for granted in the police were completely off limits to her now. 'Never mind. If this subsequently becomes a police matter I can hand them over at that point.' It grated just a bit that Brodie was effectively acting as a gatekeeper to the resource she so desperately needed to make headway with her cases. However, she could hardly blame him for doing his job.

'Do you think that the two cases are linked?' asked Brodie.

'Possibly,' said Grace. 'I'm not sure yet. So far as the stalking is concerned, I'm not even sure it's only one stalker. The love letters are loving and passionate but that noose thing was just horrible.'

'Some stalkers can flip from love to hate in an instant.'

'Yes, I know,' sighed Grace, feeling the stirrings of a tension headache. 'That's why the whole thing is so confusing. Anyway, I'd better go, I'm keeping you back.'

As they headed back to the kitchen, Grace could hear yelps of delight coming from Jack. He was sitting up at the table with Julie doing finger painting and they were both covered. Julie was laughing at his antics and even Harvey had joined in with some pawprints of his own and was submitting to having red paint wiped off his paws with a waggy tail.

'You're a natural,' she said warmly to Julie as she bent down to say farewell to her little grandson and stroke Harvey's big head. 'I'm afraid I was more blood spatter analysis than finger painting when Connor was small.'

Every time she said his name out loud in front of Brodie, she felt a little leak of air from the room like the crackle of electricity preceding a storm. Did he feel it, too, or was it only her?

'Nonsense,' he said a little too heartily. 'You were a great mum!'

Julie looked from one to the other and her lips tightened.

'Anyway, places to go, people to see,' Grace said with an over-compensatory smile to Julie that shrieked fake even as her lips stretched it out. She almost ran out of the house and had to force herself not to screech out of the estate like a boy racer.

FOURTEEN

Hannah hung up her coat on the hook at the staff entrance. She was half an hour early and still reeling from what Jean had said on the phone. If she was Katya she would be absolutely terrified. No wonder she was so snappy at the moment. It had been agreed at the outset with Sacha Komorov that Katya wouldn't be informed that Hannah was working in the house undercover and Grace had seen no reason to change that now they were working for Katya on this new matter. She shuddered at the thought of Katya finding that noose ballerina inside the decorative egg. That was super creepy. The fact that it had turned up inside Katya's room showed that her tormentor was most likely close to home. Obsessive behaviour frightened her. The fact that someone could be so out of control as to be completely unhinged.

She was about to turn into the kitchen to grab a cup of coffee when she heard the sound of raised voices. The kitchen was empty so she crept along the corridor to see what was going on. The noise was coming from Irina Petrova's room. Luckily the door was ajar so she was able to peer in before retreating to a safe distance.

'Get your filthy hands off me,' Irina hissed, her eyes black with fury.

'You're treading on thin ice, woman,' a rough voice snapped. 'We had a deal, you and I, and don't you forget it. Sacha is not the man you think he is. Your loyalty is misplaced. I'll be back when you've come to your senses.'

Feeling the disturbance of air, Hannah just had time to flee round the corner before he burst out the room, heading back the way she had just come. She caught a glimpse of him and recognised his scowling face from the photos Grace had obtained. It was Viktor Levitsky, the head of security. Tall and powerfully built, he exuded an air of danger and menace. How come he was able to push the housekeeper about? Were they in a relationship? Had he been threatening her?

She slipped back along the corridor and tentatively knocked on the door. The face that greeted her was so hard and unyielding it could have been carved from granite.

'Are you okay?' Hannah blurted out before she could stop herself. That encounter had looked as scary as hell. She could have sworn she saw fear on Irina Petrova's face. However, as she belatedly realised, there was not a trace of it now.

'You have no business snooping around,' Irina snapped. 'If you want to have the sack that can be arranged.'

'No!' said Hannah. 'I'm sorry, I didn't mean to upset you. That man, I thought he was hurting you...'

'*Viktor?*' she said scornfully. 'I'd like to see him try. You run and get on with your work now. There is no time to stand about gossiping in this house.' She clapped her hands imperiously and Hannah fled, knowing when she was beat.

She found Polly in the kitchen chatting away to the cook, Sandra Dunlop, a plump Scottish woman. The ovens already blasting away and the heat from the massive oil-fired range was soporific.

'Morning, pet, help yourself to a cup of coffee before you

get started,' Sandra said. 'There's a bit of a chill in the air this morning.'

'Thanks, Sandra,' she said and took her cup over to the scrubbed pine table to perch beside Polly, already nursing a cup of her own together with a hangover by the look of things.

'Paracetamol?' whispered Polly.

Hannah fished a packet out of her bag and slid it across to her. She envied Polly not only her freedom but also the fact that she wasn't burdened by all the secrets she had to carry.

'Sandra, I saw a man in the hall earlier,' Hannah said, not wanting to let on that she knew who he was. 'I wasn't sure if he worked here or not but he looked angry. He was in seeing the housekeeper.'

'Och, that'll be Viktor Levitsky,' she said, folding her arms over her ample chest. 'He's the head of security and also does odd jobs for Mr Komorov from time to time. Probably in to see Irina about the meal tomorrow night. It's going to be all hands on deck.'

'I swear I've never once seen Viktor crack a smile,' said Polly. 'I wouldn't like to get on the wrong side of him.'

As they made their way to the top of the house to start cleaning, Hannah tried to discover a bit more about Viktor Levitsky.

'I got the impression Viktor was being a bit rough with the housekeeper.'

'Irina can handle herself, for sure.' Polly snorted. 'Hey, maybe he's her boyfriend?'

'Er, I don't think so,' said Hannah.

'I haven't seen much of him since I started. He's fairly handy if anything breaks, though. He lives in a cottage in the grounds. He has an office on the ground floor if you need him to fix something. Just leave a note on his desk. He's not usually in there.'

As they rounded the stairs onto the top landing, they saw a

handsome man with thick dark hair tap lightly on Katya's door then disappear inside.

'Who's that?' whispered Hannah.

'Nikolai Komorov,' whispered Polly. 'He's Sacha's brother and well fit.'

Hannah had to agree. 'Does he live here, too?'

'Yes, he has a suite at the end of this corridor. You'd think he'd move out and get his own place, wouldn't you?' said Polly. 'I mean I know it's a castle and everything but Sacha acts like his father instead of his brother. He's always having a go at him for something.'

'Do you still live at home, Polly?'

'No chance. They turfed me out the minute I hit sixteen.'

'That's awful!' Hannah exclaimed. Her own mother would never have done that, no matter how bad things had got. 'What did you do?'

'No biggie.' Polly shrugged. 'That was a couple of years ago. I was put in a grotty bedsit for a while. Then I got a live-in position. I'm in a flatshare in Haddington now. It's pretty cool. You should come over next time we have a party!'

'I'd love that,' said Hannah. 'My social life is dead in the water. Don't laugh but I haven't been to a party since I was fourteen.'

Polly snorted with laughter then covered her mouth with her hand. 'Sorry, am I bad?'

Hannah mock glared at her and shook her head.

As they walked past Katya's door, Hannah heard Nikolai and Katya laughing together. It sounded proper flirty.

'Are they, you know, getting it on?' she asked Polly.

'I don't know for sure, but he seems obsessed with her. He watches her dancing all the time,' said Polly.

'What does her husband make of it?'

'I don't think he's twigged, poor bloke.'

'What's that room there?' asked Hannah, pointing to a door beside Katya's room.

'It's the nursery,' replied Polly. 'It's not on the schedule for today but you can have a quick look if you like.'

Hannah opened the door and gasped in delight. It was like something out of a fairy tale with a beautiful white carved cot and a delicate mural painted on the wall. She imagined Jack growing up with something like that and it pierced her deep inside. Was she letting him down even though she was doing the best she possibly could to provide for him?

'So, they're starting a family?' she said.

'Not so sure about that,' said Polly as she gently closed the door and they went on their way.

'What do you mean?' asked Hannah.

'Well, the nursery has been ready for nearly four years now but there's no sign of a baby. Not surprising really as she's still taking the pill.'

'How do you know?'

'She has them hidden in her knicker drawer. I found them when I was putting her laundry away. Sacha is clueless. Every month she acts all disappointed and he rushes around trying to make her feel better.'

'That's really messed up,' mused Hannah. 'Just goes to show that money can't buy everything.' She was thinking of her own little bundle of joy and knowing that nothing on this earth would make her give him up.

FIFTEEN

Grace had arranged to meet Sacha Komorov for a walk around the estate at ten to discuss the case. It was a glorious day and they strolled down by the boating lake, which was a haven for all manner of wildlife.

'Were you a city dweller before you came to live in this country?' she asked.

'Yes,' he said, gesturing to a rustic wooden bench. 'I lived in Moscow for a number of years. Life was hard. The only relief was when I escaped to Gorky Park for a few hours. It runs along the Moskva River and I found the water and the green spaces soothing.'

'Can I ask the nature of your business dealings now?' Grace asked.

'I made my fortune before coming here. There were many opportunities with the collapse of the Soviet Union providing you knew the right palms to grease. Now, with help from a top firm of accountants, it continues to increase with very little effort on my part. My collection is more of an indulgence than a desire to increase my wealth further. I come from nothing. I had to scratch about in bins to survive. The valuable things in my collection are an insurance policy.'

'Things you can secrete about your person and run?' she said.

He turned then and looked at her. 'Yes, the habit of a lifetime, I suppose.'

'So, what's next? You're still a relatively young man.'

'You don't think the lifestyle of the idle rich is appealing?'

'Do you?' she countered.

'No. Surprisingly, it lacks stimulus.'

'Your wife is very beautiful as well as being an accomplished dancer. Has she settled well in Scotland? It must have been a culture shock for her.'

A cloud darkened his face. 'I think she misses Moscow. She was a celebrated ballerina. Now, she dances alone in a room with only her own reflection for an audience. She misses her adoring public.'

'That must be a big adjustment to make. Although I'm sure that her celebrity had a downside that she won't miss.'

'What do you mean?'

'Well, some of the attention must have been a bit scary. Most celebrities have stalkers or rivals keen to do them down. She must have had her fair share of such problems in Russia?'

'Yes, she was mobbed by fans wherever she went. Most of the attention was positive. However, once or twice it took a sinister turn.'

'There's often a thin line between love and hate,' Grace said. She remembered what Katya had told her about the egg with the smashed ballerina leg. Had the injury that forced her out of dancing and ultimately away from Russia not been a terrible accident but an act of malevolence? Trying to get at the truth was like tiptoeing through a minefield.

'I'm going to need to conduct one to one interviews with all the people who knew about the existence of the Imperial Egg and also might have been able to gain access to the gallery on the night in question. I'm thinking of the curator, Oliver Compton-Ross, Harris and Hilary Hamilton, and of course your brother, Nikolai. I have already spoken to your brother once but he was rather evasive.'

'No one wants to feel like they are being interrogated and under suspicion. They are all due to come to dinner tomorrow night, aside from Viktor. Why don't you come as my guest?'

'It would give me an opportunity to mingle with them and assess their possible culpability in a more informal setting before I call on them individually.'

'Perhaps,' Sacha said with a sigh. 'However, I don't want everyone to feel they are under investigation during the evening. Can you perhaps pass yourself off as a freelance art journalist?'

Grace looked at him in some consternation. Art was something she didn't have the faintest clue about. 'I'm not sure—' she began, only for him to interrupt her.

'Come by the library later; I will have some books and magazines waiting for you that you can throw into the conversation. I will, of course, tell Katya so you can rely on both of us for support if you need it.'

Grace winced as she imagined what her former art teacher would think of the ruse. She had been asked nicely to leave the class at the age of thirteen.

'Fine, I'll do it,' she said.

'Dress is formal.' He glanced at her sideways. 'Will that be a problem for you?'

'I'm sure I can rake up something that will pass muster,' she managed, stung.

She caught a vanishingly small smirk. *So, he does have a sense of humour*, she thought.

SIXTEEN

Grace came upon Irina Petrova bent over the household accounts whilst sipping strong black tea.

'I see you're a convert to a cup of tea,' she commented with a smile.

'Not a convert. All of Russia drinks tea. It's best with a spoon of jam. You should try it.'

'I certainly will,' said Grace, surprised.

Irina looked up from her work and sighed, gesturing for her to take a seat. 'How can I help you? The matter has been weighing on me. I feel responsible. Even though the keycard is still in the safe, I worry that someone managed to get in and remove it to commit the theft before putting it back.'

'I'm sure that you took all reasonable precautions,' said Grace. 'I hope you don't mind but I'm going to have to ask you some personal questions.'

'I understand,' said Irina stiffly. 'At least you are not FSB.'

Was that a teeny tiny joke? wondered Grace. She was finding the Russians hard to gauge.

'How long have you worked for Mr Komorov?'

'Since I was eighteen. We grew up in the same neighbourhood.'

'Were you and he ever...?'

'No!' Irina shook her head so vehemently a pin fell to the floor. 'He was much older than me and had to leave neighbourhood when he was fourteen. Bad people were after him. Eleven years later he sent for me in Moscow. He had become a big man. Very important. He needed someone to run his household that he could trust. He did not forget me. A long time after that he got married in Moscow and brought me over here with them to run this household.' She gestured to her comfortable surroundings. 'He provided me with all these reminders from the Motherland.'

Grace could see the depth of her devotion to Komorov. If she had to place a wager she would guess that Irina would lay her life down for Sacha Komorov and consider it a privilege. But did that same loyalty extend to his wife? 'How long have you known Katya? Did you ever see her dance before she had her accident?'

'I was there the night it happened. Nikolai had a spare ticket and asked Sacha if I could go with him to see her dance. I knew he was mad for this girl so I was curious, I suppose. I had never been to the ballet before that night.'

Wanted to check out the woman who had stolen his heart, more like, thought Grace.

'It was better than I expected. She was more than I expected. She made me feel things I had forgotten were even possible. Then' – she snapped her fingers – 'it was all over and she lay there like broken doll. There was silence, then everything was noise. Her screams, I can still hear them...

'Nikolai and Sacha rushed to be by her side at hospital.' Her mouth twisted in more of a grimace than a smile. 'They forgot about me.'

That must have hurt, thought Grace. 'What did you do then?'

'I went to a café/bar near theatre for something to eat before taking the subway. It was early and I was dressed up and unsettled by what had happened. I sat in a booth and had vodka to steady me. Then I realise that the girls in the booth next to me were dancers from the ballet. They were trying to whisper but much vodka drank already.'

'What did they say?' asked Grace.

'They were saying that the dancer had let her go of her deliberately. He had tears running down his face. He did not want to do it. They thought someone had threatened to kill his mother if he did not do it.'

'Did he tell the authorities?'

Irina snorted in derision. 'No, he was not crazy. It is Russia, remember? He thought maybe a sprained ankle but the way she landed...'

'Were Sacha and Katya already seeing each other at that point?'

'No. He wanted to but she played hard to get. Too much choice.'

'The accident changed things?'

Irina shifted in her chair. 'Yes, for Katya most of all. Suddenly she was not high-status dancer but a woman who was damaged and without support.'

'I'm guessing a lot of those would-be suitors melted away.'

'But not Sacha,' Irina said with quiet pride. 'He stayed.'

'Can you tell me where you sleep in the house?'

'In staff quarters on the third floor at the top of the castle. My room is very big. Very comfortable. Sacha is a good boss.'

'How are they accessed? Is there a separate staircase?'

'Yes, the back stairs are accessed from the corridor outside the kitchen behind the green door.'

'I'm sorry, but I have to ask this: Do you ever have anyone to stay overnight?'

Irina's face coloured and anger flared in her eyes. 'That is none of your business but the answer is no. Mr Komorov does not permit staff members who live in the main house to have overnight guests. He regards it as security risk.'

'Are you seeing anyone, Irina?'

'Why do you ask? What has this to do with anything?' The housekeeper folded her arms and glared at her.

'I need to know whether someone could have removed the key to the safe from your neck during the night and either used it directly or had a copy made. You could possibly have been drugged.'

Grace saw a flicker of horrified recognition before Irina shut it down.

'No, I see no one,' she snapped. 'Is there anything else? I have much work to do.'

'No, that's all for now,' said Grace.

'If you are looking for someone who is a hop-the-bed, then I suggest you look no further than Nikolai Komorov,' she said, her mouth pursed in disapproval.

Pure deflection or an axe to grind? wondered Grace as she thanked her and took her leave. So, Sacha's brother was a bit of a ladies' man. It came as no surprise to her. She thought of him standing in the hallway watching Katya dance through the window. How long had he been standing there? she wondered. Maybe her stalker was closer to home than she thought.

SEVENTEEN

Hannah was definitely going off undercover work. It had sounded so glamorous but in their last case she'd been working as a waitress and here she was working as a cleaner. It had better not be long until they solved the two cases. She'd be developing housemaid's knee at this rate, she thought, as she hoovered under the bed of one of the guest bedrooms on the second floor. Her week shadowing Polly was now over. Although working on her own gave her more opportunity to snoop around for clues, it also meant she had to do all the rooms herself on quite a tight schedule. In the last week she had searched the main suites on the first floor and two of the rooms on the second floor for the missing Imperial Egg and found nothing of interest. In a place the size of the castle it could be hidden anywhere. It wasn't as though she had time to go looking for loose floorboards or anything. It felt like a hopeless task. Closing the door beside her, she turned to go back the way she had come.

When she had first applied for the job with Grace, she had been not only looking for an interesting job but trying to suss out whether she wanted her to know about Jack and be involved in their lives. Connor, in the manner of all stroppy teenagers, hadn't exactly painted his mother in a flattering light at times. However, Grace was nothing like the cold-hearted career woman she had expected. She had recreated Connor's room exactly as he left it in her new flat, looking out over Portobello Beach where he had drowned. Her daily swims in the sea had also worried both her and Jean. She would swim out until she was the tiniest speck and sometimes they would worry that she might choose not to return at all, unable to face going on without her only child. Thankfully, she was now in a much better place and Connor's room had been given a makeover for Jack's regular sleepovers with Granny. Still, she couldn't help but feel that underneath her current positivity, Grace was still quite brittle. She let out a huge sigh as she turned the corner, heading for the stairs. It seemed to be her lot in life to worry about those close to her, yet she wasn't much more than a kid herself.

'That sigh nearly blew me off my feet,' said a very posh but jolly voice.

Startled, she looked around her and discovered a young man with blond floppy hair sprawled out reading in a recessed alcove with a stunning view over the rolling lawns down to the boating pond.

'You gave me such a fright,' Hannah laughed.

He languidly peeled himself off his perch and walked over to her with hand outstretched.

'Oliver Compton-Ross.' He grinned. 'Call me Olly. You're new; I haven't seen you around here before.'

'Hannah,' she replied, shaking the proffered hand. 'Do you, er... work here, too?'

'Yes, in a manner of speaking. I'm Sacha Komorov's curator. That means...'

'I know what it means,' said Hannah with a touch of frost in her voice.

He gave her an appraising look that contained more than a hint of admiration. Hannah was cross with herself. She was here on the job and not as herself so she had no business trying to show off to this distractingly fit man.

'Of course you do,' he said with a warm smile. 'I'm sorry I underestimated you. I won't make that mistake again.'

'I love the Fabergé eggs Mrs Komorov has in her room,' Hannah enthused. 'They're SO cool! Have you seen her collection?'

The young man in front of her blushed and dropped his gaze. 'Yes, er, *no*, I haven't.'

Hannah tilted her head and looked at him. 'Which is it?' she said, her mouth curving up in a mischievous smile.

He glanced around then lowered his voice. 'I got talking to her down in the gallery when I was completing the paperwork for some new acquisitions. We got chatting and when she realised I loved Fabergé eggs she invited me to see her own collection.'

'Why didn't you just say that?' asked Hannah.

'The boss can be a little overprotective when it comes to Katya. I didn't want to get her into trouble for fraternising with the staff.'

'You're a cut above *the staff*.' She grinned. 'To do your job you must have degrees coming out of your ears.'

'One or two.' He twinkled.

'Anyway, your secret's safe with me. As I'm right at the bottom of the food chain I doubt very much I'll be doing any fraternising with the boss. I'm starting to feel like I'm acting in some period drama.'

'Well, I guess I'll see you around,' he said with a flirty look.

'Perhaps you will,' she said, with a come-hither look of her own.

As she sauntered off with her tray of cleaning products, her cheeks were burning. She liked Oliver but there was no way she would be letting him get too close to her. Although perhaps Katya was the only one he was interested in?

EIGHTEEN

Grace swung by the dance studio on her way upstairs. She had told Katya to completely shake up her routine and try to avoid anyone being able to pin her movements down. To her annoyance she heard ballet music wafting down the corridor bang on schedule as she approached. She could also hear the receding sound of fast footsteps on the tiled floor. So much for unpredictable. She looked through the window on the door, about to charge in and read her client the riot act, only to discover that she wasn't alone. To her astonishment, there was a man dancing with her who she had never seen before. He was handsome and his bearing was regal, arrogant even.

Suddenly she saw Katya pick up speed and run towards him to be borne aloft effortlessly as he spun round holding her above his head. The look on Katya's face as she held her exquisite pose was pure bliss. Who on earth was this guy?

She slipped away from the window and carried on down the corridor feeling the chequered tiles cool under her feet. Someone else had seen them, too, she remembered, as she thought back to the sound of the footsteps. Someone who hadn't wanted to be discovered watching them.

Climbing up the obligatory stairs to get anywhere in the castle, Grace found herself in the octagonal hall once more. Walking along, she heard the sound of raised voices. The commotion was coming from the library. Checking that she was unobserved, she pressed her ear to the door, keeping a wary eye out for Irina Petrova, who had the uncanny knack of materialising when least expected.

'How much is it going to take for me to buy off the reporters this time?' shouted a voice she recognised as Sacha's. 'This self-indulgent behaviour has got to stop!'

'Maybe if I had the funds to do what I want I wouldn't have to shop bargain basement for my entertainment,' Nikolai's voice shouted back.

Grace flinched at the anger in both men's voices. She hoped she wouldn't have to rush in and get in the middle of it.

'Is that what you call it?' said Sacha. 'You disgust me! No wonder I try to keep you on a tight rein.'

'You're one to talk,' Nikolai said, his voice dripping with venom. 'At least I don't hide away beautiful things and put them in a gilded cage. You put a price tag on everything, including those close to you. You know everyone's price but nobody's value.'

'You have no value; you're nothing but a liability,' shouted Sacha. 'Get out!'

Grace fled around the corner hoping he wasn't headed this way, but fortunately Nikolai headed for the main stairs muttering Russian curses under his breath. She'd been going to ask Sacha about the mysterious man who was dancing with Katya, so perhaps the fact he was so angry might make him less guarded in what he chose to reveal. She retraced her steps and tapped lightly on the door.

It was flung open and Sacha stood there, his face like a thundercloud. 'Yes?' he snapped.

'May I come in?' she said, with a tentative smile.

His mouth said yes but his eyes said no. Nonetheless, he relinquished the door with a sigh and bade her enter. He walked across to a round table and lifted a pile of glossy magazines and some books on art and passed them across to her.

'Here are the resources I promised you. Hopefully, these will help you pass yourself off as an art journalist.'

'Great, thanks,' said Grace, wondering how on earth she was going to manage in front of serious art collectors and curators.

Sacha frowned at her. 'Was there anything else?'

Grace could see he was hanging on to his temper by a thread but decided to push her luck. 'I'm sorry, I couldn't help but overhear as I was waiting to talk to you. Is everything okay?'

He sighed. 'Not exactly. My younger brother needs to be kept in check. He has expensive and rather decadent tastes without the income to support them.'

'There's quite an age gap between you. I'm guessing that translates into rather different experiences.'

'You could say that,' Komorov said, flopping into a chair and gesturing to Grace to take the one opposite. 'My mother died when Nikolai was only two and I was fourteen. It was down to me to claw our way out of poverty using whatever means necessary. Thankfully, the memories of that desperate time are mine alone. I made sure he wanted for nothing and allowed him to live in a fool's paradise. One that he is not willing to leave.' He looked so worn and sad that Grace found herself feeling desperately sorry for him.

'That was a lot of responsibility for one so young,' she said. 'You could have simply abandoned him but instead you created a prosperous life for you both. Your mother would be proud of everything you've achieved.'

'I'm not so sure,' he replied with a twisted smile. 'I mustn't take up your time with our boring family drama. Was there anything else?'

Grace decided not to push him any further today. It was essential that she win his trust. 'I was walking past the studio when I noticed Katya dancing with a man I didn't recognise. I wanted to ascertain who he was to see if he should be included in our investigation.'

Komorov looked confused and then angry. 'You must be mistaken. My wife couldn't possibly have been dancing with anyone.'

This was awkward. Too late, Grace realised that this visitor was not known to him. 'Perhaps he was there to instruct her on some technique,' she ventured.

'Her technique is flawless,' he scoffed. 'She should not be putting herself at risk in this manner. Tell me, did you see him raise her aloft?'

Grace said nothing, her downcast gaze telling him everything he needed to know.

'I will put an end to this at once,' he said, jumping up and storming out like a panther in search of an antelope.

Grace rushed after him, worried that in such a frame of mind there might be an angry altercation and feeling she had contributed to the situation by bringing it to his attention. As she followed him downstairs and along the basement corridor, she hung back just out of sight.

'Katya!' he yelled as he drew closer to the studio.

His elegant wife popped her head out of the door and gracefully walked to meet him. Only a nervous tic at the side of her mouth betrayed her nervousness. There was something else, Grace realised. Although she had been dancing there was more than a faint whiff of sweat. This was a different, rather more pungent, odour emanating from her. Grace remembered it from her time in the police. The unmistakable sour smell of fear.

'Sacha, my big Siberian bear,' she said, her expression one of amused indulgence. 'What is the big commotion? You will wake the dead with all that screeching, my love.'

'Who were you dancing with? I demand to know,' said Sacha, his face contorted into an ugly expression that Grace would not have believed him capable of. A moment's indecision flicked across Katya's face before she smiled brightly.

'Someone from the Moscow Ballet that is touring over here. He asked if he could meet with me and so I invited him over.'

'Name?'

'Igor Sokolov. I would have mentioned him but I didn't want to bore you with all our talk of dancing,' Katya said.

'How did he get in?' asked Sacha, clearly still not convinced by her explanation. 'Irina informs me of all visitors.'

'Of course she does,' snapped Katya. 'I let him in downstairs. The staff entrance is closer to my studio, that's all.'

'I look forward to meeting him properly at dinner tomorrow night,' he said in a tone that brooked no compromise.

'Of course,' she said, trying to look nonchalant. 'I'll inform him of your kind invitation.'

'I should never have allowed you to build this studio,' said Sacha, his face now creased with worry. 'You heard what the doctor said. If you fall again on that leg, you will be left permanently disabled. It is not worth the risk. You are young. You will find another passion.'

Katya sighed and moved into his embrace. He held her with such tenderness it was as if Grace had imagined the savagery in his expression only moments ago.

'It's not as easy as you think. Dancing has been my life since I was a child. Nothing else compares.' She disengaged from his arms and turned to Grace, her expression polite yet cool.

'How is your investigation into the Imperial Egg going?' she asked. 'Have you any leads yet?'

'There are a number of lines of enquiry,' she replied. 'I believe that whoever stole it is lying low for the time being.'

'So, there is still hope?' Katya said with a smile.

'Yes,' she replied with a guarded smile of her own. 'I'll leave you both now as I need to get back to the office.'

That was excruciatingly awkward, thought Grace as she walked away. *Why didn't Sacha just go in to the studio and introduce himself to the guy right away? Mind you, he'd been so angry he probably didn't trust himself not to lose his temper.* A worrying thought occurred to her. What if Katya was growing tired of living under the restrictions imposed by her older husband? Could she possibly have stolen the Imperial Egg herself and be planning to escape back to Russia with the aid of the man she had been dancing with? Someone else had been watching them together before she arrived. Could it have been Katya's stalker?

NINETEEN

The following day, Grace walked into the office to find Hannah chasing her son round the room, who in turn was chasing Harvey, who was barking in excitement, his tail wagging like a metronome. All of them skidded to a halt comically on seeing her. Jean came through from the back room holding a bunch of letters for her to sign.

'Sorry, Grace. This young man has been completely hyper since I picked him up from nursery,' Hannah said with a severe look at her giggling son.

Grace knelt down and held out her arms. As she folded his squishy little body into a hug, she thanked her lucky stars that Hannah had judged her worthy to be a part of his life. A wet nose nuzzled her. Harvey was reminding her that he was due a walk. There just weren't enough hours in the day at the moment.

The door opened once more and Hannah's mother, Darlene, stepped in with her usual air of reluctance. Although both women were around the same age, they were streets apart in life experience. Grace had had a comfortable middle-class upbringing followed by university and a fast-track career in the police. Darlene had been dragged up and forced to fight like an alley cat to keep her burgeoning family together. She had a weakness for bad boys and her choice in men was an Achilles heel that had prevented her advancing beyond the breadline. Grace had very little time for her but was willing to bite her lips until they bled not to rock the boat or cause any problems for Hannah. She was now bound to this woman for ever by a common bond: the love they shared for both Hannah and Jack.

'Darlene, come in! Welcome to the madhouse,' she heard herself say in the most unnatural voice.

'I can't stop. Just came in to pick up the bairn,' Darlene replied, her dour expression softening as she looked at him.

'Thanks, Mum,' said Hannah, gathering his things together. 'I'll be home late. I've got to waitress at this fancy dinner for work but I'm off tomorrow so I'll get up with the kids and you can have a lie-in.'

How did you get to keep your daughter when I lost my son? Grace wondered as she took in the other woman's unkempt appearance. *At least she managed to keep Hannah safe, which is more than you did for Connor*, said the mean voice inside her head, poking at the hole in her psyche.

As the door shut behind them, all three women flopped into their seats with a sigh.

'I'm shattered,' groaned Hannah. 'The thought of having to work tonight is killing me.'

'Me too. At least you don't have to get dolled up to the nines and wear heels. Sacha had the nerve to imply I might not have anything suitable in my wardrobe,' Grace said with mock outrage.

'And do you?' laughed Jean.

'I have one formal long dress. That will have to do. Hopefully, it's come back into fashion after all these years.'

'We're like Cinderella and the Ugly Sisters,' said Hannah dreamily.

Grace and Jean glanced at each other and grinned. Their youngest employee was not known for her tact at times.

'Keep your wits about you tonight, Hannah,' said Grace. 'Compared to me you will be fairly mobile. People who are that rich often regard the serving staff as so far beneath them that they are seen as part of the furniture. Use that to your advantage. Try to look efficient with a smidge of boredom and don't react to anything you overhear.'

'I wish I was going,' said Jean, her grey eyes alight with curiosity.

'We need to keep you in reserve for later, Jean,' said Grace. 'Thanks for taking Harvey home with you tonight. I really appreciate it.'

Jean stroked Harvey's ears and he leaned into her happily.

'I'll be glad of the company,' she said with just a trace of wistfulness.

Grace felt a pang of sympathy for her. Jean had been a loyal wife to a horrible man who had ditched her for a younger model without a second glance. This job, after all that time raising her family, had been a lifeline for her. Her son seemed indifferent and only contacted her when he wanted something, usually money, but her daughter seemed cut from a better cloth.

'Jean, did you manage to find anything on that Russian ballet dancer I texted you about yesterday?' asked Grace. 'He may have been able to access the castle at a crucial time with Katya's help. Katya visited the gallery the night before the egg went missing. What if she sneaked her ballet dancer friend in too?'

'Maybe dancing's not all that they've been doing,' piped up Hannah.

'Or maybe he's her stalker?' said Jean.

'Possibly,' said Grace. 'When I first approached the studio, I heard the sound of retreating footsteps, though. Someone had clearly been spying on her and didn't want to be caught.'

'Were the footsteps male or female?' asked Jean.

'Good point,' said Grace. 'I'm not entirely sure. I'd have to really think about it.'

'You'd know if it was a female,' said Hannah. 'Her heels would clack.'

'Not all females wear high heels,' said Grace, looking down ruefully at her boring flatties. 'Also, she could have slipped them off and run barefoot.'

'Not to mention some men clack, too, with those seg thingies to make them sound important,' offered Jean.

Grace and Hannah looked at each other and laughed.

'Showing your age a bit there, Jean,' said Hannah.

'What? Are segs no longer a thing?' huffed Jean. 'Anyway, I did find some information on Igor Sokolov. A bit of a strange one, actually. He's only been dancing with the Moscow Ballet for a little over three years. He did a year in the chorus then seems to have jumped to principal dancer and remained in that position ever since. The strange thing is that prior to his time at the Moscow Ballet, I've not been able to find a single thing on him. It's like he beamed down from outer space. Yet, given he's in his early thirties and at the height of his career I would have expected to find more.'

'What does his Moscow Ballet bio say?' asked Grace, leaning forward.

'It's very coy on the matter,' replied Jean, scrolling through until she found it again. 'It says he danced many major roles at regional theatres before joining the company. There's no mention of what other ballet companies he danced for.'

'Hmm,' said Grace. 'Sounds a bit deliberately vague to me. Maybe identify a list of regional theatres and email them to see what they know of him, if anything. You could say you're doing a piece on him for a UK dance magazine. No one will query that as he's over here at the moment. Send a photo as well.'

'Will do,' said Jean. 'How did you get on with your art cramming for tonight?'

Grace grimaced. 'I don't think I'll be changing careers any time soon but I hope I've assimilated enough to pass for genuine in a casual conversation.'

'Grace, I really didn't like the look of Sacha's head of security. At best he's an aggressive bully but at worst he might have been pressuring Irina to do something wrong,' said Hannah, looking worried. 'His behaviour was definitely threatening yesterday. She put a brave face on it but I really think she was scared of him.'

'It was most likely not related to the case,' said Grace. 'Irina seems very loyal to Sacha Komorov. Viktor Levitsky is very elusive. I'd have thought he'd want to be all over this investigation but he's been standoffish in the extreme. What exactly did you hear him say to her?' asked Grace.

'He was saying that they'd had a deal and it sounded like he was pressuring her to keep to it,' Hannah replied.

Grace was troubled. That did sound worrying.

TWENTY

Grace smoothed the midnight blue taffeta dress over her hips then put the finishing touch to her makeup. She barely recognised herself in the mirror. Sliding her feet into her black velvet heels, she staggered a little at the unaccustomed height.

'And that's before I've had a drink,' she muttered, pulling a face at herself.

The doorbell rang and she tutted in annoyance. Striding to the door as fast as her heels would allow, she flung it open, prepared to give whoever it was short shrift.

'Grace!' said Brodie, the word catching in his throat. 'You look...'

Grace felt her face flush with discomfort. 'Brodie, come in,' she said, feeling flustered. The last time she had worn this dress had been for him on their anniversary in happier times.

'Where are you going? Sorry, it's none of my business.'

'I'm going to a dinner party at Traprain Castle for work,' she replied.

'I remember when you last wore that dress,' he said, his gaze intense.

'Don't, Brodie...' she said, her heart beating faster none-theless.

'Sorry,' he said with a wry grin. 'You just caught me off guard, that's all. Where's Harvey? I would have taken him for you.'

'He's with Jean for the night. I figured she could use the company. What's up?' she asked. 'I've got a few minutes before I need to leave.'

'Do you remember my informant, Billy Mac?'

'The fence? Is he still around?'

'Gone up in the world. He feeds me information in exchange for me not looking too closely into his business prac-tices. We've had a few successful convictions off the back of information he has passed our way. He styles himself as an antique dealer now. He looks legitimate but scratch the surface and he's up to his neck in all manner of dodgy dealings. The local gentry love him. He's got connections in a lot of the big houses around Edinburgh. Anyone that might be willing to look the other way from time to time when acquiring pieces of art.'

'Has he heard anything about the Imperial Egg?' asked Grace.

'He knows about the theft but says everyone is keeping schtum until the heat dies down and it can be moved out of the country. All the dealers for the big private collectors are gagging for it. All this for a glorified ornament,' he said, shaking his head.

'You sound like Hannah,' she said with a smile. Brodie had never been one for the finer things in life.

'He's heard that it's definitely an inside job, though. I thought you should know.'

'You could have just phoned. Why did you really come?'

There was an awkward silence. Brodie seemed to be having trouble finding the words. Grace could feel her heart beating faster. Was he ill? Something to do with Julie?

She gestured to him to sit and joined him on the couch. It

occurred to her that they'd sat here many times when they were married once Connor was in bed. This couch was part of their shared history.

She noticed that he was staring at her, the expression in his eyes hard to read.

'What is it?' she said, raising an eyebrow.

'It's just seeing you in that dress. It's like a time machine taking me back... back to when we were happy.'

Grace shifted slightly away from him and turned her face away. She wasn't going to get sucked into reminiscing. She would take Brodie back in a heartbeat, but she was damned if she was going to let him know that.

'How's Julie?' she asked, pasting on a smile. This wasn't like Brodie. There must be trouble in paradise. She still cared enough to want him to be happy. He gave her a sad smile. He knew what she was doing.

'She's pushing for more of a commitment,' he said. 'I don't know what to tell her, Grace. I guess I'm just not ready. Look what happened to us. I thought we were bombproof and then whoosh, everything went up in a puff of smoke when Connor died. I don't know if I've got it in me to go through anything like that again.'

'So, you're trying to push her away. Brodie, what happened to us was terrible, but we survived, didn't we? You can't let fear of loss inhibit you from living. If Julie makes you happy then you have to take a chance.' What was she doing? Her mind screamed. She loved this man, so why was she encouraging him to commit to another woman?

'It doesn't help that her father is my boss.'

'And a complete ass into the bargain,' muttered Grace. Her face lit up as something occurred to her. 'If you marry Julie, you'll have to have him over for Sunday lunch. Can you imagine?'

'Not helping,' he grumbled. He stood up and so did she, the

weight of things still unsaid hovering between them. 'I won't keep you any longer. Have a good night. I hope you get some answers.'

As she drove away, Grace watched Brodie recede in the rearview mirror, her expression troubled.

TWENTY-ONE

Grace glanced over at Katya as she emitted a tinkling laugh at something one of the men vying for her attention had said. Sacha stood by himself to one side of the handsome stone fireplace, his eyes firmly fixed on his wife. Katya was wearing a long silver sheath dress worthy of the Oscars and her own dress, which had felt so fancy when she slipped it on, was decidedly pedestrian compared to the dazzling display in the room. Hannah materialised in front of her with a tray of champagne and her face set to one of polite enquiry.

'Drink, ma'am?'

'Don't mind if I do,' muttered Grace, taking one for appearances' sake.

Igor Sokolov walked in and stood on the threshold. Grace seized her chance and made her way over to him. 'Hi, Grace McKenna,' she said, sticking out her hand for him to shake so he couldn't brush past her.

'Igor Sokolov,' he said with a small bow while taking her hand and giving it a gentle squeeze.

'I hear that you're a ballet dancer with the Moscow Ballet. How long have you been over here?' she asked with her most charming smile. His eyes moved past her shoulder, hungrily seeking out Katya. He seemed distracted and his body seemed to radiate tension.

'Our opening night was on Monday twenty-eighth August,' he said. 'We arrived one week before that.'

So, he was around at the time of the theft and also could have planted that Fabergé egg in Katya's room. 'You must have known Katya in Moscow when she danced for the Bolshoi?' She smiled.

His gaze swung back to her now and a wariness had crept into his expression. 'Yes but... it is big company. I do not know her well.'

Grace doubted that. She suspected he had known Katya very well indeed and that they had unfinished business between them. 'She's done so well since her accident, hasn't she? It's a joy to see her dance. It must be wonderful for her to have a dance partner again after such a long time. So tragic what happened to her, don't you think?'

'Yes. Excuse me, I must go and greet our host,' he muttered, walking over to Sacha, who looked like he was smiling through gritted teeth.

Her next quarry was Harris Hamilton and his wife, Hilary. Harris looked to be in his early sixties but his wife's age was harder to determine. She had that freshly peeled lineless face so loved by celebrities but her waistline had slightly thickened. The diamonds at her ears and neck were clearly real. She was occupied for the moment chatting to Sacha so Grace seized her chance.

'And who are you?' Harris demanded, as she approached, his eyes weighing her up like she was a prize heifer.

'Grace McKenna.' She smiled. 'Harris Hamilton, I presume?'

'And how would you know that?' he asked, his shrewd eyes narrowing.

'You're too modest,' she said. 'I have an interest in art and your reputation as a collector of note precedes you. I read a recent article on you in *The Art Digest* and I'm delighted to meet you in person.' She could tell from the way his shoulders went back and his chest puffed out that her flattery had stroked his ego.

'Are you involved in the art world?' he asked.

'I freelance for some of the more discerning publications,' she said. 'Perhaps I could do a profile piece on you some time?' She passed across a card which she'd had made for the occasion.

'I may be able to find some time,' he said, putting her card in his inside pocket.

'I do hope that you can.' She smiled. 'Have you come far this evening?'

'My wife and I live on the neighbouring estate of Balhousie. We moved there just after Sacha bought this place five years ago.'

'Does Balhousie also have its own castle?' asked Grace, knowing fine well that it didn't.

'No. My wife and I decided to go for something a little less obvious, but each to their own.'

'So, what are your particular interests when it comes to collecting?' asked Grace. 'Are you quite eclectic or more niche?'

'Definitely eclectic,' he said, his eyes lighting up with enthusiasm. 'I particularly like pieces that are one of a kind or have a poignant history attached to them.'

'Like the missing Imperial Eggs?' asked Grace.

'Yes, precisely like that,' he said with a heavy sigh.

'I believe our host is also an avid collector,' she said.

'He certainly surpassed himself recently,' he said.

'You've seen it then,' she said.

'Not since it's been restored. There was a bit of show-and-tell scheduled but let's just say that didn't come to fruition,' he said with a sly sideways glance at Komorov.

'I'm assuming a major player like you works with someone to curate your collection?' said Grace.

'Of course. I have a great deal of knowledge myself through years of study on the subject but a good curator has international reach and knows the current market as individual pieces can fluctuate in value. They can also source the rarer pieces.'

'Like the egg?'

'That piece should have come to me, not Komorov,' he muttered, his mouth twisting with anger.

'How so?' she said, injecting her voice with as much sympathy as she could muster.

'My curator used to be that man over there,' he hissed, jerking his head in the direction of Oliver Compton-Ross. 'He's clearly been playing us both off against each other. It's absolutely outrageous! How he can sit there and smile across at me like nothing's happened, the scoundrel.'

'Does Sacha know?'

'Your guess is as good as mine,' he growled as he swivelled to glare at their host, who held up his glass in an ironic salute.

TWENTY-TWO

Hannah admired the way that Grace was managing to work the room. She hadn't realised how attractive her boss was until she saw her all gussied up. It was as though she made a choice to downplay her looks. Probably down to all those years in the police working her way up into a position of authority.

She noticed Irina slip silently into the reception room and check that all was as it should be. Her face was even sterner than usual and she looked pale and gaunt apart from a gash of red lipstick. Suddenly, her mouth fell open and she staggered back against the wall, her hand flying up to her throat. No one had noticed and Hannah swiftly made her way over and took her firmly under the elbow as she helped her from the room and into a chair in the empty library next door.

'Are you all right?' she asked urgently, as she poured a glass of water from the jug on the drinks table.

'Yes, yes, I'm fine,' Irina said, her complexion misted with a greasy sheen. 'You need to get back and do your job. Dinner is about to be served. I felt faint for a moment. That is all. Maybe I forgot to eat today.'

Hannah wasn't convinced. It looked more like she had

received some kind of shock. Was it the presence of one of the guests? Something else? She had no way of knowing and Irina Petrova was not exactly the type to cosy up for a chat. Realising there was nothing more she could do she went back to the reception room, hearing the gong to announce dinner as she went.

'Where were you?' hissed Polly as she joined her in the line of staff ready to serve once the guests were seated.

'I had to help Irina Petrova,' she whispered. 'She had a wobbly in the reception room.'

'At least it proves she's human,' said the irrepressible Polly. 'I've had my doubts at times.'

Hannah sprang into action as the first course was served. She and Polly had been pressed into service as two of the castle waiting staff were off with flu. She hoped her training at the golf club would suffice for such a fancy affair. It was all right for Polly – Irina had already trained her up for such eventualities as she preferred her staff to be versatile. The wine flowed freely, served by two attentive waiters she hadn't met before. She could feel the opening salvo of a headache as she focused on her demanding guests who were used to the very best of everything. The noise level rose exponentially, and she could feel her feet throbbing as she rushed about.

'You're doing a great job,' whispered Oliver Compton-Ross as she leaned over to serve his main course.

'Thank you.' She grinned at him, thankful to have at least one person there appreciate her efforts. Most of them acted like she was invisible. Their manners were sadly lacking.

As she moved along the table, she came to Grace, deep in conversation with Harris Hamilton, who was red in the face and starting to slur his words slightly. On her other side was Nikolai, flirting outrageously with Katya right under his brother's nose. He must have a death wish, she thought, glancing sideways at Sacha Komorov's stormy expression. Igor Sokolov, the Russian ballet dancer, was also looking daggers across the table at them.

Just what was her deal, wondered Hannah as she banged the plate down a little hard in front of Katya. Compared to her she'd had such an amazing life, yet she still seemed unhappy with her lot.

'Careful!' Katya snapped at her, her cat-like green eyes narrowed in anger.

'Sorry, ma'am,' she whispered, quickly moving on, but not before she noticed Katya had been resting her hand on Nikolai's thigh under the table.

'So, when are you going to get down to producing a son and heir, Komorov?' slurred the coarse voice of Harris Hamilton. His wife had been showing Sacha a picture of their grandchildren and her mouth pursed in a frown at her husband's comment.

'We will have a child when we are good and ready,' Komorov snapped. 'Not that it is any of your business.'

Hannah squirmed inside with embarrassment. If this was how the other half lived, she wouldn't want to trade.

'I didn't mean to embarrass you,' he said, his eyes giving the lie to that statement. 'I simply assume that you want to pass on all of this,' he said, with a gesture that took in all of their opulent surroundings. 'Otherwise, what's it all for, man?'

'Harris, you're being a bore,' snapped his wife, Hilary. Desperately, she turned to the ballet dancer, Igor Sokolov, on her other side. 'So, I hear you have been dancing with Katya? Was that the first time or have you danced together before?'

'Yes,' said Sokolov.

'No!' exclaimed Katya.

There was an awkward silence. Everyone started eating at once, making busy sounds with their cutlery.

Hannah caught Oliver's eye across the table and had to stifle a grin as he waggled his eyebrows comically at her. *Thank*

God someone here has a sense of humour, she thought. Suddenly she felt a hot breath in her ear. It was Polly. 'Stay away from him,' she hissed. 'He's not what he seems.' With that she glided back towards the table, professional mask in place once more.

Hannah watched her go. She didn't know what to think. Was Hannah warning her off Oliver because she wanted him for herself or was he seriously dodgy?

'Well, which is it?' demanded Sacha Komorov, his expression murderous as he glanced from Katya to Nikolai and back again.

Katya let out a tinkling laugh and turned the full wattage of her charm onto her angry husband. 'Darling Sacha, you must not take on so. Now that I think about it, I have danced with Igor, many years ago. It had slipped my mind. I welcomed him here not because of a prior connection but as a courtesy to the Moscow Ballet.

'I apologise for forgetting you, dear Igor,' she added, blowing him a kiss.

He inclined his head, but his eyes flashed in anger.

Wow, Katya is really doing a number on the men at the table, thought Hannah, suddenly feeling tired and that she couldn't put up with their nonsense for much longer. Eventually, she got the chance to escape for a much-needed break, once the guests had finished their desserts and moved to the library for coffee and brandy.

Standing outside the service entrance, she breathed deeply as she sipped her water and tried to clear her head. It had been a long tiring evening. All those fancy manners yet sniping away at each other whenever they got the chance. That Katya was a piece of work, yet all the men were falling over themselves to get her attention. Everyone except Oliver, she thought.

Suddenly, she jumped as a door slammed close to her. Angry voices drifted towards her through the open window. It was Irina Petrova and Sacha Komorov. *They must be in the housekeeper's room.* Hannah flattened herself against the wall and edged closer to make out what they were saying.

'How did you find out?' snapped Komorov.

'That is what worries you? How I found out?' Irina screeched. She sounded like she was falling apart, Hannah worried. Should she perhaps intervene? No, she had to stick it out. It could have a bearing on the case.

'You've wanted for nothing all these years,' said Komorov. 'I've taken care of you.'

'You take care of me?' Irina snorted. 'Boot is on other foot. I am the one who runs your house. I manage more than you will ever know so that the great Sacha Komorov has easy life like pampered poodle.'

'I pay you well,' he said, now sounding defensive.

'You stupid man. You understand nothing!' she screamed. There was a sound of something smashing. Hannah flinched. What on earth was going on? Irina was going to get her marching orders at this rate.

'I saved you from a life of squalor,' he said. 'I gave you respectability, a position and protection. I had no obligation to do any of these things. What have I done wrong apart from not burden you with the truth?'

The screams had given way to helpless sobbing.

'My father was a brute. He ruled his family with his fists. A mean drunk, he would lay into my mother and me as if we were grown men not a woman and child. He was disgusting and depraved. From a young age I burned with rage under his tyrannical rule.'

'I have no memory of him,' said Irina. 'My mother was angry and bitter. She told me nothing.'

'I remember your mother coming to our door to beg for help. You were ill and she needed money for the doctor. You were only about three and had the biggest brown eyes but you looked feverish and malnourished. Just a skinny scrap of a thing. My mother was a good woman. Despite the circumstances she gave you what she could spare. I was only ten at the time but I slipped out and followed you both home to see where you lived. When I returned my mother was weeping at the kitchen table and told me who you were. She said to say nothing to my father or he would give your mother a beating for coming to his door.'

'So, I was your father's dirty secret,' snapped Irina. 'Why did you seek me out in Moscow?'

'I would be lying if I said I felt any kinship towards you. But I did feel a sense of duty and responsibility. You had looked so small and fragile that night. It stayed with me. I resolved to better your situation and I have,' he said. 'You cannot deny it. I sent for you to work for me as soon as I was able. You were a beautiful young woman. Soon, you would have faced difficult choices in life. I gave you stability and a future you would not have had otherwise.'

'I still had the right to know the truth,' Irina said, quieter now. 'We don't even look alike.'

'You take after my father,' he sighed. 'His eyes are brown like yours and Nikolai's.'

'Nikolai,' she said, her voice laced with contempt. 'A connection I do not welcome. This changes things,' she said, her distress mounting again. 'If only I had known before...'

Hannah's glass slipped from her hand and smashed on the cobbles.

'What was that?' snapped Komorov. Hannah heard the sound of footsteps approaching the window and fled.

TWENTY-THREE

Grace glanced around the library, wondering where their host was. That had been one tense meal. Katya must have zero respect for Sacha if she was willing to flirt so shamelessly under his nose like that. It was as if he no longer mattered to her. She had read somewhere that once you started treating your partner with contempt the marriage was usually on the rocks. A cloud of exquisite perfume announced the arrival of Katya at her side. She looked extremely pleased with herself.

'Are you *crazy*?' whispered Grace. 'Shouldn't you be trying to keep a low profile?'

'I don't agree. Why not flush them out into the open? You are here. You take care of them. Problem goes away.'

'Er...' Grace began. How to explain that her role as PI did not encompass all that Katya clearly thought that it did?

'Katya, over here!' shouted Nikolai, patting a seat beside him on a leather chesterfield. She rolled her eyes at Grace then whirled towards her brother-in-law, all smiles and flirtatious banter.

'Trollop,' whispered a voice behind her.

Grace swung round and found herself staring into the hard

eyes and brittle smile of Hilary Hamilton. 'Sorry, didn't mean to say that out loud.' She grimaced. 'Let me introduce myself, Hilary Hamilton.'

'Grace McKenna. You find her a bit much?' said Grace.

'More than a bit. She has a husband who adores her. Why does she make it her personal mission to ensnare every other man in the room?'

'Including yours?' asked Grace.

'Harris is no saint, but he's devoted to his family. Nowadays, he reserves most of his mischief for Sacha. They share similar interests and compete with each other relentlessly in collecting art. Can't see the point of it myself. I'd sooner have a nice print you can put on the wall and enjoy than have something stashed away in a vault somewhere never to see the light of day.'

Grace found herself warming to her unexpectedly. 'I understand where you're coming from to a certain extent but as I make a living writing about art, without that obsession I might not have many readers. Although, I can't help feeling at times that my profession is rather parasitical with this whole industry feeding off the talent of the artist.'

'We all have our part to play in the food chain, Grace; I wouldn't be too hard on yourself. Where is Sacha anyway?' Hilary asked, looking around the room. 'He's been gone ages. I do hope Katya's flirting hasn't upset him.'

'Oh, I doubt she means anything by it,' said Grace. 'Do you work, Hilary?'

'Yes, I'm an interior designer.'

'Really? I would love to see your work.'

'Why not come over for coffee some time? I can show you the interior of Balhousie and also some pictures of other commissions I've undertaken. Here's my card. I'll be expecting your call.' With that, she smiled and glided off to network with someone else.

'Hello. Oliver Compton-Ross, Sacha's curator,' said the man

who'd arrived in front of her, sticking out his hand for her to shake. 'And you are?'

'Grace McKenna, freelance art journalist. Are you enjoying the evening?'

'Great food, scintillating company,' he said, turning on the charm. 'How could I not? I saw you talking with Hilary. Nice woman but never misses a chance to boost her business,' he said.

Grace turned to look at him. His handsome face was flushed from alcohol. 'I understand you used to work for them,' said Grace.

A shadow passed across his cherubic face. 'My, you've done your homework,' he said in a voice that wasn't entirely pleasant, giving her an assessing stare.

'Hilary mentioned it,' she lied. 'Wasn't it you who procured the Imperial Egg for our host?' she said in a low voice.

'I was one of the links in the chain,' he admitted.

'Doesn't it bother you that all these wealthy collectors effectively hide away the treasures of the world for their own private consumption?'

'I'd be in the wrong line of business if it did.' He grinned. 'For me it's all about the thrill of the chase. The foreign travel and commission don't hurt either.'

'I suppose you must have your own growing treasure trove by now. I assume you too have got the collecting bug,' she said, her smile open and friendly.

He looked at her sideways as if trying to work out if she was insinuating anything untoward then seemed to relax.

'You would think so, wouldn't you? If anything, my job has sent me the other way. Most of the people I know who collect these precious objects hide them away from view. The excitement of the acquisition soon wears off and they're obsessed with getting something else. To me, the most important thing that money can buy is unfettered freedom.'

'Don't you feel that Sacha is free?' she asked.

'There are many different types of prison,' he said, glancing towards Katya as he spoke.

'Aren't you going to join Katya and her admirers?' she teased.

'Fools, the lot of them,' he said, sending a dismissive glance in their direction.

'Why do you say that?'

'Everything about her is superficial. Crack her open and you'd find her missing a heart.'

Grace strove to hide her surprise at such a vehement reaction. Could he perhaps have made a pass at Katya and she turned him down? Could love have turned to hate? 'She's a bit out there but I guess being dramatic goes with the territory in her line of work.'

'Work?' he snorted. 'She doesn't know the meaning of the word. Not anymore.'

'That's hardly fair,' interjected Grace. 'She did sustain a terrible injury through no fault of her own. I think it's commendable that she's still dancing at all let alone capable of what I've seen her do with Igor over there.'

His head snapped round, eyes narrowed. 'She's dancing with *him*? Don't you know who he is?'

'Of course, he's a ballet dancer from the Moscow Ballet. Everyone knows that,' she replied, puzzled.

'He's only the one who dropped her and ended her career,' Oliver said, his eyes gleaming with an unsavoury glee.

'But I thought he'd disappeared after that. The person who dropped her had a completely different name and dark hair, not blond. I'm sure of it. You must be mistaken,' said Grace, puzzled.

'I overheard Katya and Viktor arguing about it. It's him all right.'

'Does Sacha know? That it was him, I mean?'

'Your guess is as good as mine.' He shrugged. 'Excuse me.'

He moved away to talk to someone else.

Grace looked around. Where *was* Sacha? There was no sign of Hannah either. Polly was bustling about collecting cups and refreshing glasses, looking a bit harassed, but Hannah was nowhere to be seen.

Slipping out of the room, she went looking for her. The cool of the stone-flagged corridors revived her and the thick stone walls swallowed up the inane drink-fuelled chatter. Her feet were killing her and she could do with going home but first she had to find Hannah. There was no way she was leaving her here alone at night. *Where is everyone?* she wondered. Somewhat at a loss, she headed downstairs towards the kitchen. Rounding the corner, she almost collided with a tearstained Hannah heading in the opposite direction. She grabbed her by the shoulders.

'Hannah. What is it? What's happened?'

Hannah collapsed against her in relief.

'It's Irina Petrova. She's dead!'

TWENTY-FOUR

Grace gave Hannah a quick hug then released her. 'Show me,' she said, snapping back into professional mode.

Hannah nodded and wiped away her tears. 'This way,' she said, leading Grace along the narrow corridors until she paused outside the housekeeper's room. The door was still ajar.

'Wait here,' said Grace. She pushed open the door and stood on the threshold, taking in the scene before her.

Irina Petrova lay collapsed at an unnatural angle in her wing-backed chair. Her eyes were wide and staring, her face stretched into a rictus of pain. Her mouth had foam at the corners. Grace quickly checked for signs of life but even though her body was warm to the touch she knew deep down it was hopeless. If she had to hazard a guess, she would say cause of death was poisoning. Before her on a side table was an over-turned cup of tea and a tumbler with a small amount of clear liquid. She sniffed it cautiously without picking it up. Vodka, most probably. Quickly she pulled her phone out of her pocket and took careful photos of the scene. There was no sign of a disturbance. Carefully she retraced her steps to the open door.

Hannah was waiting for her on the other side, her eyes dark against the pallor of her face.

'So, what do we do?' she asked.

In answer, Grace took out her phone and called Brodie. He picked up quickly.

'Brodie, it's Grace. I'm at Traprain Castle. There's been a suspicious death... It's the housekeeper, Irina Petrova, I think she may have ingested poison... No idea if it's by her own hand or not... No way of telling it it's accident, suicide or murder... Okay, will do.' She ended the call.

'Is he coming out?' asked Hannah.

'That depends, he'll need to speak to his boss who'll decide who's coming. I doubt a team will arrive for an hour or so though they might whisk out a couple of uniformed officers to preserve the scene earlier than that. They'll also need to send out the duty police surgeon to formally pronounce life extinct.'

Hannah raised her eyebrows and inclined her head. 'Isn't it... er... obvious?'

'Doesn't matter. This case will be reported to the procurator fiscal. He will then order a post mortem, which will happen in the next day or two. The body will be removed to the mortuary at the Royal Infirmary, taking care to preserve any trace evidence that may be on or around it. In the meantime, one of us needs to remain here outside the door to prevent anyone else entering. Are you able to do that?'

Hannah shivered but nodded her head firmly. 'Yes,' she said.

'I'll check on you in a little while. I need to go and find Sacha and Viktor Levitsky. Don't let Viktor into the scene, even if he throws his weight around.'

'I'll try and stop him,' said Hannah doubtfully.

Grace walked away.

'Wait!' Hannah called to her departing back. 'I heard Sacha

and Irina arguing earlier; Irina was Sacha's half sister. They had the same father.'

'What?' said Grace, startled. 'Are you sure?'

'Yes, I was outside the staff entrance taking a break when I heard Sacha and her arguing in here through the window.'

'Did Sacha reveal they were related while you were listening?'

'No. I got the impression someone else had told her and it had come as a total shock.'

'It's getting late and the guests are drunk and getting rowdy. I must find Sacha and notify Viktor before the police arrive. Although, Sacha may already know.'

'You think he killed her?' asked Hannah.

'I really have no idea.'

Running lightly up the stairs, Grace could still feel the adrenaline swirling round her body. Could Sacha really have murdered his half sister in cold blood? Who else could have had a motive? She didn't envy the police their task of trying to prise information out of this secretive household.

Her first port of call was the drawing room. Sacha was in the thick of his guests, his earlier mood apparently forgotten as he threw his head back and laughed at something his wife was saying in his ear. Before approaching, Grace stood at the threshold scanning the occupants of the room for any tell-tale signs of stress or agitation but there were none. She moved across to Sacha Komorov when his wife's attention was diverted elsewhere and asked him to follow her outside.

'I'm afraid I have some bad news,' she said, turning to face him.

'Tell me!' he commanded. 'Is it to do with the theft of the Imperial Egg?'

'No, something much worse, I'm afraid. Irina Petrova has been found dead in her office.'

He staggered back against the wall, his face draining of colour. 'What? No, you are mistaken. It's not possible.'

'Hannah found her collapsed in her seat. I'm afraid there is no doubt.'

'A heart attack? But she was so young,' he said, his lower lip trembling and his eyes moist.

Either he was a consummate actor, or his grief was genuine. 'The police have been called.'

'*You* called the police,' he said, his eyes frantic now with something else. Could it be fear? 'You had no right.'

'I had every right,' she shot back at him. 'What were you going to do? Bury her in the rose garden?'

'Of course not,' he muttered.

'Besides, at the time you were nowhere to be seen.'

'Can I see her?' he asked.

'Not here,' Grace replied. 'Once cause of death has been established, arrangements can be made for you to pay your respects. Does she have any family that needs to be contacted?'

'No, nobody,' he said, his voice cracking.

'Apart from you,' she said, her voice level.

'You know? Who told you?'

'Hannah overheard a conversation through the window when she was having her break.'

'Must I tell the police?'

'Yes, it's crucial information. Someone needs to claim the body.' *In death if not in life*, Grace thought sadly. 'It's important that no one is allowed to leave until the police arrive. They will want contact details from everyone present.'

'I had better make an announcement and end the party,' said Sacha, moving away from her.

Grace caught hold of his sleeve. 'I would wait until the police get here.'

'How can I go back in there and act as if nothing has happened?' he asked, his voice rough with emotion.

'Why not sit in the library until they arrive?' Grace said. 'I'll go in for a bit then head back downstairs.'

Grace felt the heat and noise hit her as soon as she walked back into the drawing room. She noticed Igor and Katya spring apart as she entered then relax when they saw it was only her. They weren't even trying to conceal their closeness. Oliver was flirting with the attractive young woman at the small bar in the corner and the Hamiltons were laughing at something Nikolai had said to them. She couldn't detect the slightest atmosphere. Everything was as it should be except that two floors beneath them a woman lay dead.

TWENTY-FIVE

Grace arrived back downstairs to find a shouting match going on between Hannah and Viktor Levitsky. Hannah was standing firmly in front of the closed door, refusing to budge. Neither of them heard her approach. Hannah looked close to tears.

'Viktor, the police are on their way. This needs to be treated as a crime scene meantime. Hannah was quite right to follow my instructions not to let you enter. If you persist, the police will be informed and perhaps wonder at the nature of your interest,' she added sharply.

'Fine,' he snapped, turning away from the door. The anger drained away from his face as he seemed to make a concerted attempt to calm down. 'I don't know why you didn't come and get me right away instead of involving such a junior member of staff.'

'I looked for you but you were nowhere to be found,' said Grace. 'Your boss is in the library. He's pretty cut up about it.'

'He is?' said Viktor, raising an eyebrow.

Clearly Sacha hadn't told him either, thought Grace. So, who could possibly have mentioned it to Irina?

'How did Irina die?' Viktor asked quietly now. 'Heart attack, do you think?'

'No, I doubt that,' said Grace, shaking her head. 'It's going to be a matter for the police. There will need to be a post mortem.'

Viktor went pale as though it was only now sinking in. He swallowed and Grace suspected he was fighting down nausea. She had to be mindful of the possibility he had perhaps been involved with Irina once upon a time.

'Not murder?'

Grace shrugged helplessly. 'Look, I really don't know. You're going to have to be patient for now. Why don't you leave Hannah and I here until the police arrive? They're going to want names and addresses for everyone here. As soon as the police arrive the guests are going to want to leave. Sacha will need your help until the police make it upstairs. There's nothing you can do here.'

Viktor nodded, knowing when he was beat and left them there.

'Thanks, Grace, I really think he was on the verge of shoving me aside and going in there.'

'You did really well and we didn't even have to break your cover,' said Grace, patting her arm.

'I hope the police don't take much longer,' said Hannah.

They were both seated outside the dead housekeeper's room on upright chairs Grace had brought from the empty kitchen. The cook had departed for the night before the body had been discovered. The harsh strip lighting of the passageway together with the pale green walls threw Hannah's pallor and the sharp angles of her face into focus She always looked like she was verging on malnourished, which worried Grace. She glanced at her watch.

'Shouldn't be much longer now.'

'Do you think she could have killed herself, Grace?' asked Hannah, her eyes looking almost bruised with fatigue.

'It's possible,' said Grace. 'From what you said she was in a state of heightened emotion.'

'I just don't get how someone can do that,' said Hannah, her voice rising. 'There's always another good day around the corner. To just check out and leave everyone else to deal with your mess, that's just not on.'

Grace knew that she was no longer talking about Irina Petrova. She hesitated, not sure what to say. They'd never talked about Connor's death before. It remained an impenetrable wall between them. Her phone pinged. 'That's them here,' she said. 'I told them to come to the staff entrance. Can you nip along and let them in?'

Grace could hear the crunch of tyres on gravel and see the flash of lights through the still open window. No sirens, thank goodness, or they'd all be down here in a flash creating mayhem. She shivered, her flimsy dress no match for the chill of a Scottish night. Her feet felt numb in her fancy shoes, and she thought longingly of her cosy trainers.

Seconds later she could hear Brodie's voice as he strode along the corridor. She could hear Hannah filling him in as she walked alongside him. She was relieved that he had caught the case.

'Grace, I've brought a team with me.' He paused on the threshold of the room, already attired in a forensic suit, his shrewd eyes assessing the scene. Another car drew up outside.

'That'll be the police surgeon,' he said.

Seconds later a middle-aged man rushed in. Grace hadn't seen him before.

'Dr Reynolds,' he announced. He took one look though the open door to Irina's room and shook his head. After covering his feet in plastic covers from his pocket, he approached the stricken housekeeper and felt for a pulse. Then he retreated to the others standing grouped together outside. 'Life pronounced extinct.'

'Could she have ingested poison?' asked Grace.

'I certainly can't rule it out but you're going to have wait for the pathologist on that one. If it is poison, there's no way of telling if she ingested it voluntarily or it was administered forcefully. I don't see any obvious defensive wounds though.'

'Thanks, doc,' said Brodie. 'You're free to go.' He motioned for the scene examiners to proceed and a police officer took up position outside the door to prevent any unauthorised access to the scene whilst they were busy with their painstaking work.

'Hannah, are you able to give us a brief statement now?' Brodie asked. 'It would be best to do it while it's still fresh in your mind.'

Grace looked at Hannah. She was ghostly white and shivering uncontrollably. It must be the shock of it all. 'If you don't feel up to it...' she said.

Hannah lifted her chin. 'I'm fine.'

Brodie motioned to a young female PC and an older male officer.

'The kitchen's empty,' said Grace.

They introduced themselves to Hannah and walked off with her.

'I've told Sacha; he's waiting for you in the library,' Grace said.

'I'll come up and speak to Komorov in a few minutes once things are organised down here,' said Brodie. 'We'll need to round everyone up to get their details before they're allowed to leave, including any staff members. I've posted an officer at all of the known exit points in case anyone decides to make a run for it meantime.'

'There's also Viktor Levitsky, head of security, who lives in a cottage on the estate,' Grace said. 'Someone will need to speak to him, too. He went upstairs and is probably with Sacha.'

Grace left him to get on and swiftly ascended the stairs. She took her place amongst those in the drawing room. The groupings had changed slightly since she was last in there with Katya now flirting with Nikolai while Igor glowered from a corner. The noise beat inside her head like a drum. Nikolai detached himself from Katya and wandered over to speak to her, glass in hand.

'Is everything all right? I noticed that you'd been gone awhile and my pesky brother is also missing. Should I send out a search party?' he asked, smiling.

'I saw Sacha in the library,' Grace said. 'I think he had a bit of a headache. I'm sure he'll be back soon.'

'So,' he said in a whisper. 'How's the investigation going?'

For a minute, Grace froze thinking he meant the body downstairs but then relaxed again as she realised that he meant the theft of the egg.

'I'm following a number of leads,' she said. 'Have you any information you might wish to add?'

'*Moi?*' he said in mock outrage. 'Do you really think I'd pinch my dear brother's pride and joy?' Grace looked over rather pointedly at Katya and Nikolai's face stiffened in anger.

'Of course not.' She smiled. 'I simply wondered if anything might have occurred to you since we last spoke?'

'I'm afraid not, please excuse me,' he snapped and, turning on his heel, he strode over to the Hamiltons.

That certainly hit a nerve, she thought, glancing back at Katya, whose knowing smirk showed her capacity for wreaking havoc. She was on her way over to have a word with her when the door opened and Sacha walked in flanked by Brodie and two female uniformed officers. The chatter stuttered to a halt and the guests stared at them in shock.

'What's going on, Sacha?' barked Harris Hamilton, his default setting argumentative.

Sacha ran his hand through his hair and looked to Brodie for confirmation. On receiving a nod, he stepped forward further.

'I'm sorry to tell you that Irina Petrova, the castle house-keeper, has died suddenly. The cause is not known.'

There were gasps of dismay and a flurry of chatter broke out. Brodie held up his hand for silence. 'I'm DS Brodie McKenna and I must inform you that the whole staff quarters are currently out of bounds until the crime scene investigators have finished and the body has been removed. My uniformed colleagues, PC Black and PC Reid will take brief statements from all of you in turn. After you've been seen, you may leave via the front entrance.'

Everyone sat down in silence as the first two names were called out. Grace knew that with the police presence there wasn't anything further she could accomplish tonight. She sat down with everyone else.

'Grace McKenna,' shouted Brodie, pretending to consult his notebook. Meekly, she followed him out into the hall.

'Thanks, Brodie,' she said, turning on her heel to leave.

He reached out to grab her sleeve. 'Not so fast, I might as well take your statement now, while we're both here.'

'Fine,' she sighed, following him into the dining room and taking a seat at the table.

He sat across from her and pressed record on the machine. It didn't take long as there was very little she could say beyond the formalities. That done, he switched off the recorder and sat back in his chair 'So, what else can you tell me about Irina Petrova?' he asked. 'We're treating it simply as a suspicious death for now, but I suspect it will either end up as a suicide or a murder investigation. I get the impression the family are going to be cagey as hell.'

'They're not exactly over-sharers,' said Grace. 'Irina was very stern and buttoned up. She worked for Komorov in Russia, and he brought her over to start a new life in this country when he married Katya.'

'I noticed the staff quarters were quite functional yet her room was furnished with antiques and the odd valuable painting.'

'Yes,' said Grace. 'It's quite the treasure trove. Of course, now I know why. Hannah overheard a row between her and Sacha not long before she wound up dead.'

'Spill,' said Brodie, leaning forward in his seat.

Grace looked at him. 'I've a lot I can tell you, but you didn't hear it from me. I want access to the post mortem report and toxicology results and cooperation if I need something to help me solve my own two cases. Deal?'

Brodie sighed. 'You drive a hard bargain, as always. Okay, deal, within reason. Now tell me!'

'Okay. Someone had recently told Irina Petrova that she was Sacha Komorov's half sister. Apparently, he hid it from her, and she had no idea, hence the row.'

'Hence also the special treatment perhaps? That must have hurt. It perhaps goes to a motive for suicide.'

'I think you need to consider every possibility at this stage,' replied Grace.

'The post mortem is first thing in the morning,' said Brodie, 'so hopefully I'll know more then.'

'No cooked breakfast for you then,' she teased. He'd always had a weaker stomach than her back in the day when they were both on the job.

'Quite,' he said, looking faintly queasy at what lay ahead of him.

'Of course, if Sacha Komorov kept it quiet all these years, he must have had his reasons. Maybe he didn't want it getting out that his housekeeper was his half sister and having to wait on him hand and foot despite his wealth. Think of the optics on that?' said Grace.

'Komorov has a brother, doesn't he? I wonder if he knew the truth?'

'Yes. Nikolai, Sacha's much younger brother. Spoilt and entitled though very charming,' Grace said. 'Irina certainly had a poor opinion of him. She called him a hop-the-bed. I have no idea whether he knew about his half sister or not.'

'Any other angles I should know about?' he asked.

'Well, if she has in fact been poisoned, one thing did occur to me. Given that Komorov is a Russian oligarch with a somewhat chequered past, is it possible that Irina's death is some sort of warning from an enemy within Russia?'

'I hope not!' said Brodie, looking horrified at the ramifications.

'Also,' said Grace, 'it could be linked to the theft of the Imperial Egg. Whoever took the egg needed a keycard to access the lift leading down to the gallery. Komorov had one and Irina kept the other in a safe in her room. She kept the key on a chain around her neck. I suspect she was seeing someone around that time and that person may have drugged her, lifted the key and copied it before replacing it around her neck before she woke up. It would have been some time before the theft, perhaps even before the egg arrived. Then they could have got to the keycard in the safe and replaced it after the theft with no one being any the wiser.'

'Do you know who she was seeing?'

'No, I'm afraid I don't. Hannah did tell me a while back that she was having a shouting match with the head of security, Viktor Levitsky, and that he seemed a bit rough with her. It could have been him she was seeing, or it could be someone else entirely.'

Brodie groaned and ran his hands through his hair, making it stand on end like a punk rocker. Grace hid a smile.

'The trouble with this case is that there seems to be endless possibilities and very little in the way of hard evidence,' he groaned. 'Just wait until the press get hold of it. Pure sensationalism.'

'Don't worry, I'm sure things will seem a bit clearer after the PM tomorrow. You'll let me know the findings? I'm happy to help you, Brodie, but you know that it's got to be a two-way street, right?'

'Sure,' he muttered. Grace knew he hated bending the rules to share information with her, but he was pragmatic enough to accept that he needed her help and it didn't hurt to have her and Hannah embedded at the centre of things.

Grace managed to park in a street parallel to Portobello High Street facing the sea. Turning off the engine, she slumped back in the seat and cracked open the window, the sound of the waves crashing against the shore and the salt on the air calming her. Exiting the car, she wandered down to the Esplanade, tired to her very bones. Despite the fact that she had no dog to walk tonight she slipped off her high heels and sank her bruised feet into the soft cool sand as she strolled to the water's edge. She didn't have to walk very far as it was high tide. Sometimes she ached with the need for solitude and tonight was one of those nights.

Sacha Komorov and his wife, Katya, had completely drained her. Her thoughts turned to poor Irina Petrova. She could only have been in her mid-thirties, though her stern demeanour and the rigid way she held herself had at times made her seem much older than her years. Clearly, it hadn't been Sacha who had told her. Who else could have known and what was their agenda? Could it have been a spurned lover? Perhaps someone with an axe to grind against Sacha? Her mind was going round in circles, and it was getting her nowhere. Sighing, she turned and made her way up the sand and towards her flat above the office. The huge bay window was dark as she looked up at it. Normally she left a beeswax candle lit in the storm lantern late at night. One of the last little rituals she performed for her missing son.

Opening the door, the air felt stale as if it hadn't moved for a while. It wasn't the same coming home to an empty space instead of a waggy-tailed furry menace. It felt... lonely. A strange melancholy gripped her as she inhabited the uncomfortable space between exhaustion and agitation. Another possibility was that Irina had been murdered as a means of deflecting attention from the stolen Imperial Egg. It was certainly valuable enough to incite murder. That is, assuming she was murdered. She could have committed suicide. Sighing, she poured a glass of red wine and sank onto the couch, tucking her bare feet underneath her and switching on the TV as she threw a match onto the pile of kindling and logs in the stove.

TWENTY-SIX

Grace woke up early feeling shattered. Only one thing was going to make her feel human again. She sprang out of bed and pulled on her swimsuit and dry robe with some trainers then rushed downstairs and opened the door before her brain had a chance to veto the plan.

It was a glorious September day and although it was only 7.30, the sun's rays on her skin already mitigated the soft breeze coming in from the sea. She wasn't the first to set foot on the beach this morning. There were quite a few dog walkers and runners pounding the beach but no one was in the sea yet. She unzipped her dry robe and placed it out of reach of the frisky morning tide. Shivering, she stepped tentatively into the waves, speeding up as the cold pinched her nerve endings. 'It's exhilarating,' she muttered from between clenched teeth. This would be less of an assault on the senses if she lived in Greece.

As she dived underneath the water and struck powerfully out from the shore, her thoughts drifted as they always did to her son, forever sixteen. Seeing Hannah growing and developing into such an amazing young woman, she ached for what might have been. He never even got to lay eyes on his own son.

Did he even know that Hannah was pregnant when he decided to end his life? Or was it that piece of news that tipped him over the edge? Grace never pressured Hannah for more than the few facts she had revealed. It would all come out in time when she was ready. As she settled into her natural rhythm, she wondered what her life would look like now had Connor not died. Would she and Brodie still be together if their lives had continued on the same track? If she was being honest, she had to admit to herself that she didn't know. They were both different people now. Back then she had been relentlessly career driven, whilst Brodie followed more sedately in her glittering wake, picking up the slack at home. She burned with shame when she remembered how she had resisted the idea of a second child to avoid losing career momentum. Brodie, on the other hand, had been happy to be the glue that held everything together. Grief and her subsequent breakdown had changed her, rounded off her sharp edges and humbled her, bringing a new perspective. Her heart had leapt at the thought that he might be cooling towards Julie. The way he had looked at her when she opened the door to him last night had sent a shiver down her spine. It had to be his decision though. She needed to take a step back.

As she stopped to tread water and take in the beauty of the morning, Grace felt grateful to be alive. Poor Irina Petrova would have no more sunny days to feast her eyes on. As she struck back out for the distant shoreline her mind shifted to the two cases she was working on. How would Irina's death impact on her investigations? In relation to the Imperial Egg, she'd certainly had the means and opportunity to steal it. However, if that was the case then she must have been working in collusion with someone else at the very least. Or could she have been compelled under duress? Hannah had said that Viktor Levitsky had been gripping her arm and seemed to be threatening her. Also, although overnight guests weren't permitted for the staff, she felt she had landed a blow when it came to her suggestion to

Irina that someone may have drugged her and removed the key to have a copy made while she was asleep. If only she had pushed harder at the time. If that had been the case, who could it have been? Viktor Levitsky? There was something off about him. He didn't seem as concerned as he should have been about someone stealing such a precious item right from under his nose. She sighed and then spluttered as salty water forced its way up her nose, burning the back of her mouth, causing her to break her stroke and right herself.

As her feet hit the sand, she felt a surge of determination as she shrugged on her dry robe and headed up to the Esplanade to get ready for work.

TWENTY-SEVEN

Grace arrived in the office just after Jean, who was settling down to work with Harvey at her feet. He was so excited to see her that he nearly knocked her over as he zoomed round her in circles, wagging his tale like a windscreen wiper, making small noises in the back of his throat. She dropped down to his level and made a fuss of him.

'Thanks so much for looking after him, Jean. I hope he wasn't too much bother?'

'A model house guest.' Jean grinned. 'He's welcome any time. How did it go last night?'

'A complete and unmitigated disaster,' groaned Grace.

'Why? What happened?' Jean asked.

Grace rapidly caught her up on the evening's events.

'Well, that rather complicates things, doesn't it? Poison, you say?'

'It appears likely. But whether she was poisoned or whether she took it herself in light of Sacha's revelation, I have no idea.'

'At least Brodie has caught the case. You know you can work with him and he'll share information if he can.'

'Yes,' said Grace.

The door opened and in came Hannah. The tired, pinched look of last night was gone from her face and she looked raring to go. *The resilience of youth*, thought Grace. Harvey did another meet and greet as Hannah sneaked him a bit of sausage she had saved from her breakfast.

'What can I do to help?' asked Jean, looking desperate to be involved.

'I know it's frustrating, Jean, but you're already helping us by keeping everything going here. I promise that if anything else occurs to me you'll be the first to know,' said Grace.

'I've plenty to keep me going here,' said Jean, with a forced smile.

'I'm heading off to the castle now. I want to catch them when they're still feeling vulnerable. I'll see you at the castle later, Hannah,' she said, stroking Harvey's silky ears before fleeing from the office in a manic burst of energy.

TWENTY-EIGHT

Grace slipped in the staff entrance and made her way up to the ground floor without encountering anyone. The house felt silent, like it was holding its breath after the terrible events of last night. She could hear the sounds of clearing up and the clink of glasses and clatter of crockery being loaded onto trays.

She arrived at the library where she tapped lightly on the door.

'Enter!' shouted an imperious voice. She walked in and her heart went out to him. Never had she seen a man look quite so miserable. 'You may as well sit down,' Sacha muttered.

She quietly sat opposite him in front of the fireplace, which contained an unlit fire that had been set by the staff. It was cold in the room, but he seemed oblivious. It seemed to match the winter in his soul.

'I'm so sorry about Irina,' she said gently.

'I like to keep my private business to myself,' he sighed.

'So do most people but it's not always possible,' she said, remembering the huge invasion of privacy she suffered herself when her son went missing, presumed drowned.

'Yes,' he said. 'You know.'

'I do,' she replied with a slight twist to her lips. 'Irina didn't know that she was related to you?'

'No,' he sighed. 'She was only my half sister. We had the same father. When I was seven, he had a child with another woman. He left her after a couple of years and came back to my mother. Then Nikolai was born three years after that. My mother died a couple of years later. My father immediately left, leaving Nikolai and I to starve in the gutter, just as he had done with Irina and her mother. Although I was only fourteen, I had to find a way to support us and stop Nikolai being taken away. It wasn't easy. I didn't forget Irina. I never felt kinship to her as our only connection was through my father but I felt she was another casualty from his actions therefore I felt a sense of duty, if not love, towards her.'

'So, when you became wealthy?'

'There was no question in my mind. I had a responsibility to her. Initially I did not envisage the situation to be long term. I sought to give her employment and train her well so she could have a sustainable future and become self supporting. I wanted to keep my distance.'

'So how come she was still with you at the time of her death?' asked Grace.

'She turned out to a quick learner and also ambitious. I decided to promote her to managing my household. She was paid a salary commensurate with her responsibilities and I arranged for her to have small touches of luxury in her private quarters. It was a satisfactory arrangement for both of us.'

'Except, you knew something that she didn't?' said Grace.

'Yes,' he sighed. 'In my defence, I really didn't see her as my half sister. It was a sense of duty that bound me to her as much as anything else. I could have left her to the careless predations of tourists but I chose to step in and mop up my father's mess. I also provided for her in my will.'

They both fell silent as they contemplated how little use that would be to her now.

'The last words I said to her were so harsh,' he said, his voice breaking.

His anguish was real. Grace was sure of it. That didn't mean that he hadn't killed her in a fit of rage. Or that he hadn't cast her into such despair that she had lost the will to live. She couldn't suggest poison though. Brodie would no doubt be along with a search warrant soon and she didn't want to tip him off so he might hurry to dispose of any evidence.

'Did Nikolai know?' she asked.

'No,' he sighed. 'He does now. He had plenty to say on the subject last night once our guests had finally left.'

'How did Katya take it?'

'She was furious. Irina and her did not get along at the best of times.' He put his head in his hands and groaned deeply.

Grace felt an urge to comfort him, but she resisted it. She had never seen Sacha display such vulnerability before but for all she knew he could be trying to manipulate her with a view to getting her on side. This was a police investigation now and she had to maintain a professional distance so as not to muddy the waters even further.

'Maybe she died of natural causes,' he said. 'It's possible, isn't it? After receiving such a painful shock perhaps her poor heart stopped beating.'

Grace very much doubted that, but it wasn't her place to speculate now that Brodie's team was involved. She was about to get up and leave when something occurred to her. 'If it wasn't you who revealed the truth to Irina, then who was it? And how on earth did they find out?'

'I have no idea,' he replied. 'Not even Viktor, my head of security, knew.'

TWENTY-NINE

Grace wondered who to tackle next. She didn't have long before the police arrived to conduct further interviews, no doubt with a search warrant in hand. For a crazy moment she wondered if the Imperial Egg could possibly still be within the confines of the castle. Imagine if Brodie uncovered it through his search. She'd have to show him the photo of it she had obtained from Sacha when he arrived.

There was something else nagging at her. Hannah had mentioned that earlier in the evening when they were all at the table eating, Irina had walked in and then suffered some kind of reaction which she had attributed to feeling a bit faint or dizzy. Looking back on that, it could either have been evidence that she was already suffering from something ingested which would lead to her death or a reaction to someone being in the room that had caught her off guard.

She paused in the hallway as she thought back to everyone who had been there. The only person that she likely hadn't come across before was the ballet dancer. But why would he evoke such a strong reaction? Irina was hardly an aficionado of the ballet. It had to be something else. But what? No, it could only have been that the seeds of her doom had already been ingested and were starting to work their way through her system. Poor woman.

A faint sound of classical music wafted towards her from the floor below. Katya must be practising again. She swiftly headed downstairs, the music becoming louder as she neared the studio. She could hear more than one pair of feet jumping. Igor must be dancing, too. She glanced in just as Katya jumped into his arms to be borne aloft above his head as he slowly spun her around. This time she concentrated on Igor rather than Katya. According to Oliver, he was the one who had dropped her in her very last public performance. She'd watched the video again earlier and now she could see it. He'd had dark hair before, not blond, and of course a different name, but the nose was the same. Katya must surely be aware. Why on earth was Sergei Nanov here and executing the very same move that had had such catastrophic consequences for her before? It made no sense. Grace was able to slip away unseen as they were too wrapped up in their dance even to notice her.

Irina had possibly recognised Igor Sokolov as she had been there that fateful night. Nikolai had been there, too, but Sacha had not. What dangerous game was Katya playing? If Igor Sokolov had harmed her once, who was to say that he might not do so again?

If Nikolai had recognised the dancer, why had he not told his brother? She didn't trust Nikolai. He exuded an air of entitlement and his feelings towards his brother seemed ambivalent at the very least. She had to ascertain what he knew before the police arrived and shut her down. She ran lightly up the stairs once more. Thank goodness she was as fit as she was. Reaching the second floor, she walked noiselessly along the plush carpet and paused outside the door leading to his suite of rooms. Hearing no sound coming from inside, she rapped lightly on the door. Not a sound in response. Hesitating, she looked around her then tried the handle. To her surprise the door gave way and she slipped inside. Swiftly ascertaining that the suite was indeed empty, she started looking around urgently. Opening his bedside drawers, she found the usual tangle of chargers, remote controls and other paraphernalia that might be expected. A handsome ottoman was stacked with designer clothes and underwear. No baggy tracksuit bottoms and scruffy T-shirts in this guy's life. Despite feeling that it was hopeless, she searched every drawer until the last one yielded a surprise. Some very expensive female lingerie and a silk kimono that had not come from the high street. So, who was his lady friend?

She rushed to the large marble bathroom to continue her investigation. Out of the open window she could hear two cars advancing up the driveway. A quick glance revealed Brodie at the wheel of one and a squad car following. She'd better be quick. Opening the medicine cabinet, she rifled through the contents, noting that it contained a selection of expensive male and female toiletries. There was nothing she could identify as implicating him in Irina's death. However, she did find a beautiful replica Fabergé egg in his desk drawer. She fiddled about to open the catch, which took longer than it should have due to her haste. There was nothing inside, although something had clearly been carefully removed as she could see where it had been previously attached. A gift for Katya? Or was he intending to leave her a twisted message?

Quietly she let herself out and went in search of Katya, hoping she was back in her room by now. She tapped lightly on the door. Katya opened it a crack and peered out. Her eyes narrowed when she saw Grace standing there as though she was a most unwelcome intrusion. She was still wearing her practice clothes and her forehead was beaded with sweat.

'Now is not a good time...' she began. 'I need a shower...'

'Quick,' whispered Grace, trying to create a sense of

urgency as she glanced behind her. 'The police are here. I need to talk to you.'

Katya sighed and opened the door. 'Sit,' she said, trying but failing to hide her impatience. 'What is this about?'

'You know that Irina Petrova was found dead last night during the party?'

'Yes, of course. But what does that have to do with me?'

'Did you know that Irina Petrova was Sacha's sister before last night?'

Katya laughed. It was an unkind sound that spilled out of her mouth. 'Of course not! I could hardly believe it.'

'If it's any consolation Irina had no idea either.'

'I saw the way she looked at me, like she hated me for existing. Well, I hated her, too,' she burst out. Katya clamped her hand over her mouth as though aware she had said too much. 'I didn't mean it,' she said, her voice trembling.

'I expect it's the shock,' said Grace, pouring her a glass of water from her nightstand. She changed tack. 'Is Igor still here?'

'No, he left a few minutes ago.'

'Do you know where his company are staying?'

'Yes. The Royal Hotel. He dances tonight at King's Theatre.'

'I know who he really is, Katya,' Grace said, with utter conviction in her voice if not her heart.

'Igor Sokolov, that is who he is,' she said, her eyes narrowed and watchful.

'Sergei Nanov, the dancer who dropped you and ended your career.'

'How dare you say this!' Katya shouted, eyes flashing with rage. 'It's not true.'

Grace folded her arms and just looked at her. 'Does Sacha know his real identity?'

'Sacha does not like me to dance much. He worries. Igor is gone now. Nothing to discuss.'

'These incidents you told me about, the ballerina with the smashed leg, the funny-tasting wine, the letters. Is it not possible that Igor is your stalker?' asked Grace. 'Certainly, if he's the one who dropped you, he's already hurt you once. Might he be prepared to do so again?' Grace caught a flash of worry chase across Katya's beautiful face. She pressed home her advantage. 'Did you know that Irina was in the audience that night? The night that he dropped you?'

'No. I didn't,' she snapped. 'What is your point?'

'Irina is dead. Perhaps she recognised Igor when she saw him?'

Katya's face drained of colour as she took in the implications of what Grace was saying. 'It wasn't Igor. I'm sure of it. Irina probably took her own life due to finding out she was Sacha's half sister. That makes more sense.'

'I need you to level with me, Katya. Your life may depend upon it. Has there been any more contact from the stalker since we last spoke?'

'I will only tell you if you accept Igor had nothing to do with it. Yes, it was him who dropped me, but he had no choice. I have forgiven him.'

'Tell me,' Grace demanded, her pulse accelerating.

Katya walked over to her wardrobe and, reaching into the back of it, she pulled out a plastic bag. It contained a green Fabergé egg with a gold criss-cross pattern and a ballerina doll with smashed legs.

'When was this left for you?'

'Last night,' she admitted. 'It was on my pillow when I returned to my room after giving my statement.'

'I'm going to need to give this to Brodie to have it dusted for prints,' said Grace in a voice that brooked no argument.

'I told you, no police!' Katya shouted.

Grace realised that she wasn't just having a strop, she was genuinely terrified. 'We can't keep this to ourselves any longer.

A murder may have been committed. The two crimes may or may not be connected but the stalker seems to be escalating.'

'I feel he draws close now,' Katya muttered.

'Exactly. We need to utilise the resources of the police. DS McKenna can be very discreet. We have worked together before many times. You can trust him.'

'Very well,' Katya sighed. 'But I know that you are wrong about Igor.'

Grace wasn't so sure.

THIRTY

Hannah sat in the kitchen beside Polly, her hands wrapped round a mug of hot strong coffee. Sandra, the cook, came and sat across from them at the long wooden table with a mug of her own.

'I still can't believe it,' the older woman said with a sigh. 'We may have had our differences but to die like that, completely out of the blue. It's just so sad.'

'Did you know her well?' asked Hannah.

'As well as anyone, I suppose. She liked to keep her distance from the rest of us. I often thought she must be lonely. This job was all she had in life really.'

'Did she not even have a boyfriend?' asked Hannah.

'Chance would be a fine thing,' Polly sniggered.

Hannah shot her a look and Polly looked cross.

'Look, just because she's dead doesn't mean I have to pretend like we were besties or something.'

'There have only been two gentlemen callers as far as I can recollect,' the cook said. 'One of them was Viktor Levitsky, the head of security. That only lasted a few months before she dumped him. I don't think he took it too well. The other was a local teacher from North Berwick. Nice man, she'd have had a good life with him.'

'How did they meet?' asked Hannah.

'I believe he came to give her and Katya English lessons when they first got here.'

'Can you remember his name?' asked Hannah.

'Why so interested?' asked the cook, narrowing her eyes.

'My mum volunteers at a refugee centre. They're always looking for English teachers there.'

'Let me think,' said the cook, scrunching up her face with effort. 'It was a while ago now. Graham something. Graham... Mackie, that's it.'

'Thanks,' said Hannah. 'I'll pass his name on to my mum.'

'That head of security is downright creepy,' said Polly, shuddering and giving a fleeting glance over her shoulder.

'I believe he used to work with the FSB,' whispered Sandra.

'Who are they when they're at home?' asked Polly.

'The modern version of the KGB,' replied Sandra.

'Who told you that?' said Hannah, widening her eyes.

'My last employer, Harris Hamilton. I'd give Viktor a wide berth if I were you.'

'I bet he could strangle you with his bare hands,' whispered Polly.

Hannah didn't doubt it after witnessing his encounter with Irina. 'I didn't know you used to work there. What were they like to work for?' she asked.

'Mrs Hamilton wasn't bad. She treated you like a human being when he wasn't there. Her husband was so pernickety I couldn't stand it. I would cook a perfectly good restaurant-quality meal and he would send it back on some pretext when it was just the family dining. He always had to have the upper hand. Made my blood boil, he did. In fact, I once dreamt I cut him up, stuffed him in a casserole and put it in the oven.'

Both girls burst out laughing.

'You're scaring me now, Mrs D.' Polly grinned.

'What about the wages?' asked Hannah.

The cook's mouth curled in a sneer. 'You're better off here, put it that way. Polly used to work for the Hamiltons, too,' said the cook.

'You never said.' Hannah turned and stared at Polly, who had turned red and looked irritated.

'Why would I? We just work together. It's not as though we're friends.' With that, she muttered about having work to do and took herself off, leaving Hannah staring after her in astonishment.

'Just ignore her, love. Got a bit of a short fuse, that one. Me and my big mouth. I forgot there was a bit of a problem at the Hamiltons'. I assume it was some kind of man trouble. They still gave her a reference so it couldn't have been all that bad. I don't think she likes to be reminded of it.'

Hannah got up to go. 'Thanks for the coffee, Mrs D. I'd best get on, too, though it's hard to think about work with all this drama going on.'

'I know exactly what you mean, lass. They'd best not be expecting anything fancy for their lunch or they'll be sorely disappointed.'

THIRTY-ONE

Grace was walking along the landing after leaving Katya's room when she heard the sound of approaching footsteps coming up the stairs. It must be Brodie and his team. Her first instinct was to cast about for somewhere to hide. The last thing she wanted was for him to accuse her of meddling in his investigation. Hurriedly, she slipped into the room beside Katya's at the end of the first floor, preparing an excuse should it be occupied. Her breath caught in her throat as she realised that she had stumbled into the nursery that Hannah had mentioned to her. It was excruciatingly sad. A room crafted with such love and expectation, waiting for a child that would never arrive. It was one thing for Katya to decide she didn't want a child but to lie to Sacha by taking the pill behind his back seemed cruel. She walked around admiring everything. There were beautifully crafted wooden toys including a toy train, an exquisite hand-painted nest of dolls and a ballerina doll in the costume of the Sugar Plum Fairy. How sad to think that none of these items would ever be played with. She listened but all was quiet and the temptation proved irresistible. She pulled the string on the mobile above the cot and sat dreamily in the hand-carved rocking chair, her mind drifting off to when Connor was just a baby. He'd been so tiny but feisty with it. He'd quite worn her out with his constant crying in that first year, but she'd give anything now to repeat the experience, not realising what a short time she would have to love him.

There was a quiet tap at the door and Brodie entered, closing the door behind him. 'Grace, what are you doing in here?' He took in the tear tracks that she hastily wiped away. 'Are you all right?'

She nodded, slowly standing up. 'I'm fine. It catches me off guard every now and again, that's all.'

Brodie took in his surroundings. 'What's all this about? I thought Komorov didn't have any children?'

'He doesn't. It's an expression of hope, I suppose. Hannah discovered that his wife is on the pill, but she's hidden it from him.'

'You never know what's going on behind closed doors in a marriage.'

They stared at each other. Grace was the first to look away. Time to get this conversation back on track. 'What happened at the post mortem this morning?'

'Grace, you know I can't...'

'Yes, you can, Brodie. Quid pro quo, remember? I have just as much skin in the game as you have here. I have two unsolved cases and a reputation to consider. I don't doubt that one or both of these cases may have some bearing on the murder, if indeed that's what it was.'

'If it were to get out that I'd been feeding you information, Grace...'

'I'll keep my mouth shut, Brodie. You know I will.'

'Fine,' he sighed. 'We've opened a murder investigation. The toxicology results aren't back yet but the pathologist said all the signs are consistent with poisoning.'

'Could she have killed herself?'

'Unlikely. There was no note. If her motive was due to being upset by Sacha's revelation, she had no time to source the poison. It's unlikely, though not impossible, that she had some simply lying around.'

'Defensive wounds?'

'None. It appears that she was completely unaware when she ingested the poison. It was probably in the tea but tests are ongoing.'

'Poor woman,' said Grace. 'We need to figure out a motive.'

'You think?' he said drily. 'What have you got so far from your dealings with the household?'

'Well, one possibility is Sacha Komorov himself. The night she died they were heard arguing because Irina had found out from an undisclosed person that she was his half sister. He obviously hadn't told her for a reason. Maybe he didn't want it coming out?'

'A bit of a risky strategy since he didn't know who had spilled the beans in the first place,' said Brodie.

'I know. Perhaps he simply panicked?'

'Who else?'

'There was no love lost between Irina and Katya. Perhaps Katya killed her to prevent Sacha finding out that Igor Sokolov's real name is Sergei Nanov.'

'Is that name supposed to mean anything to me?' asked Brodie.

'Sorry, he was the ballet dancer who ended her career. Irina was there that night in Moscow when it happened.'

'Nothing concrete, then,' said Brodie.

'Not yet,' said Grace. 'It could also be linked to the cases I'm working on. Perhaps Irina discovered something incriminating and someone killed her before she could reveal it,' said Grace.

'It would happen on the night of a dinner party,' said Brodie. 'So, we have to add everyone present into the mix.'

'I'd look at the head of security, Viktor Levitsky,' said Grace.

'He may have committed the murder on someone else's orders. He's rumoured to be former FSB.'

'That's all we need,' said Brodie, 'but thanks for the tip. Watch your back, Grace.'

'You, too,' she said, leaving the tranquillity of the nursery before him. Probably best if she wasn't seen being too chatty with the police.

THIRTY-TWO

Grace sat at her desk deep in thought nursing a hot chocolate. Jean and Hannah sat across from her holding mugs of their own. Harvey snored gently on her stockinged feet, keeping them warm.

'I feel like the investigations need to branch out a bit,' said Grace. 'We need to try and connect with people from outside the castle walls. It will give us a wider context within which to place the household to give us a chance of evaluating how truthful they are actually being with us.'

'If I was at work and people were asking me questions about my employers, I would be worried about my answers getting back to them,' said Hannah. 'I'd be more likely to open up, have a moan or whatever, if I was somewhere I felt comfortable.'

'Duly noted,' said Grace, frowning at her.

'I didn't mean...' began Hannah.

'I know.' Grace grinned. 'Just messing with you.'

'I hate it when she does that,' muttered Hannah to Jean.

'Igor Sokolov is a bit of a mystery, isn't he?' said Jean. 'He seemed to vanish off the face of the earth after the accident five years ago then all of a sudden he's back with the Moscow Ballet dancing in Edinburgh.'

'Not to mention dancing with Katya again doing the exact same lift from which he dropped her and ended her career,' said Grace.

'Right under her husband's nose,' said Jean.

'If *he'd* wound up dead, I could understand it,' said Hannah, 'but what connection does he have to Irina? Although, she did take a bit of a turn when she walked in the dining room that night. Maybe she recognised him?'

'That would give both him and Katya a motive to silence her,' said Grace grimly. 'Have you had any luck filling in the blanks where he's concerned, Jean?'

'I've been in touch with an investigative agency in Russia,' said Jean. 'I was struggling to find anything about him under either name online. It appears that Sergei Nanov left the Bolshoi the night of the accident. He doesn't crop up in any of their subsequent performances, nor is he listed as a member of the company after that date. A few weeks later, Igor Sokolov makes an appearance in a regional theatre dancing in the chorus. His hair is blond and after a year he starts being given principal roles and ultimately joins the Moscow Ballet two years ago where he has been ever since. No one seems to have made the connection due to the different name and altered appearance.'

'So, hiding in plain sight,' said Grace. 'But was he hiding because he was guilty of causing harm to Katya or because he thought he might be harmed as well?'

'The Moscow Ballet are still in town,' said Jean. 'It's their last performance at King's Theatre tonight before they return to Russia. He's never met me. What if I go along to the performance and try to get backstage afterwards as a devoted fan or a reporter for some high-brow magazine? It would be easy to fake a press pass.'

'I could come along as well but we'd not let on we know each other. Separate seats etc,' said Grace. 'That's if we can pick up a couple of single seats at this late stage.'

'There's usually a few single seats speckled about. I'll book them,' replied Jean.

'Phew! I thought for a minute you might want me to go as well.' Hannah grinned. 'Watching ballet for two solid hours would be torture.'

'Philistine,' said Grace, pulling a face at her. 'No, Hannah, you've done enough for today. You get off home. Jean, you'd best get off and put your glad rags on. I'll pick you up at seven.' Both members of her team scooted off with a spring in their step for different reasons.

'Right, boy, chop chop,' said Grace, nudging her sleeping dog awake. 'Time for a walkie before your supper.' Locking up the office, she headed down to the beach with Harvey in tow. She was bone tired but knew she would get a second wind later. This case was taking it out of her, not least because Brodie was involved. Part of her loved him being around but the wiser part knew that it made it harder for her to heal; she had to accept that he was with Julie now and likely always would be.

As Harvey frisked along the beach at the water's edge trying to kill a piece of seaweed, she breathed in the cooling salty air and tried to relax her shoulders. The sun was setting earlier now and the evenings were crisper as autumn started to take hold. Her tummy suddenly rumbled, embarrassingly loud. Best not do that at the ballet. It wasn't just Harvey who was ready for something to eat.

Grace had selected a seat that afforded her a bird's eye view of the theatre stage and audience. As her eyes scanned the stalls, she suddenly noticed Katya sitting in an aisle seat in the stalls close to the stage. What on earth was she doing here?

A few rows further back she spotted Komorov's head of security, Viktor Levitsky, his head hidden between the glossy pages of a programme. Was Katya aware that he was here or was Komorov having her followed? That idea made Grace very uncomfortable.

The opening strains of the orchestra started up and the lights dimmed. At least Viktor had no idea that Jean was working with her. They'd agreed to give each other a wide berth at the interval. As Igor leapt onto the stage and was joined by the stunning prima in the lead role, Grace wondered just what was going on inside his head. Was Igor obsessed with Katya and plotting her downfall? Was he trying to win her trust so he could dash her to the ground again and complete the destruction he'd visited on her in Russia? Or were they simply star-crossed lovers?

THIRTY-THREE

Jean normally loved nothing more than going to the ballet but tonight she was here to work so resisted the undertow as the music and dancing sought to pull her into another world. Her phone vibrated and she stole a surreptitious look at the text Grace had sent her. Apparently, the head of security was in the audience, as was Katya. Her pulse quickened. What did it mean? She suspected it was no coincidence. A crazy thought slipped into her head. Could Igor Sokolov be going to defect from Russia and claim asylum here? It was the last night of the performance, after all. Her stomach churned and she felt a little sick. She doubted whether this had occurred to Grace. It was only the fact she had been such a fan of Rudolf Nureyev, who had defected himself, that had put her in mind of it.

At the interval, to keep up appearances she wandered about clutching a glass of wine. She sent Grace a text about her theory but heard nothing back. Whenever she saw Grace coming, she studiously turned her gaze in the opposite direction. She felt like her body language was morphing into furtive despite her best efforts. Normally she had no difficulty appearing incon-spicuous, if not downright invisible, but tonight she felt she stood out like a sore thumb. At least no one should suspect a middle-aged woman of being up to no good.

Suddenly, she spied Katya, who she recognised from her picture on the internet. Casually, she drifted closer.

'Excuse me? Aren't you Katya Federov?' Jean asked, using her maiden name. The woman spun round to face her, looking startled and... something else. Afraid?

'I saw you in *Giselle*. It was broadcast over here. You were fabulous!'

'You have a good memory,' said Katya, with a small tight smile.

'Are you enjoying the performance?' Jean asked brightly.

'Yes, very much,' said Katya with a look that belied her words.

'I've seen better primas but the male lead is simply stunning. Such a powerful dancer. What's his name again?'

'Igor Sokolov,' Katya muttered, eyes casting round for an escape.

'Do you know him?'

'No!' Katya said vehemently. 'Excuse me, I have somewhere to be...' And she rushed off.

Jean followed her at a discreet distance, welcoming the cooler air outside the bar area but soon Katya had disappeared into the ladies' toilet. It wouldn't be long before the interval was over. She had to find Sokolov. Fortunately, she had been on a tour of the theatre some years ago so was able to head towards the backstage area. She'd nursed a notion she would be able to slip backstage without anyone noticing her. Ballet goers were a sedate lot, so she was shocked to see two heavy security types effectively guarding the door backstage. From the bulges in their jackets she would bet that they were carrying weapons too. How on earth was she going to get past them? Maybe she could get in from the outside. She walked outside the theatre and turned up the side street where she knew the fire exit from backstage to be. As she had expected, it was locked. She was turning to head back to her seat when a large white lorry turned into the street and drew up outside the door. It had no logo on it. Jean paused on the corner to see what it was going to do. The doors to the rear of the lorry were pinned back and four people dressed all in black got out from the cab and walked towards the fire door. Jean glanced down at her plain black dress and sensible shoes. They were also wearing lanyards but she still had one in her bag from a recent visit to building control. Someone opened the fire door outwards and pinned the two sides. Rails of costumes were passed out and loaded into the lorry. Jean managed to slip inside when they were distracted. It was dark and gloomy inside. She walked quietly but with confidence. She made her way to the dressing rooms. She had just spotted Igor's when the loudspeaker announced the interval was drawing to a close. She could hear raised voices behind the door. Suddenly, the door burst open and she was almost knocked to the ground as two men in dark suits that screamed former military personnel came flying out the door. Behind them came another two, both gripping Igor Sokolov by the upper arm. He looked anxious but not like he was being removed against his will. Once she'd recovered her balance, Jean ran after them to see where they were going.

'One minute to curtain,' came the voice from the loud-speaker.

An angry woman carrying a clipboard of papers came running down the corridor.

'Igor! Stop! Where are you going? Come back!' She grabbed her walkie-talkie and began screaming into it in Russian. The two security goons came running, guns in hand. The screech of tyre tracks could be heard approaching. Jean ran out the open fire exit a few seconds behind them as they bundled Igor into the back of the car. The lorry was just closing its doors, blocking her view of the car drawn up in front of it. She managed to see part of the registration number but not all of it as the sleek black car accelerated, turned the corner and was gone.

Jean made it back into the auditorium, breathing heavily, just seconds before the lights went off. However, she was in time to notice that both Katya and the head of security were not in their seats.

'Due to principal dancer Igor Sokolov regrettably becoming ill, his understudy Vladimir Baranov will dance in his place,' said the announcement.

Her watch vibrated.

Meet me in Bennet's Bar in five minutes, said the text.

Jean slipped out of her seat in the dark and made her way towards the exit. What on earth had just happened?

THIRTY-FOUR

Grace brought two glasses of soda water and lime over to the round table in the corner. As she sat down, she glanced around her, reassured to see that there had been no major changes to Bennet's Bar since her last visit some time ago. She had worked here as a student and had many happy memories of the place, which remained popular with the theatre crowd. It had a sizable collection of malt whiskies up on the carved wooden gantry and was also known for its real ale. She also had a bottle of Coke and a glass and ice. Jean eyed the third drink.

'Are we missing someone?'

'Brodie will be along shortly. I thought it might save him fighting his way to the bar. He's making some phone calls to see if Immigration are involved.'

'You think Igor might have been defecting?'

'I hope so. He wouldn't be the first Russian ballet dancer to have jumped ship in Europe. Life is trickier than ever in Russia now. If he wasn't defecting with a view to claiming asylum then his life is probably in jeopardy,' replied Grace, taking a sip of her drink.

'Do you think Katya was in on it?'

'Hard to say at this stage. She certainly didn't come back to her seat after the interval, nor did the head of security.'

'If it wasn't a defection then maybe she flew back to Komorov to get him to call in favours to find out where he's been taken and what they intend to do with him?'

'For all we know, Komorov is the one behind it,' said Grace. 'After all, he may think that they're having an affair, particularly if he's discovered their prior connection. He's certainly got the contacts and resources to pull off a stunt like this. By the way, ten out of ten for improvising, Jean.' Thanks to her, Brodie had descriptions of the men with Igor, the two goons with weapons and also a partial plate on the sleek black car.

'Thank you.' Jean beamed.

At that moment Brodie pushed open the swing door and walked over to them, pulling up a seat. Grace pushed his drink over to him. 'I thought you'd probably be driving.'

'You thought right,' he said, picking it up and taking a long swallow. 'I've phoned my contacts and this appears to be an abduction rather than a defection.'

'Have you arrested the two guys with guns who were guarding the door backstage?' asked Grace.

'Not yet. They weren't employed by the company or the theatre. No one has seen them since. The security guard who should have been guarding the door backstage was discovered bound and gagged in a cupboard.'

'What about Katya?' asked Grace. 'Has she been taken, too?'

'Some officers have gone out to the estate to try and locate her whereabouts,' said Brodie. 'I'm just heading to Igor Sokolov's room at The Royal Hotel now to search his belongings, assuming I can manage to get access as the Russians will have a major flap on. However, the accommodation is leased to the theatre so it should be fine.'

'Want some company?' She grinned, knowing what the answer would be.

'Sorry, Grace, no can do. But, if you're still up, I might be able to update you in passing later on.'

'That would be good,' said Grace. 'I'd like to know if you find any hair dye. We believe his real name is Sergei Nanov so it will be interesting to see if he has any paperwork with him in relation to his actual identity.'

'So, he could be travelling under a false passport?' asked Brodie.

'Perhaps,' said Grace, 'unless it has been changed legally in Russia, which I doubt.'

'Great job by the way, Jean,' said Brodie. 'At least you've given us something to work with.'

'Was the lorry picking up the costumes implicated at all?' asked Grace.

'No, it checks out. With it being the final performance, they were simply loading up the costumes from the first act ready to be packed away for transport back to Russia,' said Brodie. 'The timing might have been deliberate though as it did cause a bit of a diversion and increased the confusion and busyness at the scene.'

Brodie downed the last of his cola and left as quickly as he had arrived.

'If this gets out it will cause a major diplomatic incident. I hope Katya is all right. I've tried calling her but she's not answering or picking up my texts.'

'Do you really think Komorov might be involved?' asked Jean.

'I wouldn't put it past him,' replied Grace. 'When it comes to Katya, he would do anything to hang on to her.'

'He sounds almost frightening the way that you talk about him,' said Jean.

Grace considered what she had said. 'I think if you stripped away that veneer of sophistication, he's very possibly still that feral boy who would go to any length to achieve what he considers is his due in this world.'

THIRTY-FIVE

Grace glanced at her watch and sighed. It was after midnight. Brodie was unlikely to come round now. Harvey was snoozing away in his basket after his evening walk. She looked down at her comfy pyjamas and worn slippers. She'd nearly succumbed to vanity and put on something nicer but realising that she would be doing it for him had panicked her.

'You need to get a grip, Grace,' she muttered. Harvey's leg twitched. Life was a lot simpler if you were a dog. She would stay up a bit longer to unwind, maybe watch an episode of *Heartland*. Opening the stove, she threw another log on and gave it a poke, causing the flames to leap up again. That was better. Pouring herself a small glass of red wine, she wrapped a woollen throw around herself and sank onto the couch. She had just pointed the remote at the TV when the doorbell rang. Brodie.

Shuffling to the door in her ramshackle slippers, she let him in. He looked shattered, his face grey with exhaustion.

'Tea?' she asked.

'Please,' he said, flopping onto the couch she had vacated.

Harvey let out a low woof and staggered over to collapse onto his feet, shutting his eyes again immediately.

She brought Brodie a mug of tea through with a bowl of crisps, which he fell upon.

'I'm starving,' he muttered.

'I can make you a sandwich?'

'No, it's fine. Julie will have left me something in the fridge.'

There was an awkward silence.

Grace sat beside him on the couch. 'Any news? Did you get in to Sokolov's digs?'

'Yes, fortunately he didn't share with anyone. Principal dancer perks. The company were booked into a couple of small hotels in Lauriston Place, just a few minutes' walk from the theatre.'

'Nice little bolthole for him and Katya, perhaps? Did you find anything to suggest that she had been there?'

'There were a few feminine items there but as to whether any belonged to her? Impossible to say.'

'Did you take photos?' asked Grace.

'Yes, a few,' he said, passing his digital camera across to her.

The double room was plain and unremarkable. The bed was unmade as though he had got out of it in a hurry. Both sides looked as though they had been slept in. In the bathroom there were two toothbrushes and a small dish with some earrings and a hairclip and bobble.

'So, he was sleeping with someone, we just don't know who yet,' said Grace.

'We might be able to pull DNA from the toothbrush,' he said, 'but that will take time.'

Grace scrolled further. 'What's that object on his bedside table?' she asked, zooming in.

'I thought you'd spot that. It's one of those cheap Fabergé egg things. It's been logged as evidence. I scooped it up in case it had implications for Katya or someone at the castle being involved.' Brodie shrugged, taking a sip of wine.

Grace's pulse quickened. 'Katya is obsessed with them. Igor may have bought it for her. I need to see what's inside it. Please, Brodie, it could be really important.'

'Let's not jump to conclusions,' he cautioned her. 'He might have simply brought it with him from Russia as a small token to remind him of home.'

'There's another possibility,' said Grace. 'Katya's stalker left her that Fabergé egg with the mangled ballerina inside. Maybe it was intended to be left to frighten her, but he never got the chance.'

'I'll take a look at it tomorrow,' said Brodie.

'I can show you how to open it. If it's just some cheap tourist tat, then it won't take us much further forward but if we're lucky it might contain a clue as to what has been going on. I'll make us a fresh pot of tea and some toast.' Energised, despite the late hour, Grace stood up and placed another log in the stove before heading to the kitchen.

When she returned with the tray, Brodie was slumped to one side and breathing heavily with his mouth open. She gently laid down the tray on the coffee table and turned to look at him.

'Brodie,' she said softly. Nope, he was fast asleep. What to do? She rolled Harvey off his feet and gently removed his shoes. Swinging his feet up onto the couch, she laid his head on the cushion and draped a couple of blankets over him. Glancing at him once more by the light of the dying flames, she tiptoed out of the room and left him to sleep.

THIRTY-SIX

Grace was woken by the sound of a delighted Harvey barking his head off and crashing around the living room. So, Brodie was still here. She had rather thought he might wake up during the night and slip away but apparently not. Crikey, this was a bit awkward. Feeling grumpy due to not having had enough sleep, Grace threw on her tatty dressing gown and nudged her feet into slippers that Harvey considered were his.

She stuck her head round the door. 'Coffee and a bacon roll?'

Brodie rubbed his eyes. He still looked shattered and worry lines snaked across his forehead. 'Thanks, Grace, but I'd best get off. Julie was at my house last night. I can't believe I fell asleep. What's she going to think?'

'Brodie, nothing happened. You did nothing wrong apart from drive yourself to complete exhaustion. Julie will understand. Look, why don't you freshen up in the bathroom? You can even use my toothbrush. Don't say I'm not good to you! Meanwhile I'll do coffee and bacon rolls so you can hit the ground running.'

He stood there in an agony of indecision before snapping into action. 'Okay, sounds like a plan. Thanks, Grace.'

She turned towards Harvey, who was sitting at her feet with an expectant look. 'Sorry, boy, can you wait a few minutes? Once I've sorted out Brodie, I'll take you out then give you your breakfast. I'll even throw in some bacon to sweeten the deal.' She took his answering woof for a sign he was willing to cross his legs for a few more minutes. Thank goodness he had a big tank.

Fifteen minutes later, they were sitting at her kitchen table. As Grace topped up their coffee from the cafetière and tucked into her bacon roll, she was acutely aware of his presence opposite her. God, how she missed him. This wouldn't do.

His phone rang. He glanced at the screen, looking stressed. It was obviously Julie.

'Go ahead,' she said. 'I've got some things to sort out for work anyway.' Grace left him to take the call but it was a small flat. She could hear Julie's voice buzzing like an angry wasp as she shoved papers into her leather satchel.

'Julie, it wasn't planned. It'd been a long day and I nodded off on the couch. She's my ex, for goodness' sake. We're just friends. There's nothing between us.'

Just a dead son and a grandchild, thought Grace. *Clearly throwing me under the bus.* It made her really cross that Julie was sniping about her like she was some femme fatale when the truth was that she had been his wife for nearly half his life before they split up. As far as she was concerned, it was Julie who was the other woman.

Hold up, that wasn't really fair, she admitted. Julie had met him fair and square quite some time after they separated. Also, as she had only recently started admitting to herself, she would take Brodie back in a heartbeat. If only she hadn't been so shattered by grief that she had let him slip through her fingers in the first place.

In her more rational moments, her head jumped in and told her that they had got divorced for a reason and that perhaps loneliness was skewing her judgement. Anyway, there was no point driving herself mad thinking about it. She had cases to solve.

Brodie came through, shrugging on his jacket and stuffing the last of his bacon roll into his mouth. 'Grace, sorry about that, I've got to go check in with the team at the station.'

'What about the Fabergé egg?' she pleaded. 'I really need to examine it, Brodie.'

'If you pop over to the station after twelve, I'll borrow it out from the evidence room and we can look at it properly then.'

Grace bit her lip in frustration but didn't want to make things any harder for him. He patted Harvey and then he was gone, the air somehow flattened by his absence.

Harvey glared at her.

'Right, boy, out we go,' she said, picking up his lead from the hook beside the door. It was still only 6.30 but she felt like she'd been up for hours.

THIRTY-SEVEN

Hannah was still reeling from what Grace and Jean had told her about Igor Sokolov's abduction. It sounded like something out of a spy novel. As she trudged upstairs with her cleaning materials, she wondered if Polly would be in today. Hopefully, she wasn't still in a strop. Walking along the first-floor landing, she stifled a scream as Polly leapt out at her from behind a statue.

'Are you trying to give me a heart attack?' she gasped, clutching her chest.

'You're such a wimp, Hannah,' Polly laughed, seemingly back in good form.

'At least you're speaking to me again,' Hannah said, glaring at her.

Polly lowered her gaze and bit her lip. 'Yeah... about that... I'm sorry. It really wasn't anything to do with you. It was Sandra Dunlop stirring up trouble.'

'Why? What happened?' asked Hannah, pulling her into an empty room. They sat on the bed. Now that the housekeeper was gone it was unlikely anyone would be checking up on them for a few days.

Polly looked a bit torn but then sighed, clearly deciding to unburden herself. 'Look, it's not something I'm proud of, okay, but I stole something in my first job.'

'With the Hamiltons?' asked Hannah, trying not to look shocked.

'Yes. I left school at sixteen and ended up working for them in the kitchen under Mrs Dunlop.'

'What happened?'

'Well, remember I told you I had fallen out with my parents?'

'Yes,,' said Hannah.

'I was a bit of a handful back then but... it still hit me hard. All that unconditional love shit? Don't believe it. Anyway, I managed to get a live-in job with the Hamiltons, which got me out of a real jam.'

'So, what went wrong?'

'Well, Mrs Hamilton always treated me well, but her husband was horrible. He acts like the big family man and his wife hasn't a clue but, amongst the staff, he's got a reputation for being a bit handsy, if you get my drift.'

'What a creep!' Hannah shuddered.

'Anyway, one day he caught me on my own and backed me into a corner. I started to yell but he put his hand over my mouth. I managed to bite it and he swore and let go of me so I got away. Olly had heard the commotion and found me crying in the pantry. He was proper mad at what his boss had done.'

'I'm not surprised,' murmured Hannah.

'Anyway, he asked if I was interested in a little payback and needless to say I was so upset I jumped in with both feet.'

'What did you do?'

'You've got to promise not to tell anyone – I mean it, Hannah,' said Polly, glaring at her now.

'Of course!' said Hannah. 'It goes without saying...'

'Well, there was this horrible painting in Mr Hamilton's bedroom. Oliver had got it for him and he was over the moon with it. He had it copied then got me to switch the paintings over. It was small so it fitted in the cleaning trolley I used on the day the sheets were changed. It wasn't like it is here. Oliver wasn't able to stay over and sneak about. He came by appointment only. He needed someone with access to the bedrooms.'

'What happened to the original?' asked Hannah.

'He sold it.' Polly shrugged. 'He bunged me a few thousand, but he got a lot more. I planned to go off travelling.'

'So you got away with it?'

'We would have done but Mr Hamilton got an assessor in to audit all his pieces for insurance purposes and we got found out. Oliver returned the money. He threw me under the bus saying I'd ensnared him and he'd done it for love. Talk about an Oscar-winning performance. He leaned on me to give my share back, too, but I said I'd spent it all. I also told Mr Hamilton that if he didn't let it go, I'd report him to the police for assault and tell Mrs Hamilton what he'd been up to.'

Hannah strove to keep her expression sympathetic but she was actually really shocked by Polly's behaviour. 'So how come you both ended up here and not in jail?'

'Mr Hamilton wanted shot of us so his creepy behaviour didn't get found out so said he would give us good references. I think he was really happy Oliver came here as he envies Mr Komorov and hoped Oliver would rip him off, too.'

'So that's why you warned me off him.'

'I could tell he was trying to reel you in. He can be very persuasive. I thought he was genuine once, but he turned on me.'

'Were you and he...?'

'Yeah, for a while. More fool me,' she said with a twisted smile that showed it still hurt.

'You'd never think it to look at him,' sighed Hannah. 'He looks so... wholesome.'

'Mrs Dunlop never knew all the ins and outs of it. She just knows I left under a bit of a cloud.'

Hannah left to get on with the rooms on her list, her mind reeling as she took in all that Polly had told her. One thing was clear. Oliver was a dangerous and manipulative fraudster. Had he pulled a similar stunt here to the one he'd pulled before? Had he stolen the Fabergé egg?

THIRTY-EIGHT

Grace lifted her chin and pulled her shoulders back as she entered the police station on Leonard Street where Brodie and his team were based. She hated coming here but needs must. She couldn't believe it had only been three years since she had been railroaded out. Before Connor had died, she had been harder. Someone who saw the world in terms of black and white and had little tolerance or understanding for what she saw as weakness. It had taken her son's death to humble her. She was no longer the same person, and she suspected others might see that as an improvement of sorts.

This time she was recognised by the young man behind the desk and buzzed through immediately. She really hoped that she didn't run into her old boss, Detective Superintendent Blair. It wasn't as if she could even tell him what she thought of him as he was now Brodie's boss and, worse still, Julie's father.

Sighing, she walked down the corridor towards Brodie's office. It really bummed her out being here. She much preferred being her own boss. Suddenly, his head poked out of his office. Looking left and right, he beckoned to her to hurry.

'Hey, Brodie,' she said, amused.

'Sorry.' He grinned, closing the door smartly behind her. 'Blair is on the prowl and you know he's not exactly your biggest fan.'

'True,' she said with feeling. 'Have you got the egg?'

'Sure,' he said, removing it from a drawer. 'I haven't opened it. I thought it best to leave it for you since you're used to tinkering with these things and I didn't want to break it.'

'Has it already been dusted for prints?' she asked.

'Yes, nothing back yet. They did the inside as well. You can take it out of the evidence bag.' He handed over a pair of gloves and she slipped them on before taking the egg out to examine it. Looking for the tiny opening mechanism, she pressed her nail to it and the hinge swung open.

'I don't believe it,' she murmured. 'An engagement ring?'

'I thought that would surprise you,' he said. 'The question is, who was it intended for? Katya Komorov is the most likely possibility. They've been spending time together and have a shared history.'

'Maybe,' said Grace. 'However, he did end her career. I can't figure out their relationship. I'm concerned about the ring being in the Fabergé egg. Her stalker uses them to leave creepy messages for her, too.'

'There was a bottle of champagne in the fridge,' said Brodie. He pulled out the photos to show her.

'Perhaps he was intending to pop the question tonight after the performance,' said Grace. 'I take it you're no further forward with the abduction?'

'No. There's been no contact to support an intention to defect. No contact at all.'

'I take it there are alerts at all the major transport hubs?'

'Of course! But if he himself is orchestrating this then he'll no doubt have secured new identity papers and changed his appearance in some way again so will slip through our fingers.'

'Have you been able to question the rest of the company, the other dancers?'

'No, they're pleading diplomatic immunity and have been shepherded away to an undisclosed address by the Russian ambassador to await their flight.'

'It could be Komorov himself, of course,' pondered Grace. 'He's obsessed with Katya.'

'Kind of goes with the territory. He is her husband.'

Grace gave him a look then continued, 'Sacha Komorov was just one of many suitors crowded about Katya's feet when she was a prima ballerina. By all accounts she paid him no more mind than any of her other would-be suitors.'

'Where are you going with this, Grace?'

'He swooped in when she was injured and her glittering choices and prospects were suddenly diminished, but what if...?' Grace shook her head as if to clear it.

'What if he was the one who forced Igor Sokolov to drop her? You really think he's capable of that?' asked Brodie, letting out a whistle.

'Who knows what he's capable of? And if that was the case, he wouldn't shrink from instructing some heavies to abduct Igor if there were any signs of him rekindling an old passion.'

'Grace, this is pure speculation, not to mention that he's your client.'

'I know,' she sighed. 'But Katya is my client, too, and I'm worried I won't be able to keep her safe. Have you made any progress with Irina's cause of death? Was it poison?'

'Like I said before, it would seem so but we're still waiting on a poison being identified by toxicology. There's also currently no way to determine if it was murder or suicide. She could have ingested it herself after the big reveal of Sacha being her brother.'

'I mean, if you had done that to me, can you imagine? I

wouldn't have killed myself though. I'd have torn you apart limb from limb and mounted your head on a stick.'

'Good to know,' he said with a small smile. 'That's not worrying at all.'

'I mean, I can't imagine Irina taking that news well. She would be furious as well as upset. Surely, she'd plot some sort of payback rather than ingest poison there and then. After all, where would she even get it?'

'We found no obvious trace of poison in the house, but it would've been easy enough to get rid of it after it'd served its purpose.'

'Nothing on her fingers, clothes or in her office?' asked Grace.

'Nothing. Obviously once we know the exact poison then it will be easier to focus our search. If she'd killed herself impulsively in a fit of anger or sorrow, you wouldn't expect her to be so forensically aware,' said Brodie. 'That's why I'm leaning towards murder.'

'Unless she was so angry, she wanted to frame Komorov for the murder and bring about his ruin from beyond the grave,' said Grace.

'Remind me never to fall out with you,' said Brodie.

'You already have,' she reminded him.

There was an awkward pause.

'So, it looks like Igor, at least, isn't Katya's stalker,' said Brodie.

'No... assuming the ring was for Katya and that's a pretty flimsy theory without Katya confirming their relationship.'

'You're going to have to lean hard on both Komorov and Katya if we are going to get to the bottom of this,' said Brodie.

'What about the head of security, Viktor Levitsky? Now all these government types are involved, can't you give them a poke to give us some background on him given that he, too, is conceivably a person of interest in Irina's death. After all, rumour has it he worked for the security forces in Russia at the highest level.'

'I can only try,' said Brodie. 'Poisoning is quite a common thing over there. I imagine Komorov made more than a few enemies on his climb to power.'

'Russia has a long reach and an even longer memory,' said Grace, chills of foreboding running down her back.

THIRTY-NINE

Grace made it outside to the pavement without encountering Superintendent Blair. She moved to cross the road to where her car was parked when she heard the sound of running footsteps behind her. Glancing round, her heart sank. It was Julie and her expression was one of sheer fury. Grace sighed and turned round to face her.

'Julie, nothing happened. Brodie was worn out and fell asleep. That's all, I promise you.'

'You didn't think to text me to tell me what was going on?' Julie snapped.

'No, I didn't, but I probably should have done. I went to bed and assumed he'd be gone by the time I woke up.' She didn't have time for this. 'I'm sorry that you were upset but you should know by now that Brodie and I are simply friends.'

'You might be able to pull the wool over his eyes, but I know that you want him back.'

'Excuse me?' said Grace, her face flushing in anger. It didn't help that her accusation had some merit in it. She'd been so careful to hide her feelings and not interfere in their relationship. Or she thought she had.

'Oh, don't act the innocent. You think you're so much better than me, don't you? Miss hotshot detective.'

Grace was startled. Where was all this coming from? 'Of course I don't, why would I?' she said.

'If Brodie goes back to you, I'll see to it that his career is ruined!' Julie hissed.

'Oh, come on,' said Grace, exasperated now. 'We're two grown women. Surely you don't need to run to Daddy? Brodie is free to be with whoever he wants.'

'And who he wants is me!' Julie shouted. 'So back off, you dried-up old witch.'

An elderly couple turned and gawped at them then walked on, shaking their heads.

Grace walked off, her back ramrod straight. Once she was out of sight, she found a café and sat in a corner shaking as the reaction set in. She had always thought that Julie was a bit hippy-dippy but fundamentally well intentioned. It had never occurred to her that she could nurse so much bile and spite inside her. Mind you, given who her father was, she shouldn't have been all that surprised. All because Brodie had flaked out on the couch. Admittedly she hadn't been thrilled when Julie had first rocked up on the scene, but she'd seemed to make Brodie happy and she had tried hard to accept the situation and develop a cordial relationship with her, especially once Jack had come along. The fact that she was so good with him had gone a long way.

Maybe she should have woken Brodie but she just couldn't bring herself to do it. It had felt so good having his presence there. Now that she was starting to heal after losing Connor, she had been shocked to catch herself feeling lonely every now and again. She supposed in the circumstances she could hardly blame Julie for lashing out although threatening to tank Brodie's career had been a low blow. Grace finished her coffee and stood up. She'd already decided not to tell Brodie about Julie's outburst. She didn't want to make matters any worse between them.

She glanced at her watch. It was 11.30. Nikolai had been conspicuously absent of late. He was also a contender for being Katya's stalker. Just how far would he be prepared to go to drive a wedge between his brother and the wife that he clearly desired? How might he have reacted to the news that Irina was his half sister? Or did he already know?

FORTY

Rossiter and Roebottom, art and antiques specialist auction house, was located in a cobbled street in the heart of Edinburgh's Old Town, in the midst of a graceful crescent of Georgian houses. Grace had phoned ahead to check that Nikolai was there and willing to meet with her.

A beautifully polished young woman welcomed her with cool restraint and bade her take a seat in the waiting room, which looked like it had formerly been a drawing room; it had a beautiful bay window looking onto a walled garden at the rear of the property. There were a couple of others waiting who Grace pegged immediately as part of the county set with their distressed-through-age tweed jackets and lace-up leather brogues. She felt a little conspicuous, clearly the odd one out in a room that reeked of money.

'Grace?' A head poked round the door.

'Nikolai, thanks for seeing me at such short notice,' she said as she followed him out the door and down through the bowels of the building to a small office cluttered with antiques of all shapes and sizes.

'Sorry about the mess,' he said as he uncovered a seat for her in front of his desk and squeezed in behind it. 'All this lot has to be catalogued for an auction next week. You look surprised.' He smiled. 'Didn't think I had a real job?'

'No, it's not that exactly,' she said, looking around her with curiosity.

'Sacha always acts like I'm some kind of hedonistic playboy,' he said with a flash of anger. 'I've worked here since I graduated. The hours are flexible, which is why I'm around at some times more than others.'

'I take it you've heard what happened to Igor Sokolov,' she said.

'I wasn't there but I heard about it. Has he defected?'

'Apparently not, according to my sources,' she said, watching him closely. 'Can you think of anyone who would wish him harm?'

'My brother for one,' he said with a twisted smile. 'He was furious with Katya for allowing him to come over and dance with her.'

'And you?' said Grace with a slight smile. 'It's no secret that you're one of Katya's biggest admirers.'

'What do you mean by that?' he snapped. 'She's my sister-in-law.'

'I've seen you watch her dance a number of times.'

'So? She's very talented.'

'You were there in Moscow the night that her career ended, weren't you?'

'Yes, I will never forget it. It was horrible beyond words,' he said, still looking haunted as he recalled the memory.

'I take it then that you recognised Igor Sokolov as the other dancer when he came to the house?'

'Not at first. It wasn't until I saw them dancing the following day doing that same risky move that I made the connection. I'm sure his name and hair colour were different back then, but the face is the same.'

'When she was so gravely injured your brother proposed to her even though her other suitors disappeared. Were you not tempted to do so, too?'

'No. I think a large part of my admiration was how she soared when she danced. When her legs were cut from under her it seemed that she'd never dance again. I melted away and conceded victory to Sacha. I couldn't have confronted her crushed body and spirit every day. I wasn't strong enough to will her back to life,' he said with a sigh.

Grace was impressed by his admission, which hardly reflected favourably on him. She was starting to feel a little sorry for Katya, a woman so determined to be in charge of her own destiny yet who had ended up being discarded by her admirers and forced to settle for a dull existence walled up in a cold castle in the Scottish countryside.

'But now that she is dancing again?'

'Perhaps I was a little too hasty,' he said. 'In any event, she might be dancing again but she wouldn't be up to the gruelling schedule of a dance company.'

'Did you get the impression that it was truly an accident, or do you think that Igor dropped her deliberately?'

'I've always assumed it was nothing more than a terrible accident though you do hear of such things happening from time to time, usually as a result of rivalries within the company.'

'Irina was there that night, too, I understand?'

His face darkened at the mention of her name. 'Was she? I can't even remember.'

'Has Sacha spoken to you yet... about Irina?'

'That she was my half sister? Yes, it came out in an argument the night she died,' said Nikolai. 'Nice way to find out. I went to his room. Katya had called me as she didn't know what to do with him. He was distraught. I'd never seen him like that before.'

'Like what?' Grace probed gently.

'Sobbing and smashing things. He was literally tearing his own clothes. I've never seen him lose control like that. I'd no idea he could even feel things to that extent. To be honest, I've always seen him as cold and robotic.'

'How did you feel about it?'

'Angry, I suppose, that I'd been deprived of a relationship with her. She didn't approve of me, you know.'

'I rather gathered that,' said Grace with a small smile as she recalled some of Irina's diatribes against him.

'I always knew she was devoted to Sacha. Somehow, he manages to treat people like they're rubbish yet they love him for it,' Nikolai said bitterly.

'Even you?'

'My feelings for my brother are... complicated. Why could he not have told her? Given her a cottage nearby? To have her slaving away for him all these years, why would he do that?'

'I think only Sacha can answer that,' she said diplomatically. She had no intention of getting drawn into their feud with each other.

'Just as well I knew we were brothers or I might have ended up being the butler,' he said with a forced grin. 'It's not as if he isn't loaded, yet he treats every bloody penny like a prisoner.'

'Early trauma can affect people like that,' said Grace. 'Also, your life doesn't look too bad to me.' She swept a hand round to encompass the office. 'You have a career, financial security, not too shabby.'

'It's all relative, I suppose,' he said. 'I hear you used to be married to DI Brodie McKenna. Has he asked you to spy on us for him?'

Grace laughed. 'No, but I'd tell him where to go if he did. I'm only asking questions in case Irina's death has any relevance to my other investigations.'

'Investigations, plural?' he said, raising an eyebrow.

'Oops, am I bad?' said Grace, rising to her feet and giving him an enigmatic smile.

As she walked down the road, she could sense eyes on her from the front window of the office. Hopefully, she had managed to rattle him sufficiently. Interestingly, in his workplace he had no trace of a Russian accent. It was as if he had shaken off the mantle of his Russian heritage completely. It looked like he wasn't quite as much of a waster as Sacha had implied. Perhaps some of that was simply him trying to pierce his brother's armour by enraging him.

FORTY-ONE

Grace and Hannah sat at the stripped pine table in Jean's sun-filled kitchen. It was a handsome mid-terraced sandstone house in one of Portobello's quieter streets. She'd invited them for lunch to break up the day. Harvey was sitting on the patio, apparently asleep but ready to spring into action if any morsel dropped from the table, which was spread with all manner of delicious cold eats.

'You're so lucky, Jean,' said Hannah, looking all around her. 'There's so much space, and to have a garden as well!'

'Fortunately, we bought it when the area was quite rundown,' said Jean, smiling. 'I certainly couldn't afford it now.'

'I reckon I'm going to end up living in a shed at this rate,' said Hannah, glumly. 'It's so hard for my generation to get onto the property ladder.'

Grace and Hannah exchanged a concerned glance. Hannah had seemed quite down in the dumps recently. Her housing situation was getting her down. Now that she was working and had a toddler, the cramped conditions and fights with her mother, not to mention looking after her younger siblings more than she should, was wearing her down. Grace only had a two-bedroomed flat and Brodie was involved with Julie now.

'It won't always be like this, you'll see,' said Grace, determined to speak to Brodie and see what else they could do to help her and their grandson, Jack.

They all helped Jean clear away the plates and stack the dishwasher then settled back down at the table with some coffee to discuss their cases.

'I don't suppose there could be a secret passage or anything like that?' said Hannah. The other two burst out laughing.

'This isn't the Famous Five, Hannah.' Jean smiled.

'Laugh all you want but when I was in Katya's room I really did feel as if there were eyes on me. It was creepy,' said Hannah.

'I suppose it would explain how people seem able to get into Katya's room and leave stuff without being seen,' said Grace.

'I could look into the history of Traprain Castle at Portobello Library,' said Jean.

'I *could* ask Sacha but he might have a vested interest in hiding it from us,' said Grace.

'You'd think an architect would have found it when they were constructing the gallery space,' said Jean.

'Not necessarily,' replied Grace. 'It's in a different wing of the castle.'

'I'll see what I can turn up,' said Jean.

'I must remember to text Brodie to see if the toxicology report is back yet,' Grace said. 'I wish they didn't always take so long.'

'Why are you so interested in Irina's murder?' asked Hannah. 'Isn't that Brodie's job?'

'Well, yes, but none of these crimes have necessarily happened in isolation. There could well be links between them that we haven't even guessed at yet. For example, the theft of the Fabergé egg has links to Irina as she was keeper of the key.

The stalker left a crude message for Katya inside another Fabergé egg. Katya is known to be obsessed with Fabergé eggs.'

'Are you saying you think the same person is behind all three crimes?' asked Hannah.

'Not necessarily, but I do think that there are connections beneath the surface that we need to expose to get to the truth.'

'What do you think has happened to the Imperial Egg?' asked Jean. 'Surely, it could have been spirited away to the other side of the world by now?'

'I still think that it's in the castle,' said Grace.

'But where?' said Hannah. 'We've looked everywhere. I've been all over the castle by now. I can't think where else to look for the wretched thing.'

'If only Katya hadn't made her obsession with Fabergé eggs so public,' said Jean, looking worried. 'Any Tom, Dick or Harry could easily find out about it. Every interview she's ever done mentions it at some point.'

'I know,' sighed Grace. 'It's something it would be easy for a stalker to latch on to. But the men in her life have also purchased them for her to win favour.'

'Yeah, Sacha had to go large with his big whopper Imperial Egg, didn't he?' said Hannah. 'A lot of good it did him, though. Katya seems proper high maintenance.'

'Even if the woman Igor was about to propose to isn't Katya, they have spent time together so hopefully she'll be able to tell us who she is. If Katya was planning on leaving Sacha, I think it's quite likely that she'd be looking to secure a nest egg for her new life, no pun intended. Igor isn't wealthy and Katya can no longer do the one thing she was trained for, which is to dance,' said Grace.

'She could have rationalised stealing the Imperial Egg by thinking it was intended as a present for her in any event,' piped up Jean.

'Can't you find out what she told the police?' asked Hannah. 'That might give us a clue.'

'It's not that simple,' said Grace, squirming inwardly as she remembered her earlier confrontation with Julie. 'Anyway, I'd rather hear it from her in person. She's meeting me for coffee at North Berwick at 3.30pm, away from prying eyes.'

Jean got to her feet and started stacking the dishwasher as the others helped her clear away the lunch things.

'That was a lovely lunch, Jean,' said Hannah. 'I ate so much I think I might just burst.' She patted her stomach with a sigh. 'Your kids were lucky to have a mum like you.'

'I doubt they would agree,' Jean said with a small smile. 'My husband used to find fault with everything, and they rather followed his lead.'

Grace squeezed her shoulder. 'They'll come around in time,' she said. 'It's a maturity thing.'

It suddenly hit her. She should follow her own advice. Connor had been a typical stroppy teenager and they had clashed endlessly. Perhaps, if he hadn't become so overwhelmed that he took his own life, they would have one day been able to laugh about the many fights they'd had. She had a sudden flash of them sitting by the sea enjoying breakfast together, his face crinkled in a smile, lit by the sun...

'Earth calling Grace,' said Hannah, her voice seeming to travel a long way.

'Sorry, you caught me daydreaming.' She smiled.

'Hope he was tall, dark and handsome,' Hannah quipped, then stopped when she saw the stricken look on Grace's face.

'What is it?' asked Jean, alarmed.

'Nothing,' said Grace. 'I just remembered something I need to do. I'd best head off to North Berwick. Thanks for lunch, Jean. It was great to get away from the office for a bit.'

She bit her lip as she reached her car. Hannah had intruded

on her reverie in the worst possible way as Connor was not only the girl's first love but the father of her child. If Connor had only got to hear Hannah's news, would he have been able to hang on long enough to accept help for his mental health? They would never know.

FORTY-TWO

Nudging her car into the busy traffic of Portobello High Street, she put some music on to calm her. In a matter of minutes, she was driving alongside Longniddry Bents, with the North Sea glittering like diamonds on her left. She cracked open the passenger window and filled her lungs with the fresh sea air.

Arriving in the beautiful coastal town of North Berwick, she parked in the car park of the impressive Marine Hotel and quickly made her way through the opulent reception lounge to the bar where she ordered coffee for two. She slipped into a table in the conservatory set away from prying eyes. The lawn at the back of the hotel gave way to West Links golf course with the sparkling sea beyond. The sun was shining and she had a clear view of the Islands of Lamb and Craigleith and across to Bass Rock. She was soon joined by Katya, who looked ill at ease compared to her usual air of flawless confidence. They exchanged pleasantries until coffee had been served in a silver pot by an immaculate waitress in a tartan waistcoat and bow tie. Then, as she walked away, Katya leaned across the table and grabbed Grace's hand, making her jump.

'You've got to help me. I've no one else to turn to.'

'What's happened?' asked Grace, alarmed.

'Are you crazy?' Katya hissed, her dark eyes narrowed. There was something almost feline about her, mused Grace. 'Everything has happened. I find out that insufferable woman was my husband's half sister?'

'You had no idea?'

'No! Then I go to ballet and Igor disappeared. Do you know who took him?' she asked, unable to hide her anxiety.

'No, I don't,' said Grace. 'I saw you there that night.'

'I went to watch ballet. That was all,' said Katya, lifting her chin as though anticipating an attack.

'Look, Katya, I have to ask. Were you conducting a romantic affair with Igor Sokolov?'

Katya bristled with anger. 'That is none of your business. You find stalker. That is all.'

'Can't you see?' said Grace. 'Things have gone beyond that now. A woman has been murdered. You have a stalker. What if they are the same person? I need to know how Igor Sokolov fits into this complicated puzzle. There must be no missing pieces if we want to stop further harm. I need you to tell me the truth about him. All of it!'

'But you work for Sacha, too. How do I know you will not tell him everything I say to you?'

'Because if it doesn't relate to the theft of the Imperial Egg, it's not relevant to the case I'm instructed on,' replied Grace.

Katya thought for a moment and then sighed as though she had reached a decision. 'Igor and I reconnected recently. He has been over here six weeks with the Moscow Ballet.'

'Had you remained in touch once you had left Russia?'

'No. It all happened so quickly. The accident. I was in shock that my career had suddenly ended and worried about the future. One minute I was soaring high. All the men wanted to throw diamonds at me and win my heart. Then, just like that' – she snapped her fingers – 'all over. I was just a broken doll and suitors vanished overnight. I became desperate,' she said quietly. 'Dancing was my life. I had no other way to earn a living. It had consumed me from a small child and now I was destroyed.'

'And then Sacha asked you to marry him?'

'Yes. I did not love him, but it was a lifeline and I took it. In Russia life is about survival. My parents are both dead. They worked many jobs to pay for my ballet lessons to help me escape the poverty they had been born into. I could not let their sacrifice be for nothing.'

'Sacha must have loved you very much,' ventured Grace.

'Love?' Katya shrugged. 'Who can say? It felt more like a transaction but I did not care. My heart was broken. Dance was my one true love, and I was desperate to escape. Hidden away in a Scottish castle seemed a fitting end to my fairy tale.'

'There were rumours that Igor dropped you deliberately?' said Grace.

'He did,' she said simply.

'But why?' asked Grace, astonished by Katya's calm demeanour. 'I've seen you dance with him since then. How can you ever trust him again?'

'He had no choice. Someone threatened him. They abducted his mother and younger sister. He doesn't know who it was. All he knew was that if he did not drop me at the end of the first act they would be murdered horribly. If he told anyone they would be murdered horribly. They sent him a photo of them both bound and gagged. He showed me this when he came over here.'

'So, you forgave him,' said Grace.

'I had to. In his shoes I would have done the same thing. He prayed I would not be seriously injured. Many dancers fall and recover. I was unlucky.'

'Were you together at the time?' asked Grace.

Katya tossed her hair and tilted her chin. 'No, I had bigger suitors with better prospects. Back then I thought love is not everything.'

'And now?'

Katya's eyes unexpectedly filled with tears. 'Now, Igor is all I can think about. I am sick with worry. I want to ask Sacha for help, but he hates Igor. He is jealous of our close bond. It pains him to see us dance.'

'You were at the theatre that night. Was Igor planning to defect?'

'Yes. He was planning to slip away at the interval, and I was going to drive him to police headquarters where he would claim asylum. I waited and waited round the corner from the theatre but he did not come. Then, I heard a screech of tyres and a black car flew past the end of the road where I was parked and I knew. I knew it in here,' she said, clutching at her heart, 'that he was gone.'

'Do you know who took him?' Grace asked.

'I have reached out to someone in the company, a friend of his who knew what he was planning. It was not the Russians. They are furious and have now locked down the company and removed all communication devices until they are able to fly home. They have brought in more security and the dancers are never left alone with guards posted outside their rooms. It is like being in prison. They are all wretched.'

'If your plan had succeeded and Igor gained asylum here, were you going to leave Sacha to be with him?'

'Yes. I may want for nothing in material terms, but Sacha is a cold man. Now that Igor has gone, I have no one to turn to. The morning after Igor was taken, I found this in my room on my pillow,' she said, her hands shaking as she drew it out of her handbag.

It was another Fabergé egg but not the one she had seen in Nikolai's room. Katya placed it on the table and popped the catch. As the egg sprang open, Grace's heart missed a beat.

Inside was a crudely fashioned noose with a male ballet dancer swinging from it, his neck clearly snapped. He had been fashioned to bear more than a passing resemblance to Igor.

'Was there anything with it?' Grace asked.

'A wedding ring with a tiny padlock,' said Katya, rummaging around her bag. 'Here it is.'

Grace pulled on a pair of the disposable gloves she always carried and took it from her to examine it, turning it this way and that. It was of an unusual design and looked like an antique, only spoiled by the padlock and chain.

'Can I pass this on to the police?' asked Grace.

'Please do, 'said Katya with a shudder. Always ethereal, she looked even slighter now with dark shadows under her eyes. Clearly, events were exacting a toll on her.

FORTY-THREE

The following day Hannah threw herself down at the table in the kitchen for her afternoon tea break. Her stomach was rumbling again. The cost of living crisis was biting hard at home. Most nights she and Mum made do with a slice of toast and a can of beans between them so the kids could all have a proper meal. Sometimes it felt as cold in the house as it did outside but they didn't dare switch on the heating now that the bills were soaring as well. It was all very well for Grace and Jean. They might not be loaded but they weren't poor either. Hannah was sick of her clothes smelling fusty even when clean because of the time they took to dry without the heating on. At times it all got a bit too much and she could see the road to her future stretching out endlessly into some dystopian landscape. Morosely, she sipped her coffee and ate some biscuits from the plate set out for them. She'd been working at the castle now for the best part of four weeks with no end in sight. They were now into October and still nowhere close to solving the two cases for which they had been hired. All this other stuff had happened with Irina and now Igor. She just wanted to be done and get out of here.

'Blimey,' said Sandra Dunlop, drying her hands and squeezing her bulk behind the table opposite her. 'What's up with you today?'

'Just a bit fed up,' Hannah said, with a crooked grin. 'You know, work, sleep, eat, repeat. No matter how hard I work, I don't get anywhere. Sometimes it doesn't seem fair, that's all.'

'I get where you're coming from,' said the cook. 'I see this lot upstairs with all that money and those bitter faces and I want to tell them to wake up and appreciate what they've got sometimes. They really are a miserable bunch.'

'Imagine if there was a thunderstorm or something and we got to switch roles with them like some kind of messed up *Freaky Friday*.' Hannah grinned. 'How cool would that be?'

'Which one would I be?' mused Sandra, her jowls folding in contemplation. 'Katya, that's it. Always fancied myself as a bit of a ballet dancer when I was a kid.'

Hannah tried not to burst out laughing at the thought of Sandra gliding across the stage in a tutu.

'All those gorgeous clothes,' Sandra continued, her expression dreamy, 'and the figure to wear them, that would do me.'

'I'd be Sacha,' said Hannah. 'He has all that money and power, and no one gets to tell him what to do. He's a proper king of the castle.'

Sandra glanced at her watch and drained the remains of her coffee. 'That's odd. Polly hasn't been down yet.'

'I thought she wasn't in today,' said Hannah. 'I haven't seen her at all. We usually bump into each other at some point.'

As they were carrying their mugs over to the sink, they heard a bloodcurdling scream. It made the hairs at the back of Hannah's neck stiffen in horror.

'That's Polly!' she said, her mug falling to the floor. Turning on her heel, she ran for the stairs, her body surging with adrenaline, leaving Sandra puffing far behind in her wake. Assuming the scream had come from the main rooms on the first floor, she ran first to Katya's door. Throwing it open, she paused in horror. Polly was lying on her back on the floor to the right of the bed. Her face was drained of colour, and she appeared to be unconscious.

Sacha came running in behind her, pushed her aside, and knelt down beside the young woman. He quickly felt for a pulse. He tried again and leaned across her to feel whether any air was being expelled. Then he shook his head, stood up and turned to face them. Oliver and Nikolai had arrived too by now.

'She's dead,' he said as though he couldn't quite believe the words.

'Are you sure?' demanded Hannah, her fingers poised to dial an ambulance.

'I'm positive,' he said, his expression closed off. 'I will call the police. I need two of you to stand outside this door to ensure that no one enters the room until the police arrive.'

'I'll do it,' said Hannah.

'I'll stay, too,' said Oliver.

Hannah really didn't want to be alone with him but felt she couldn't say anything.

'Thank you. Everyone else, downstairs to the study. I think a measure of brandy and some tea might help.'

'I'll get that organised,' said the cook, her lip trembling.

'Thank you. You may join us there as well,' said Sacha. 'This is no time for standing on ceremony.'

Oliver went off to fetch them two chairs to sit on so Hannah took the opportunity to fire off a text to Grace to let her know about Polly. Fortunately, her mum was collecting Jack from nursery today. She was still in shock. Polly had been so outgoing and carefree. Hannah had envied her at times when she felt weighed down by her own responsibilities. How could it be possible that she was dead? Who could have possibly wanted to snuff out such a young vibrant life? Her teeth started chattering as the shock set in.

Oliver emerged from the nursery with two upright chairs and a couple of blankets to ward off the chill from the draughty hallway and they sat side by side. He'd also brought a hip flask with some brandy and a couple of shot glasses, which he filled, passing one to her.

'Here, drink it,' he said as she shook her head. 'It'll help.'

Still shaking with shock, she was about to take it from him when she stopped herself, remembering what had happened to Irina.

'No thanks, I don't drink,' she said.

'Suit yourself.' He shrugged and knocked his own drink back in one.

'Are you okay?' she ventured. 'I know you and Polly were close.'

'What did she tell you?' he asked, the shutters coming down.

'I know what happened when you both worked at the Hamiltons',' she said.

His face hardened. 'I wouldn't believe everything that she told you. If her life wasn't interesting enough, she'd make stuff up. Proper little drama queen, she was.'

'Oliver, she's lying dead on the other side of the door. How can you...?' She stopped abruptly as tears threatened once more.

'What did she tell you anyway?' he asked, his mouth like a steel trap.

Hannah was seeing a different side to him now. One that she didn't like. She decided to let him think that Polly hadn't told her the whole story.

'She just said you and her used to go out together before you worked here.'

'That's a bit of an exaggeration.' He grimaced. 'We went out once or twice but that was it for me. Probably best if you don't mention it to the police. I don't want them crawling all over my life for the sake of a cheap fling.'

'Polly had moved on,' said Hannah, feeling compelled to defend the dead girl. 'She was saving up to go travelling. Her life would have been amazing.'

'Talk is cheap,' said Oliver. 'I doubt very much she would have made it happen. She went through her money as fast as she made it.'

He seemed to belatedly realise how badly he was coming across. 'Look, I'm sorry she's dead, of course I am. But I'm not going to pretend to be more broken up about it than I am. We were distant work colleagues, that's all.'

Hannah gave him a small insincere smile and nodded. She had to hide her true feelings and crack on with the job. If he had had anything to do with Polly's death, she was going to do whatever it took to make sure that he faced justice.

FORTY-FOUR

Grace burst into the agency to find Hannah sitting typing with a hot chocolate at her side and Harvey on her feet.

'Are you all right? What happened, Hannah?' Grace dipped down to pat Harvey, who thumped his tail but couldn't be bothered to get up.

'Oh Grace, it was awful! I was the one who found the body. Again! I was downstairs when all of a sudden there was this bloodcurdling scream like something was really, really wrong. Everyone raced up there but I arrived first. I found her in Katya's room. She was already dead. There were signs of a struggle but no sign of anyone else. I volunteered to guard the door till the police got there and Oliver stayed, too.'

'You said that a number of people raced to the room. Can you remember where each of them came from?' asked Grace.

'I'm not sure, I wasn't really thinking about that at the time.'

'Try,' said Grace. 'It might help if you close your eyes and imagine yourself there from when you first heard that terrible scream. Try and notice your surroundings as you head towards the room. It's only a memory so you can slow it down as if it is happening in slow motion. Use all of your senses. Think about what you can see, hear, smell and touch. If it gets too much then simply open your eyes and we can stop. It's important to do this whilst it's still fresh in your mind.'

Hannah closed her eyes and screwed up her face in concentration. 'Sandra Dunlop was in the kitchen with me when I heard the scream. I went up the staff stairs to the ground floor and there were a number of doors that were opening. I could smell the open fire from the library and saw Sacha standing there looking up towards the stairs. As I ran past him, he reached out an arm to stop me but I shook it off and ran on. I remember my breath rasping in my chest and my calves hurting as I ran up the main stairs to the first floor. I heard two doors opening on the landing as I ran up but people were just standing there as though they didn't know where to look or what to do.'

'What people?' prompted Grace.

'Nikolai's suite is at the far end of the landing as he has a corner suite. I saw him walking towards me. His face was white. He shouted something. "Katya!" That's it, he shouted "Katya!" then he broke into a run. Oliver arrived just after me. I don't know where he came from.'

'Think,' said Grace. 'Did he appear on your right or your left when you first became aware of him?'

Hannah closed her eyes and concentrated once more. 'It was my left,' she announced then looked puzzled. 'But there's nothing down to the left. The only room we clean down there is the nursery... mind you, that's where he went to get the chairs for us to sit on after... What would he have been doing in the nursery?'

'Does he ever stay over?' asked Grace.

'Sometimes,' said Hannah, 'but the guest bedrooms are all on the second floor. He doesn't have a special room. Anyway, I opened Katya's door and I saw Polly.' A hiccoughing sob escaped her. 'She was lying on her back. Sacha checked for a pulse, but it was obvious she was dead. Her eyes were just sort of staring. She had marks round her neck like someone had squeezed really hard and her eyes were all bloodshot.'

'Do you know why she'd been in Katya's room?'

'She'd been promoted to be Katya's personal maid so it wasn't her job to clean in there anymore. Maybe she was sorting through her clothes or something?'

'The fact that it occurred in Katya's room rather muddies the water in terms of motive,' said Grace. 'It could be that Polly was the intended victim all along. But, equally, perhaps Katya's stalker was in her room getting up to more mischief and Polly caught them by surprise and they panicked and killed her.'

'I've given my statement to Brodie,' said Hannah, collapsing in on herself as the reaction to the day's events set in. 'As it's a second death at the castle, his team have been assigned. I've typed up my statement for you and Jean and I'm just going to add in those extra details you got me to remember.'

'Then it's straight off home,' said Grace. 'I see Jean's not back yet. She probably went straight home from the library. I'll catch up with her tomorrow. Hopefully, her hours of research have borne some fruit.'

Grace felt a deep weariness settle in her bones. What had started off as a straightforward case of theft had morphed into a complex tangle of interlinked crimes. However, while she knew the links were there, it was proving almost impossible to determine which ones were relevant and which were a blind alley. Now, two women had lost their lives and a third woman, Katya, remained in jeopardy. Igor Sokolov was also still missing and she fervently hoped his abduction did not become another murder case. What was at the root of all this seething discontent amongst these fabulously wealthy clients? What was the prime driver and catalyst? To what extent was Harris Hamilton's household involved? Everywhere she turned she found links between the two households.

Clipping on Harvey's lead, she left the office, turning left to walk along the Esplanade towards Leith.

'Grace, wait up!'

She turned to see Brodie walking towards her. The lead jerked out of her hand as Harvey barked in delight and pounced on him. Brodie picked up the lead and handed it to her, making a fuss of him.

'I was just going to walk him before heading up to the flat,' said Grace. 'I can go back to the office if you'd prefer?'

'And get the sad eyes from him?' laughed Brodie. 'No chance. Happy to walk and talk if that's okay with you?'

'Sure,' she said. They wandered along in companionable silence for a few minutes. Grace thought about telling Brodie about her meeting with Julie but decided against it. The last thing she wanted to do was come between them although she was less sure than she had been that Julie could make him happy. 'So, another murder, then? Have you got the toxicology report back in relation to Irina yet?'

'Yes, it came in yesterday. She was poisoned, all right. Although there was none left in the cup itself. Fortunately, she'd made the tea in a pot so there was still some to test.'

'And the poison?'

'Apparently, one used by Russian security services, *Gelsemium elegans*. It's known as heartbreak grass.'

'That's a new one on me.'

'Apparently, it grows exclusively in south-east Asia. She died from respiratory distress. Not a good way to go.'

'Poor woman,' sighed Grace. 'I don't suppose she could have taken it herself? She was very upset after the big revelation from Sacha.'

'Unlikely. She'd have had to have it lying around to act on a sudden impulse. We've upgraded the case to a murder investigation and due to the potential overlap, my team has been assigned to the murder of Polly as well. I had to go and tell her parents. As you can imagine, that did not go well.'

'Hannah said they were estranged?'

'Yes, they said she'd been out of control, so they thought they'd try a bit of tough love. She never spoke to them again. They're going to be tortured about that choice for the rest of their lives,' Brodie said.

There was an awkward pause as they each remembered how they had felt on receiving a similar knock at the door in relation to their own son.

'If it's used in Russia and grown in south-east Asia, then that should help with narrowing down the list of suspects,' mused Grace, stopping while Harvey sniffed a lamppost.

'I'll get a warrant for all their travel plans over the last year,' said Brodie. 'I want to know which of them have travelled to Russia or Asia in particular.'

'I suspect that whoever stole the Fabergé egg is well travelled,' said Grace. 'Something that valuable is in a class of its own and it would be pointless stealing it unless you had the knowledge and experience to move it around the world to elite underground auctions for private collectors.'

'Perhaps such a person also picked up some *Gelsemium* while they were there,' said Brodie grimly.

'I just wish that Fabergé eggs weren't the communication method of choice for Katya's stalker,' said Grace. 'It really muddies the waters.'

'I know. Especially as the latest one left for Katya clearly was meant to imply that Igor Sokolov has been murdered.'

'It could be based on certain knowledge, or it could simply be a crude attempt to frighten and intimidate her. Impossible to know at this stage,' said Grace.

'What I don't yet understand,' said Brodie, 'is what motive there could be for murdering Polly. She's just a local girl. Her parents said that as far as they were aware there was no boy on the scene.'

'It could simply be that she was in the wrong place at the wrong time,' said Grace. 'Perhaps she stumbled on the stalker in Katya's room?'

'Is that you trying to make sure I have to solve your case first in order to clear up my own?' said Brodie with a tired smile.

'I'll take any help I can get.' Grace smiled back.

'Oh, I gather you met Julie the other day?' said Brodie.

Grace stiffened, striving for a neutral expression. 'Yes, I did.'

'She said the pair of you had a right old chinwag. It means a lot to me that you're making a big effort to get along, Grace.'

Oh, Julie was good, thought Grace. What a manipulative little madam. Well, she had her number now and wasn't going to stand by if her antics impacted Brodie. She nodded and smiled, trying not to look as though she was gritting her teeth, though she was. She really was.

FORTY-FIVE

Grace slipped into a comfy armchair in a coffee shop on Portobello High Street. It was still early so they had the massive table to themselves. Jean was off today but had asked to meet her for coffee to share what she'd learned at the library yesterday.

Jean removed a lever arch file from her large shopping bag and opened it up as they sipped from their lattes. Grace was happy to see her so lively and engaged. Personally, she always felt research was a necessary evil but it was interacting with the individuals on a case that sustained her interest. Jean, on the other hand, was glowing. Who'd have thought hours toiling away in a library could have such a marked effect?

'The research into the castle was fascinating,' Jean said. 'The current building was restored in the late twentieth century.'

'So the bulk of the renovations weren't done by Sacha Komorov?'

'No, his renovations were extensive, to be sure, but they seem to have been more cosmetic than structural. However, there *is* a secret passage!' Jean produced a copy of glossy sales particulars. 'These were how the property was marketed for sale ten years ago. It alludes to it clearly here, though it doesn't indicate the full extent of it.'

'Thanks, Jean. Hannah will be thrilled. It looks as though it runs behind the back wall in the first-floor rooms. It's odd that no one has mentioned it to us, don't you think?'

'Maybe they don't know,' replied Jean. 'Sacha must know but he may have simply regarded it as a quirky feature and had no real interest in it.'

'Perhaps,' said Grace. 'It's not as though they're stuck for space. If it was me, I wouldn't necessarily want to advertise what could be regarded as a vulnerability. I'm going to ask him about it. His reaction might be revealing. I assume his head of security, Viktor Levitsky, knows about it, too. That man is practically invisible yet clearly wields considerable power behind the scenes.'

'I'm hoping my research on the household will bear some fruit today,' said Jean. 'It hasn't been easy to find out about what they all got up to in Russia before they came here to live.'

'Outsource parts of it to a Russian agency, if necessary,' said Grace, 'but be sure to double check their legitimacy first. We also need an express service. Don't let them fob you off.'

Jean looked at her.

'Sorry,' said Grace with a rueful smile. 'I know I can be a bit of a control freak.'

'Just a bit.' Jean smiled to take the sting out of her words. 'If that's everything for now, I'm off to do a food shop.'

Grace headed to the castle. She was determined to make progress today as the need for answers was starting to burn a hole in her psyche. They were now into October. It couldn't go on. Sacha Komorov was paying her for results and Katya was in clear and present danger. The sensation of pressure building within her was becoming intolerable. Decisive action was called for.

The first thing she did on arrival was slip upstairs to the nursery as no one should disturb her there. Feeling a thrill of excitement, Grace moved to the back of the room and tapped on the wall. Nothing. It was rock solid. Puzzled, she tapped it all over. There was no difference. There was a mural depicting scenes from Narnia painted on the wall. More on a feeling of whimsy than anything else, Grace went to the part where the wardrobe scene was depicted. It was portrayed in 3D and messed with her sense of spatial awareness. Feeling gently along each painted panel, she could feel no seam or hinge. On the verge of giving up, she pressed the knob on the wardrobe handle and jumped back in fright as the two halves of the wardrobe slid apart, leaving a gap big enough for her to enter sideways. A dank musty smell crept out of the gash of darkness. She could do with Hannah to back her up but if she called upon her now then people might learn that they were working together. However, just in case she fired off a quick text to her.

> Secret passage behind nursery. Press wardrobe door. Going in.

There was no reply. She must be caught up in something. Grace felt inside her shoulder bag for the small powerful torch she always carried and switched it on. Heart in mouth, she slipped through the gap. The door slid noiselessly shut. *Please don't let there be rats*, she thought as she shone the beam around her. There was a wooden stool and a small table with a flask on it. She unscrewed the lid and sniffed. Vodka. Something occurred to her and reluctantly she switched the torch off. No light came from the room. She'd suspected there might be a spyhole so that someone could see into the room without being seen. She switched the torch back on and moved it over the wall she had come through inch by inch. It didn't take her long to find the spyhole, which was opened by moving a knob open or closed. It was closed now, which was why she hadn't seen any light coming through. She left it switched to open so that she could see into the room if she returned this way.

The tunnel wall stopped a few feet away from her on the left, which made sense as the nursery was the last room along here. Turning the other way, she shone her torch into the dark void ahead of her and moved forward. The next room along here was Katya's. Knowing what to look out for now, she soon found the slider and peered into the room. It, too, was empty. Could Polly's killer have left Katya's room in this manner then exited through the nursery? She had to ascertain where the tunnel ended. As she continued along, she felt for the sliders to enable her to count the rooms. When she reached Nikolai's suite of rooms, she thought the tunnel had come to an end once more but soon discovered it veered to the left.

Suddenly, her foot met with empty space and she tumbled down some steep, roughly hewn stairs. Clattering to a halt, she gingerly felt for broken bones but came to the conclusion she'd got off lightly with a twisted ankle, a couple of staved fingers and some bruises. Feeling horribly claustrophobic now, she decided she needed to find a way out pronto. She'd completely lost her bearings and couldn't work out where in the castle she was. It didn't help that the castle was round rather than rectangular with all of the rooms having slightly curved walls. She'd hoped that the stairs might go all the way down to the ground floor but it looked as though she would have to walk along this next floor to find out more.

Feeling hot and clammy, she continued. It felt like there wasn't enough air to breathe. After a while, just when she was about to turn back the way she had come, she heard the sound of voices raised in anger. Following the sound until it was at its strongest, she groped along the wall until she stumbled on the slider, not daring to turn on her torch in case someone in the room noticed it. Opening it, she placed her eye to the hole and realised she was looking into the library from the corner of the massive bookcase.

Sacha Komorov was shouting at Viktor Levitsky. The head of security's face was impassive, but his fists were clenched by his side. Grace tried to focus in on what was being said. From time to time there was an angry outburst in Russian, which was most likely strings of expletives.

'I am under siege in my own castle. A castle which is meant to be impregnable!' he yelled. 'We are being picked off one by one and you dare to tell me you have no idea who is behind it all? If you had failed like this in the FSB, you would have suffered a long slow death.'

'If you had listened to me before we might not be in this situation,' snapped Levitsky.

'You dare to tell me this is my fault?' spluttered Komorov, clearly on the verge of losing control.

'You call me head of security. I am head of nothing,' fired back Levitsky, squaring up to his boss. 'I have no team. I am one man. No man can be everywhere and see everything. You throw silly parties. No CCTV is allowed in case shady business associates don't like it. Your wife skips about anywhere she likes. She invites strangers in to dance with her. It's laughable. The curator can wander down to the gallery unescorted when-ever he feels like it. This isn't a security operation. It's a shambles!'

For a minute, Grace held her breath, fearful that they might come to blows, then Komorov deflated and poured himself a drink. He didn't offer one to Levitsky, though she rather thought he might throw it back at him if he did.

'So, what do you want from me?' Komorov asked, his voice now flat.

'If you want to get this situation under control, I need to hire a team of four mercenaries with military and operational credentials. Your wife doesn't leave the castle without a bodyguard. I have tried to keep tabs on her, but I can't be in multiple places at once. You allowed the housekeeper to secure one of the keycards to the gallery. That was a mistake. She was not security trained. It would've been child's play to take it from her. Your brother, Nikolai, is also a weak link. He is dissolute and a security risk. He should be stopped from coming and going as he pleases. He has also been known to sneak in women under cover of darkness. All visitors must sign in and out and be escorted from the premises. You will need to employ additional house staff as well to meet these requirements, all applicants to be vetted by me.'

'This will cost a fortune,' spluttered Komorov.

Levitsky's face was inscrutable. 'You have a fortune. Your choice.'

'Very well,' sighed Komorov. 'Do it.'

Viktor Levitsky was clearly intent on turning the castle into a prison, thought Grace. She stifled a sneeze brought on by the dust. Irina Petrova would have had a blue fit if she'd seen the mess back here, thought Grace with a small smile. She came to another flight of stairs and managed not to fall down them this time. She stopped once more when she heard the haunting strains of ballet music on the other side of the wall. This time the slider was still open and as she peered into the room she could see Katya dancing, lost in her own enchanted world. Her gaze drifted towards the door. Nikolai was staring straight at her through the glass. She ducked reflexively, her heart pounding but then, she reasoned, he couldn't possibly have seen her; the hole was tiny. Even if he didn't see her, did that mean that he knew about the secret passage? Had he been sneaking about the castle spying on Katya when she was alone in her room? The thought made her shiver. She dared to look again but he had vanished. What would happen if she bumped into someone in here? She knew that it most probably wouldn't end well for her. The thought of that spurred her on to find a way out.

Finally, she found herself in the wine cellar underneath the kitchen. The bad smell that she had detected on this level was at its height now and she couldn't help but gag. She pulled off her cardigan and put it over her nose and mouth. It smelled of putrefaction and the hair on the back of her neck stood up in horror. Daring to shine her torch around the enclosed space, she saw a body slumped against the opposite wall. Forcing herself to bend closer, she could see it had once been human. Stifling a scream, she realised it was Igor Sokolov from the scraps of dance clothing and the ballet shoes on his feet. She jerked back and frantically stabbed her fingers over the wall until she found an exit mechanism. The door swung open, and she hurriedly closed it again, gasping in relief. A puff of fetid air pushed out behind her but soon started to disperse. She rushed up the steps to kitchen level and made her way out of the staff entrance. She didn't want to cause a panic by raising the alarm until the police were here. Also, she didn't want to alert the murderer until the last minute that the body had been discovered. Feeling light-headed, she called Brodie and told him what she'd found then she texted Hannah, who was at work somewhere in the castle. There was no reply.

Her mind went to Katya. This was going to come as a terrible shock. She was most likely still in danger herself. She needed to tell her before someone else did.

FORTY-SIX

Hannah was now on her break and had read the text from Grace in astonishment. Igor Sokolov was dead! She had barely spoken to him the night of the dinner so hadn't really formed a view of what he was like as a person. The body count was rising and she was starting to get scared. Polly's death, in particular, had really freaked her out. Jack had already lost one parent; she couldn't have him lose another. It didn't help that it now appeared there was a creepy secret passage so, for all she knew, the killer could already have clocked her snooping around. What if they thought she was on to them and decided she needed to be silenced? She was feeling a bit woozy. She looked at her mug of tea in horror. What if it had been poisoned? Her throat felt like it was closing up and her heart was thumping. She couldn't get enough air. Half standing up, she clutched at her chest. What was happening to her?

'Are you all right, pet?' asked Sandra Dunlop, turning from the stove in alarm.

'C... can't... breathe,' she stammered, collapsing onto the seat again, trying and failing to suck in mouthfuls of air. Everything was looking black around the edges and she could hear Sandra's voice getting farther away. What was this?

Grace suddenly appeared in front of her, taking both her hands firmly in hers.

'She's taking a funny turn,' shouted the matronly cook. 'Does she need an ambulance?'

'Hannah, look at me.' Her anguished eyes met hers. 'You're having a panic attack. Breathe with me. In... one... two... three.'

'I... can't...'

'Out... four... five... six. In... one... two... three... Out... four... five... six.'

Slowly Hannah's breathing came back under control and the blackness faded from the periphery of her vision.

'Atta girl,' said Sandra, flapping her dish towel in relief. 'You had us proper worried with everything else that's gone on here. Just as well Grace landed on the scene.'

Hannah, to her chagrin, burst into tears. She'd be getting the sack from both jobs if she kept this up. What the hell was wrong with her?

'There, there,' flapped the cook, clearly out of her comfort zone. 'Best you get off home, pet. You're overwrought and can't say as I blame you.'

'I'm sorry,' sobbed Hannah. 'I don't know what's wrong with me.'

'Don't worry,' said Grace, squeezing her hand. 'It's just your body's way of recalibrating. You'll be right as rain in no time. I'll walk you around in the fresh air for a bit and then when you feel steady enough you can drive home.'

Hannah grabbed her bag and jacket, and they left through the staff entrance.

'Grace, I'm so sorry, I don't know what came over me.'

'Has this happened before, Hannah?'

'Once before.' It had happened when she heard about

Connor's death having just discovered she was pregnant. She wasn't about to share that with her though. Grace didn't pry. She liked that about her.

Grace headed for the walled garden and they sat there in silence for a while as Hannah recovered her equilibrium. They then walked round for a while before heading for the car park.

Hannah glanced more closely at her boss as they approached the cars. She was bleached of colour and there was a faint trace of an unpleasant odour coming off her. 'Grace, I got your text. What happened to Igor Sokolov?'

Grace looked conflicted.

'You can tell me, I'm feeling heaps better now,' she protested. A slight exaggeration perhaps but not knowing would worry her more. Hannah turned her head at the sound of tyres crunching on gravel. There were two marked police cars and a van making their way up to the castle they had just left.

'Okay,' said Grace. 'That secret passage winds all the way from the first floor of the castle down to the cellar. I found the body of Igor Sokolov behind the cellar wall.'

'That's awful!' Hannah gasped. 'He was murdered?'

'Yes, for sure,' replied Grace. 'I got out of there as quickly as I could and called Brodie without alerting anyone. When I knew they were on their way, I came to find you. It would appear that our killer is a member of this household.'

They'd now reached the car park but Hannah turned on her heel and started walking back the way they had come. 'I can stay. I want to help,' she said.

'No,' said Grace, pulling on her arm. 'I'm putting my foot down as your boss. Go home. I need you fit and rested tomorrow. That's an order.'

Hannah felt a bit miffed, but she knew that Grace meant well so she capitulated and moved back to her small red car. She waved at Grace as she drove off. She loved working for the agency most of the time but this case was really getting to her. Polly's death had brought home to her that she wasn't invincible.

FORTY-SEVEN

Grace hurried up to Brodie, who was waiting for her at the side of the castle.

'Was that Hannah? Is she all right?' he asked, his forehead creased in concern.

'Yes, she's fine. She's not a witness, so I told her to head home.'

'Does Sacha Komorov know about this?'

'Not yet, unless *he* put Igor's body there. I thought I'd better get you in there before I spoke to him. I'll need to show you how to get into the secret passage to recover the body. It's behind the cellar wall and already putrefying, I'm afraid.'

'How are you wanting to play this, Grace?'

'I can hardly say I was snooping around to the extent of discovering a body in his secret passage,' said Grace. 'I can perhaps mention that to Katya but not him.'

'I'm happy to indicate it was a tip-off from an anonymous source, if that would help?'

'Yes, it would help enormously,' said Grace, relieved. 'I'll take you to see him now then I'll slip away to speak to Katya.

She's going to be devastated about Igor's death, let alone the circumstances in which his body was found.'

They approached via the front door. Grace felt the formality of the occasion called for it though she knew that Brodie already had all the other exits covered. She could hear the bell echoing around empty space. Eventually the door was flung wide and Sacha Komorov appeared, looking haggard.

Wordlessly he showed them into the library. The fire hadn't been lit and the room felt cold and unwelcoming.

'I'm afraid we've had a tip-off that there's a dead body behind the cellar wall,' Brodie said.

'You cannot be serious,' said Komorov, running his hand through his thick black hair. 'How did it get there?'

'That has still to be determined,' Brodie said. 'Do we have your permission to search the castle and recover it?'

'I can hardly say no, in the circumstances,' Komorov said wearily. 'Do you know the identity of the body?'

'We've an unconfirmed report that it's the missing dancer, Igor Sokoloff,' replied Brodie.

Komorov let loose a couple of Russian words that were undoubtedly an oath. 'Do what you must,' he said and stood up in front of the fireplace with his back to them. Clearly, they were dismissed, thought Grace.

'Before we go, sir,' said Brodie as he, too, rose to his feet with Grace. 'Can you tell me the full extent of the hidden passageway behind the castle walls?'

Komorov went very still then turned round to face them. 'It extends from the nursery to the cellar and beyond that to the woods on the other side of the walled garden.'

'You didn't think to mention it to anyone before?' said Grace, exasperated.

'It would have compromised our security. Only myself and Viktor, my head of security, know about it. Nobody else.'

Did he realise he'd just landed himself in a suspect pool of two? wondered Grace. Or was he so accustomed to bending people to his will that he thought there was no mess so big that he couldn't be extricated from it? Although if Jean had managed to find out about it then no doubt other people could have as well.

She led Brodie down to the entrance to the cellar where his team were assembled. They all filed down the wide roughly hewn stone steps. Grace put a handkerchief over her face and opened the secret door. The smell burst into the cellar, and she retreated to the steps as the forensic team got to work under Brodie's direction. Turning on her heel, she left them to it. There was nothing more for her to do here.

She went in search of Katya, uncertain as to whether Sacha would have had time to break the news to her. Running lightly up the stone stairs and all the way to the first floor landing, she tapped lightly on her door. There was no reply. She tried the handle but it was locked. Grace then ran back down to the dance studio. There were no strains of music drifting along the corridor so initially she thought that she wasn't there but when she stuck her head round the door, she found her hunched in a corner in the semi-darkness, weeping quietly. She went over to her and sank down onto the floor beside her.

'I take it you've heard,' she said quietly.

Katya nodded. 'Sacha came and told me. He pretended to be sad but he's glad, I know he is!' she burst out.

'Did you know about the secret passage?' Grace asked.

'No, of course not! I hate the fact that someone has been spying on me in my bedroom. It makes my skin crawl to think some maggot has been creeping around behind my wall with their tongue hanging out. How could Sacha not tell me?'

Grace had no answer for her. Maybe Sacha had been the one wandering around the castle walls spying on everyone to make sure he was not being betrayed?

'Is it possible anyone lurking behind the wall might have seen anything that could lead to Igor's murder?'

Her hand flew to her mouth and anguished eyes beseeched her.

'Igor and I... well, you can guess the rest,' she whispered. 'Do you think that Sacha saw?'

'I think that someone did,' said Grace, patting her on the arm as she got up to go. 'Is there anywhere else you can go?' she then asked the broken ballerina.

'No, the only life I have is here within these walls.'

'Has there been any more communication from your stalker?'

'No, nothing more.'

'Igor had an imitation Fabergé egg in his room at the hotel. It contained an engagement ring. I assume it was for you, Katya. I'm so sorry.'

'Our love was true,' she said, tilting her chin and wiping her eyes. 'If I tell you something, will you promise not to tell another soul?'

'I promise,' Grace replied, 'as long as it doesn't impede the police investigation.'

'I'm pregnant,' she said.

'And the father?'

She shrugged, helplessly.

'Are you sure you don't want me to find you somewhere else to stay?'

'No. I gambled and lost. I accept my fate is to remain here. In time, Sacha will forgive me, I am sure.'

But can you forgive him, if it turns out that he murdered the love of your life? wondered Grace.

FORTY-EIGHT

Grace made her way up the central staircase once more. The more she thought about it the more likely it seemed to her that if the Fabergé egg was still in the castle, it would be hidden somewhere in the nursery. That was where the secret tunnel commenced and it was the only one of the rooms with doors opening out from the passage that wasn't currently in use. Hannah had also mentioned she had seen Oliver coming out of the nursery when she reached Katya's room the day that Polly was murdered. If he knew about the secret passage, he could of course have murdered Polly in Katya's room and then come out of the door into the nursery looking like an innocent bystander. The same could also be said for Nikolai, who had come dashing along from his suite. Sacha had been downstairs in the library, which would have been a much tighter timescale, though not impossible. As for Katya herself, hadn't she been dancing at the time? Something occurred to her. A few times when she had gone looking for Katya, she had heard the ballet music, seen the lights on and simply assumed she was in there dancing. If she knew about the secret passage, perhaps she, too, could have been prowling around watching people behind the wall before returning to the studio once more as if she had never left. As for Viktor Levitsky, the shadowy head of security, Sacha had shared the existence of the secret passage with him. Her mind was churning different possibilities round and round, unable to settle on a single coherent theory.

Letting herself into the nursery, she started to search it in earnest. There were so many beautiful toys and exquisite pieces in here. She hoped that Katya's child would get the opportunity to enjoy them one day. Dropping to her hands and knees, she looked inside the three-storey doll's house and her heart skipped a beat in shock. Each of the crime scenes for the three murders had been crudely re-enacted in detail. From the body behind the wall in the cellar where a false wall had been added and was gaping open, to Irina Petrova sitting in her wing-backed chair frothing at the mouth with her tea cup upended. Finally, there was Polly, a floor above lying on her back, a red mark staining her neck. Even their clothes were a nod to what each had been wearing when they were murdered. Igor was in dance clothes, Polly had her maid's uniform on and Irina was in her black housekeeping dress. Opening up the doors, she photographed the contents. The other rooms were empty, awaiting decoration. Waiting for the next victim? Grace closed the door and spun round. The sun had moved round, and the room was filled with shadows. She had a sudden feeling she was being watched and raced over to open the secret door, straining her ears for the sound of footsteps hurrying away but there were none. It must have been her imagination. Either way, she needed to get out of here.

It was now clear to her that they were dealing with a psychopath with a severely twisted mind, which put everyone, including her and Hannah, in grave danger. It was most likely someone she knew but whose mask was so firmly in place she had been unable to detect the monster behind it.

Opening the door, she hesitated. She was going to have to

get Brodie up here pronto to see this, which meant she wouldn't get another opportunity to search for the missing Fabergé egg until his team were done with the room. They might even bag everything up and take it with them.

Although it was the last thing that she felt like doing, she turned back into the room and started examining every item there to see if it could conceal the egg. She felt all around the cot, under the padded chairs, every drawer in the bassinette and changing unit. Nothing. She turned her attention to the toys, prodding gently as the last thing she wanted to do was damage them. Again, nothing. Exasperated, she looked round again. This time her attention was caught by a large nest of dolls, which she suspected had cost a fortune as it was covered in intricate gold leaf patterns. She unscrewed it and discovered another doll. She removed and looked inside three of them. When she pulled out the fourth, it rattled and felt heavier. Scarcely daring to breathe, she unscrewed it and sat back on her haunches, gasping in disbelief. She had found it. She had found the missing Fabergé egg.

Hurriedly, she wrapped it in a soft coverlet from the cot and placed it into her satchel. She had to get it to Sacha and then that would be one of her cases concluded at least. Reaching for the door handle, she glanced in the mirror to her right and what she saw in it chilled her to her core. The door to the secret passage was open like a gaping mouth. She pulled on the handle, but it was too late. Someone was behind her and before she could react the back of her head received a heavy blow. Everything went black.

'Grace! She's coming round! Over here, officer.'

Nikolai. What was he doing here?

Grace blinked uncertainly. What was going on? Her head hurt like hell.

'What time is it?' she asked groggily, struggling to sit up.

'Easy does it, Grace.' Brodie swam into view. 'Someone bashed you on the head. You were out stone cold. I don't know for how long.'

What had she been doing... before...? It felt as though an opaque fog was swirling in amongst her thoughts. Suddenly, the fog cleared. The Fabergé egg, it was in her satchel. She'd been on her way to return it to Sacha. Where was it now? Hurriedly, she pulled the satchel towards her. It was right next to her, thank God. She fumbled with the straps then groaned loudly. Whoever had attacked her had made off with it.

'We need to get you to the hospital,' Brodie said. 'They'll want to give you a scan to check there's no internal damage.'

'No way, Brodie, that's not necessary,' she protested weakly.

'No point arguing, Grace, it's a done deal. They're on their way. It looks like you were hit with this.' He held up a baseball bat with blood on it.

'That definitely wasn't there before,' she said, then she turned her head towards Nikolai, looking at him with narrowed eyes, 'Where did you come from, Nikolai?'

'I was at the top of the stairs when I heard the crash and came to investigate,' he said. 'I stayed with you and texted Sacha to get the police up here.'

'Did you see who attacked you, Grace?' asked Brodie.

'Unfortunately not,' sighed Grace. Her head was banging with pain now and she was feeling more than a little nauseous.

Sacha tapped on the door then entered, followed by two paramedics.

'Really, I'm sorry they called you, there was no need...' began Grace, then yelped as one of them probed her poor head.

'Sorry. She needs to go in,' said the paramedic to Brodie. 'She could have a subdural haematoma. Not worth the risk. She'll most likely be admitted overnight from A & E.'

Grace knew there was something she needed to tell Brodie

hovering at the periphery of her consciousness, but she couldn't find the words. She motioned to Sacha Komorov and he bent down to listen to her. Her voice seemed to be weaker and it was an effort to push the words out. 'I found the Fabergé egg in the nest of dolls. I was bringing it to you but the person who hit me got it. I'm sorry...'

Sacha's face had lit up only for hope to be extinguished once more. His face receded. Brodie's reappeared. She gripped his arm and brought his face down to hers. 'Fabergé egg in castle,' she managed. 'I had it but now it's gone. Don't let it get out of the castle. Doll's house... look in doll's house...' Then everything went black once more.

FORTY-NINE

Grace woke up in hospital to find Jean and Hannah beside her bed, staring at her with anxious eyes. She tried to speak but her tongue felt stuck to the roof of her mouth. Jean lifted a plastic cup of liquid with a straw to her lips and she took a few sips. Much better. 'What time is it?' she asked. 'How long have I been here?'

'Don't freak out, but it's 2.15 on Wednesday,' said Hannah.

'Wednesday?' said Grace with a start. 'How did that happen?'

'You had a subdural haematoma,' explained Jean. 'Your brain was swelling so they needed to put you in a medically induced coma until it returned to normal.'

'In other words, I'm fine,' said Grace. 'Where are my clothes? I need to get out of here.' She pulled herself up to a sitting position.

Jean and Hannah exchanged meaningful looks.

'You tell her, Jean, I'm too scared,' said Hannah.

'You're not getting out until tomorrow at the earliest and that's final,' said Jean firmly.

'But...'

'Not another word, Grace,' said Jean. 'You scared us all half to death. Brodie has been beside himself. He's already been here this morning. Your whole family have been here at different times. You need to cooperate with the doctors and rest until they're completely sure that you're well enough to be discharged.'

'Okay,' said Grace meekly. 'Can I at least talk about the case?'

'No!' they both answered in unison.

'It's all under control,' said Hannah, exchanging an enigmatic look with Jean.

'What about Harvey?'

'I took him home with me,' said Jean. 'I'm catering to his every whim. He may not want to leave.'

'She's not joking.' Hannah grinned. 'I'm starting to wish *I* was her dog!'

'But the Fabergé egg... I held it in my hand. The person who whacked me must have it by now.'

'Everyone who leaves the castle has to have their bag searched,' said Hannah. 'Viktor Levitsky set up a checkpoint and there are guards at all the exits funnelling people towards it. The secret passageway is also blocked off. A temporary wall has been put in place so they can't travel past the cellar so they can't get out that way.'

'So, with a bit of luck, it's still in the castle,' said Grace, falling back on her pillow. Despite herself she could feel exhaustion stealing over her.

'You need to get some sleep.' Grace was dimly aware of Jean patting her hand then faded away again.

She didn't know how much time had passed before she became aware of another voice by her bed. It was Brodie. She tried to focus in on what he was saying. Her eyes felt as though they were stuck together. It was too hard to try and open them.

'You nearly gave me a heart attack, Grace. When I entered

that room and saw you lying there unconscious, I thought I'd lost you for good. It felt as though the world had stopped. It made me realise how much I still love you. I want us to be a family again, Grace. What I'm trying to say is I want you back, every last cranky, stubborn, unreasonable part of you. I don't know if you'll have me. I don't know how I'm going to manage things with Julie, but I'm working on it. God, you're so much easier to talk to when you're unconscious. I've tried to talk to you several times but given up.'

He subsided into silence though kept holding her hand, which she was dying to scratch, but she couldn't let him know she'd heard all that. She had to sort out her own feelings first, though she definitely knew *one* thing. She loved him, too.

After a suitable pause, she opened her eyes. 'Brodie?'

'You're awake! I hear that you're getting out tomorrow.'

'Yes, I feel heaps better,' she lied.

There was an awkward pause and he let go of her hand on the pretext of looking at his watch.

'Did you see inside the doll's house?' she asked.

'Yes, I did. It gave me grave cause for concern. It appears we may be dealing with a psychopath who enjoys messing with us. I didn't get back in the room until later as our main priority was getting you to hospital and recovering the body behind the wall. However, when I popped back up, I saw this.' He showed her a photo on his phone that made her suck in her breath in disbelief. An empty room in the doll's house had been redecorated as a nursery. It showed her prone body by the door with blood in her hair.

'That's crazy!' she said, shaking her head in disbelief. 'His need to complete his ritual was greater than his need to avoid being caught.'

'The thing is, Grace, I suspect he might not rest until he's finished the job. At the time he completed this he may not have known that you'd survived.'

FIFTY

Hannah was sick to death of the castle but felt she owed it to Grace to continue to show up and do whatever she could to solve their cases so they could all get their lives back. Poor Grace could have died. It was infuriating to think that she'd managed to find the egg only to have it snatched away again. At least she was getting out of hospital today. As Hannah arrived at the car park, she saw a couple of police cars parked nearer the castle, then she spotted two officers patrolling the perimeter. One of them stopped her on the way in but when she showed her driving licence, they ticked her name off a list and let her proceed. Hannah felt reassured by their presence. She trudged into the castle and headed along the corridor to the kitchen. When she had first started here the place had been spotless and had run like a well-oiled machine. Now to say there was a skeleton staff would be an understatement. There weren't enough bodies to get the job done and it showed. The whole castle seemed to droop with neglect. Sighing, she turned into the kitchen before stopping in her tracks. Sandra Dunlop was slumped at the kitchen table sobbing, twisting a large cotton hanky round and round in her puffy hands. She looked up and saw Hannah and beckoned her in, making a huge effort to stop crying, her chest heaving with the effort.

'Don't mind me, lass, in you come and have a seat.'

Hannah went to the sink and poured Sandra a glass of water then went to sit opposite her.

'Are you okay?' she asked, worried in case something else had happened.

Sandra Dunlop shook her head, her face flushed with emotion. 'I just can't stop thinking about poor Polly. I can't eat. I can't sleep.'

'I know,' sighed Hannah. 'Me neither. I just can't wrap my head around the fact that she's gone. It's like I expect her to walk in the kitchen any minute or jump out at me from behind a pillar like she used to do.'

Sandra gave a wobbly smile. 'She was so full of life, that one. Never a dull moment when she was around.'

They both paused and the silence seemed somehow excruciating, emphasising Polly's absence.

'All kids think they're invincible,' Sandra sighed. 'Polly was clearly in over her head. All she wanted was a bit of a start in life but there was no one to give it to her. Her parents turfed her out at sixteen. Didn't want to know. She was all on her own in the world.'

Hannah tensed but said nothing, not wanting to disturb her train of thought. It was as if Sandra was almost talking to herself.

'She was desperate to get away from here. She must've been or she wouldn't have done it. She was a good lass at heart.'

'I know she was,' said Hannah, softening her voice. 'What did she do?'

'She tried to blackmail someone. That's what got her killed.'

'How do you know?' asked Hannah, surprised. This was the first she'd heard of it.

'I found the letter in one of her uniforms when it was

returned to me for washing after her death. She was only asking for £500. Imagine killing a young girl for that amount of money. What monster would do that?'

'Do you still have the letter?'

'Yes. I was in two minds what to do with it. I thought there was no point in sullying her reputation. Nothing I could do would bring her back. I only wish she'd confided in me.'

'Wait a minute, you said the letter was in the pocket of her uniform,' said Hannah. 'Maybe the person she intended to blackmail never even saw it?'

Sandra put down her drink and stared at her. 'You're right! I never looked at it like that. I've been too upset to think straight. So, it might not have been Oliver who killed her. He was the one she was attempting to blackmail. She thought he'd stolen something. Something worth a lot of money. I've been keeping quiet in case he came for me next. We've never gotten along.'

'Maybe now you can tell the police?' said Hannah. 'They won't let on it was you.'

'But if it wasn't him, then who killed her?' Sandra asked, turning anguished eyes upon her.

'It might still have been him. She could have sent him another version of the letter. Or, if he really didn't see it, then it might not be important. Either way you need to tell the police. We need to get justice for Polly,' said Hannah determinedly.

FIFTY-ONE

Grace was impatient to crack on with the case and drove out to the castle first thing on the Friday. Her sister Cally had picked her up from hospital yesterday and dropped her back home at Portobello. Aside from a headache, it was business as usual. Hannah had told her about her conversation with Sandra Dunlop, the castle cook. Grace still wasn't convinced that Oliver was out of the frame as her killer, though. The letter in the uniform was unsigned and could simply have been an early draft.

Once at the castle, she immediately noticed the police presence. No doubt there would be a couple of officers stationed inside as well. Brodie was no doubt annoyed that Sacha had refused to relocate the household but he seemed determined to tough it out. Mind you, if the killer was already part of the household, then relocation was hardly likely to solve the problem. Her first port of call was Katya. Grace was becoming more and more concerned for her safety given the pace of recent unfolding events. She managed to find her in the magnificent lounge where she was curled up in the corner of an enormous sofa in front of a huge stone fireplace. The fire was lit and the logs were giving out a pleasant warmth. Her client looked pale and withdrawn. Glancing up, her eyes widened in surprise, and she motioned for Grace to join her on the sofa.

'I didn't expect you. How is your head?'

'Still attached,' said Grace with a smile. She lowered her voice. 'Have you told Sacha about the baby?'

'Yes,' she said with a wan smile. 'He is over the moon.' She, too, lowered her voice. 'He says he will not question the provenance as long as I have another soon after.'

Grace grimaced. 'How do you feel about that?'

'I have come to accept that feelings are a luxury I can do without. It is best option for baby so that is best option for me.'

'And you're both going to continue living here? After what happened?'

'The secret passage will be blocked off completely soon. I will be safe from prying eyes. I can keep my dance studio but no more partners. However, in my heart I still dance with Igor. He is my shadow partner and I hold him close to me when I dance.'

'And that is enough for you?'

'It will have to be.' She shrugged. 'Once belly is big with child I cannot dance anyway. Once investigation is concluded all staff will be sacked and replaced so it will be a fresh start.'

'Even Viktor?'

She shook her head. 'Not him. He stays. My husband needs him. He is, how do you say, security blanket?' Katya gave a little laugh, pleased at her own joke.

'Do you know why the two of them have such a strong bond?' asked Grace.

'No, he has never told me. Viktor has been with him for many years. That is all I know.'

'Have you told Sacha about your stalker yet?'

'Yes. He was angry with me for not telling him before. He says if he finds them before you, he will kill them for terrifying me so much.'

'Did you tell him you asked me to investigate?'

'Yes, he knows you were only trying to help, so you do not need to worry.'

'Have you been into the nursery recently?' asked Grace. 'Is the doll house still there?'

Grace thought it would probably have been removed as evidence by the police but thought she'd better warn her just in case it had been left behind.

'The police took it but I saw it before.' She shuddered. 'Mad bad person done this.'

'Did Sacha mention that I had found the Imperial Egg?'

'Yes, but now it's gone again. Sacha is angry all the time. He stomps about this way and that way. I keep out of his way.'

Grace regarded the beautiful young woman. A dancer who could only dance alone trapped inside a stone castle. 'And you're sure that this is the life you want? I can get you help, somewhere to go. You have options,' said Grace.

'I am decided. No more talking.'

Grace nodded. 'Understood. It has got to be your decision. No more nasty messages from the stalker?'

'Nothing since you went away. Maybe now the passage is to be blocked and everyone knows, he is scared to creep about in case he is caught? I am afraid still. Maybe my fear is enough for him?'

Grace took her leave, her mind filled with foreboding.

Her next port of call, before she announced herself to Sacha, was the nursery. She stood outside the door, her heartrate increasing as she gently turned the handle, determined to confront what had happened to her and shine some light on it. There was still a smear of her blood on the floor. The castle was clearly still in need of staff.

She tutted in annoyance as she saw the doll house. Why hadn't the police secured it as evidence like Katya said? She went over to it and opened the door only to gape in astonishment. The house contained four completely empty rooms with white lining paper on the floors and walls. A blank canvas again. But for what? She took a step back and her eyes flew round the room in case someone was hidden there, waiting to pounce. The killer clearly wasn't done yet.

Grace prowled around the beautiful nursery that now had the feel of some Gothic horror film about it. The nest of dolls was missing, which was to be expected. They would be examining that for prints and DNA. Glancing at the crib, she noticed a new addition. A baby doll was now under the coverlet. She lifted the cover off the doll but there was nothing nasty underneath it. Maybe Katya had put it there for the new arrival? Then she lifted the doll itself and dropped it like a hot potato. Forcing herself to pick it up again by the arm, she gingerly turned it around. Instead of the back of the doll's head being normal, it had another quite different face. One face had blue eyes and the other had brown. Somebody knew about the affair between Katya and Igor Sokolov. Grace felt sick to her stomach. She had to figure out exactly what was going on before someone else lost their life, or she would never forgive herself.

FIFTY-TWO

Grace went in search of Sacha Komorov. He wasn't in the library or any of the magnificent public rooms opening off the octagonal inner hall. She balked at tapping on the door of his suite upstairs but listened carefully at the door and heard nothing. She was pleased that Katya had taken his advice and now slept in there at night so was less likely to come to harm than if she slept alone. He must be outside somewhere.

Feeling as though the energy had drained out of her feet and into the floor, she headed out. Finally, she found him in the walled garden where he was sitting on a bench looking morose.

'Please,' he said. 'Sit.'

Grace joined him on the bench. The garden was a riot of colour as the leaves put on their autumnal display. A small fountain tinkled in the central bed and animated birdsong punctuated the air.

'Have you recovered from your injury?' he asked, turning to scrutinise her.

'Yes, I was lucky. I could have died.'

'I'm sorry. The Imperial Egg. It is tainted for me now. No object is worth all this suffering.'

'Especially when it's fake,' said Grace, turning her head to look at him.

He stiffened then nodded. 'How long have you known?' he asked, his voice flat and stripped of all emotion.

'I suspected for a while. You're so careful and controlled, it seemed increasingly unlikely that you would allow such a treasure to be stripped from you. It was a test of loyalty. You suspected that you had a traitor in your midst.'

'A traitor, yes. A murderer, no. If I had known how things would turn out, I would never have put all of this into motion.'

'That's why you were so reluctant to involve the police at the beginning,' said Grace flatly. 'You hired me for appearances and because you expected me to fail. You did your research all right. Probably concluded that I was a washed-up mess?'

Sacha looked uncomfortable. Two pink spots flared in his pallid complexion. 'Clearly, I was wrong,' he said with a small tight smile.

'I take it the real Imperial Egg is in a bank vault somewhere?'

'Yes, it has been authenticated and insured.'

'Unbelievable,' said Grace, shaking her head with a sigh. 'Did Viktor know, too?'

'No, I told no one. I still need you to ascertain who stole the replica,' he said.

'Whoever it was clearly believes that it's authentic as they were willing to take the risk of killing me to get it back,' said Grace.

'We must let them continue to think that,' said Komorov. 'Otherwise, they will go to ground, and this will all have been for nothing.'

'The police have made you aware of the likelihood that a psychopath is behind the spate of killings?'

'Yes, they showed me the doll's house before they took it away. It was... disturbing.'

'I've just been up there,' Grace said, watching him closely. 'There's another identical doll's house been put in its place. It has four rooms that remain bare.' She decided not to tell him about the double-faced doll. She suspected his decision not to question the parentage of the baby had been a hard one for him to make and she didn't want to disturb such a volatile arrangement if it brought both him and Katya some measure of peace.

Sacha sprang to his feet and began pacing up and down. 'What does this person want from me? I don't understand!'

'Well, he or she has certainly got our attention,' said Grace. 'I don't think it's any longer as simple as a visceral hatred for you or anyone under the mantle of your protection.'

'You think it could be a woman?'

'It's impossible to say. However, the killer has now got a taste for killing. It may be that this desire was dormant but has been reactivated.'

'You think it's likely that they have killed before all this?'

'Perhaps,' said Grace. She wished that she had more to offer him, but she couldn't conjure evidence out of thin air and it might be harmful to speculate about something so important. She looked at the closed expression on his face.

'Who in your household has killed before?' she asked.

'Nobody!' His mouth protested but his eyes told a different story.

'Your brother, Nikolai. Did he do his national service in Russia?'

'Yes, as did I. He acquitted himself well, by all accounts. He could have escaped the draft. He had been educated in England at a boarding school, but he chose to do his duty before he went to university.'

'Did he choose it? Or did you choose it for him?'

Sacha's mouth tightened in anger. 'I always acted in Nikolai's best interests. Sometimes he did not understand exactly what those were.'

'Did he see any action?'

'Some. Before you ask, Viktor and I were also in the military. I did what you would term my national service but Viktor had a military career.'

'And then joined the FSB?'

'That is not for me to say. None of this has anything to do with the situation we find ourselves in.'

'Viktor Levitsky seems particularly loyal to you. Is there a reason for that?'

Sacha gave her a twisted smile. 'Am I so terrible in your eyes that I cannot possibly inspire any loyalty without owning a man body and soul?'

'That's not what I meant,' she protested.

'When he was in the FSB, he made a very dangerous enemy. That person was also trying to destroy me and obliterate my standing in the regime. What is that expression?'

'My enemy's enemy is my friend?' supplied Grace.

'Exactly. I helped him take down a dangerous foe and escape with his life and reputation intact.'

Grace nodded thoughtfully and excused herself. Russia could cast a long shadow and what was going on in the castle spoke of real resentment if not out and out hatred. It might not be Viktor, but someone was harbouring a very real and dangerous grudge.

FIFTY-THREE

Grace waited until the police removed the second doll's house. She suspected another one would appear before long. The nursery door had been locked but it was going to be over a week before an appropriate contractor could seal off the secret passage effectively. All of this was taking its toll on the occupants of the castle and also on her own staff. She needed to double down and get results and the sooner the better. There were two angles of the case she hadn't fully explored yet. One of these was the occupants of the neighbouring Balhousie estate. The other was Viktor Levitsky, who, far from showing an active interest in her investigation, seemed to disappear whenever she was around. Now she thought about it that was rather odd in itself. If she was in his shoes, she would be dogging his footsteps. Maybe it was time that she paid him a visit rather than waiting for him to show up at his office.

She knew that he lived in a cottage in the grounds, but she hadn't anticipated it would be quite so hidden away. The cottage was dark and brooding with the woodland trees at its rear cutting out a lot of light. The small garden was paved with a few tubs of flowers and a couple of wooden benches and a table. She opened the wooden gate and walked up the path before pressing the doorbell. The sound echoed down the hallway but there was no sign of life forthcoming. Glancing around, she walked to the back of the house, keeping her posture upright. Nothing to see here. Behind the fence of the rear garden, which contained only a small lawn with a washing line, the densely packed trees loomed. Anyone could be watching her from in there. She knocked on the back door. Nothing. She turned the handle and to her surprise the door opened. *What kind of a security man goes out without locking his door?* she wondered. Was it a trap?

'Hello,' she called out, opening the door and stepping inside into the kitchen. It was comfortably equipped but the style was pared back and minimal although what was there was of good quality and impeccably clean. She walked over to the kettle and touched the side, drawing her finger away quickly. Still boiling hot. She flushed as adrenaline flooded her system. He was still in the house. Why hadn't he come to the door? What was he playing at?

Armed with the knowledge of his presence, she didn't open the drawers or cupboards and snoop around as she longed to do but continued through to the lounge where he was sitting in a leather armchair beside the fireplace. He gave her a cold smile with no warmth in it, raking her up and down from head to toe. He looked like a cobra poised to strike and Grace scented danger with every fibre of her being. An Alsatian dog sat to attention beside him, baring its teeth, a low growl deep in its throat. Awaiting an instruction to attack?

'Hello,' she said. 'Didn't you hear me knock? I thought I'd best come in when I noticed the back door was open, check that you were okay, given recent events.'

He gave a mirthless laugh as if he admired her cheek. 'Please, won't you sit down? Or perhaps you would like to examine the rest of my home, in case there might be... casualties?'

'You're aware that I'm only here to look into the missing Imperial Egg,' Grace stated. Sacha had said that Viktor wasn't in on the fact that it was a fake so that was the way she would have to play it.

'I'm aware that you have been crawling all over the castle looking into whatever takes your fancy. I am head of security. This is my job, not yours.'

'If you had done your job well then none of this would have happened.' Grace hardened her voice. He was not the kind of man who would respect weakness.

'I cannot do the job with one hand tied behind my back,' he snapped. 'No cameras in the house, he says, apart from in the gallery itself. For someone in his position, his wife should not leave the property without a dedicated bodyguard. Instead, she floats here, there and everywhere on a whim and I am left to pick up the pieces and hide the bodies.' He laughed unpleasantly, seeing Grace's startled expression. 'I did not mean this in literal sense. Even you cannot conduct yourself properly and ended up in hospital! I am surrounded by amateurs. One man can only do so much.'

'Quite the pity party you have going on there,' Grace said drily. 'I can see why. There have now been three murders and one attempted murder at the castle. I'm surprised you haven't been sacked for incompetence.'

'You poke the bear with a stick then maybe you get eaten alive,' he snapped.

'Is that a threat?' she asked. 'Didn't threats use to be your stock in trade? I heard that you used to work for the FSB. Like debt collectors on steroids. Did poison come as standard in your kit?'

His knotted muscles gave away his tension, but his face

remained impassive. 'I do not have time to play silly games,' he said.

'What? Like with doll houses? Do you enjoy playing with *them*?'

At first, he looked confused. *Maybe he doesn't know*, she thought, but then a flicker of recognition was followed by a flash of revulsion. He knew. Moreover, he had at least an idea as to who was behind all this.

'Tell me!' she demanded.

'I have nothing to tell.' He stood up, his face a perfect blank. 'I need you to leave now. I have work to do. If I hear anything about the Imperial Egg, I will come and tell you.'

Grace left, her mind spinning. If he had an inkling of who was behind the murders, why didn't he tell her? Who was he protecting? Could it be Sacha himself?

FIFTY-FOUR

Grace hadn't known what to expect of Balhousie estate. Harris Hamilton certainly hadn't impressed her as someone with taste and discernment. However, clearly his interior designer wife, Hilary, was extremely talented. The beautiful drawing room could have materialised straight from between the pages of a *Home & Country* magazine feature. The ceiling was high with ornate rose cornicing and the furniture was beautifully uphol- stered in fine materials in strong autumnal colours that ought to clash but instead flowed together beautifully. Grace thought of her own basic décor and sighed wistfully. Mind you, she couldn't imagine Harvey chilling on the couch in a place like this either, and a dog was what made a house a home in her humble opinion.

The door opened and Hilary breezed in with a welcoming smile followed by a young woman about Hannah's age hefting a tray of tea with what smelled like freshly baked shortbread. She was wearing a uniform of a plain grey dress with a white lace-trimmed pinny tied in a bow at the back.

'Grace, this is a pleasant surprise,' Hilary said, like she meant it. 'Thank you, Rosie, that will be all.'

'I remembered your kind invitation to show me around your beautiful home,' Grace said, smiling. 'This is quite the calling card you have here.'

'You like it? Next time you come it might be quite different. I like to ring the changes. Fashion never stays still.'

There was an awkward pause.

'I heard about what happened to you. I can't believe you're already up and about. If that was me, I'd have milked it for all its worth,' said Hilary, pouring the tea.

Grace laughed. 'If only I could. Hilary, I think it's time that I levelled with you. I'm actually a private investigator hired by the family in relation to certain difficulties they're having.'

'Good heavens! Tell me more,' she said as she handed over a cup of tea in a delicate china cup.

'Have you heard anything at all as to the potential where-abouts of the missing Imperial Egg?' asked Grace, nodding her thanks as she accepted a piece of shortbread.

Hilary laughed and took a sip of tea before replying, 'My husband and Sacha are bitter rivals on the collecting front. They enjoy nothing more than snatching some valuable piece from under the other's nose. It's a bad case of arrested development. However, I think both of them would draw the line at outright theft from the other's home.'

'Are you aware that there's a secret passage in Traprain Castle?' asked Grace.

'Yes, I've even been in it,' she said.

'How come?' asked Grace, wondering why Sacha hadn't mentioned it.

'Because we were trying to buy it at the time and Harris insisted they showed us round every nook and cranny,' she said. 'I think that's what kicked off their rivalry, to be honest. Harris had his heart set on the castle. Personally, I prefer it here but for Harris, nothing quite says you've arrived like owning your own Scottish castle.'

Grace realised that she really liked this woman with her ironic sense of humour. How she coped with being married to such a bombastic snobbish bore was anyone's guess. 'There seems to be quite a lot of crossover between staff amongst the two estates,' she said.

'Hardly surprising, really,' said Hilary. 'The grass is always greener and we're the only two employers offering this kind of work for several miles.'

'What can you tell me about Oliver Compton-Ross?' asked Grace.

'Strictly between us?'

'Of course!'

'He's a thoroughly bad egg. His references were impeccable, but we later found out they were completely fake. He'd supposedly worked for the Duke of Buccleuch down in Dumfries and Galloway, which, as you can imagine, impressed my husband no end. We telephoned the number on the letter and spoke to the head curator, who was very complimentary but it transpired she was an actress.'

'What about his degree and schooling? Was any of it real?'

'His degree in fine art is real but he grew up on a council estate in Easterhouse. He got a scholarship to Fettes and then through the school friends he made there managed to catapult himself into the world of country houses and fine dining.'

'It's... almost admirable,' said Grace.

'I felt similarly conflicted until I factored in the fact that he'd stolen from us and also inveigled young Polly into his plan.'

'How did you find out about his background?'

'After he stole from us, I started with the headmaster at Fettes. Our boys went there and we've been staunch supporters of the school. They were keen to avoid any scandal attaching to a former pupil.'

'Were there any signs of other unusual behaviours whilst he

was working for you? For example, cruelty to animals?' asked Grace.

'Good heavens, no! Or not that I'm aware of,' she said, looking alarmed now. 'I know that we should never have given him a reference, but we were desperate to have him out from under our roof and he threatened to go to the tabloids and make up stuff about my husband.'

'And, of course, if he also ripped off Sacha that would be the cherry on the cake?'

Hilary sighed. 'Sacha can take care of himself. Or at least we thought he could. You can't think Oliver is behind all these killings? He's just your garden variety conman as far as I'm aware.'

'Honestly, I have no idea,' said Grace, now munching on a buttered blueberry scone. 'All I know is that the occupants of the castle, including those who work there, remain in terrible danger until the killer is apprehended.'

'You must let us know if there's anything we can do to help?'

'Do you have a similar gallery set-up to the Komorovs?'

'Why yes, we do. We employed the same firm of architects. It's rather specialised.'

'Would it be possible to see down there?' Grace asked.

'What, now?' Hilary asked, looking rather perplexed.

'If you wouldn't mind,' Grace said, almost holding her breath.

'Fine, why not? Follow me and don't let on to my husband. You'd think we kept the crown jewels down there. I hardly ever bother going down.'

There was no lift but, instead, a separate staircase leading down three flights of stairs. At the bottom was a door which was opened with a keycard that Hilary had obtained from a built-in wall safe on the way down. As the door opened, the gallery flooded with light. Both women looked at each other in stunned silence. There, on a raised plinth glinting in the spotlight, was no other than the missing replica Fabergé Imperial Egg in all its fake splendour.

Footsteps clattered down the stairs behind them.

'Hilary, what are you doing down here?' a querulous voice demanded. As he came through the door and saw them both standing there, Harris Hamilton's thunderstruck expression was something to behold.

Grace was furious. 'Was it you who put me in hospital?' she demanded.

'Harris, what have you done?' his poor wife faltered.

'What? No, of course not! Don't be ridiculous,' he blustered.

Both women folded their arms and glared at him, stony-faced.

'Fine,' he sighed, motioning to some elegant chairs grouped at one end of the gallery. 'I'll come clean. First of all, I did not attack you or anybody else.'

His wife sank onto a chair but Grace remained standing. It was all she could do not to completely lose control and yell at him.

'Have you been gaining access to the castle through the secret passageway?' asked Grace.

'No! I knew it was there, of course, but it wouldn't occur to me to go rampaging round someone else's house. Why would I? He invites me there often enough as it is.'

'So,' said Grace, 'explain why you have *that*?'

'Someone contacted me by email and said that they had the Imperial Egg but it was too hot to handle. They said they were getting ready to cut their losses and run and would take £100,000 in cash.'

'Tell me you didn't, you stupid, stupid man...' groaned his wife, putting her head in her hands.

Harris looked embarrassed. 'I'm afraid that I did, my dear. It seemed too good an opportunity to pass up. Of course, my intention was to admire it for a while then give it back to Komorov, provided he paid my expenses. But... then I discovered...'

'It was a fake,' the two women finished for him. Their eyes met. Hillary was clearly shocked and angry. *No wonder*, thought Grace.

'Um... yes. I tried to have it authenticated and the truth was revealed. I thought I might as well hang on to it...'

'Is this some kind of mid-life crisis?' asked his wife. 'Have you gone completely barking mad? You do realise that if this gets out, I'll never work again? Who would allow me the run of their house now? You've ruined everything!'

'The person who sold it to you,' snapped Grace. 'What can you tell me?'

'Not a great deal. He met me at the entrance to the passageway in the woods. He was dressed in some kind of forensic suit with a hood and wore a mask. He also had a gun. I don't know if it was real, but I wasn't going to take any chances. He didn't speak. He just gestured what he wanted me to do.'

'Maybe he thought you might recognise his voice,' said Grace, frustrated. 'How tall was he?'

'Taller than me.'

Harris was about five foot ten, she guessed. 'Slim, fat?'

'About average.'

'Did you catch a glimpse of his hair colour?'

'No, it was covered by the mask.'

'Any distinguishing marks, tattoos, anything at all that might mark him out?'

'Nothing,' said Harris, looking despondent at being unable to redeem himself. 'He knew what he was about.'

'What are you going to do?' asked Hilary, looking worried.

'Well, if you let me take the copy away, I'll tell Sacha what happened and that you intended to give it back to him after enjoying it for a while. You've taken a financial hit as a result, so he might not want to involve the police but that will be entirely up to him. If the theft of the egg is in any way related to the murders of Irina, Polly or Igor then your actions may have prevented a killer being caught sooner. That's something you might have to live with.'

'I didn't think,' he muttered, looking worried.

Grace looked at him in distaste. His greed and petty rivalry with Sacha could have had far-reaching consequences. She pitied his poor wife, who seemed to be cut from a superior cloth.

'Can you forward the email to me? I suspect the sender will have covered his tracks but you never know.' She handed over a business card to him.

Harris pulled out his phone and a couple of seconds later the email pinged into her account. He then disarmed the security and helped Grace pack the fake egg away into a padded box for transport.

'I'm so sorry, I don't know what to say,' said Hilary, squeezing her arm. 'He seems to have taken leave of his senses. I suspect it was Sacha's gloating that got to him. I really don't know where we're going to go from here.'

'You deserve better,' said Grace with a last scathing look at her husband on the way out.

FIFTY-FIVE

Hannah traipsed up the stairs, feeling on edge. She was only just starting work but she felt hot and bothered already. It creeped her out that there were so few people about the castle now. It was starting to feel more like a crypt than a home. Why couldn't they all just decamp to the nearest Premier Inn or something? Hannah thought they were mad for continuing to stay here. Her phone pinged, making her jump. It was a text from Grace.

> Do NOT go in the nursery under any circumstances.

What was that about? wondered Hannah, her interest piqued. Grace could be a bit overprotective at times. She was nearly nineteen after all. Hardly a kid. She carried on with her duties, trying to put the nursery to the back of her mind but it felt like an itch she had to scratch. To take her mind off it, she resolved to search each room again thoroughly. No one would be checking up on her, she reckoned. Apart from the crazy person who was murdering people, she thought with a shiver. She desperately wanted these cases to be over so she could get her life back. Another text pinged. This time it provoked a smile. It was from Hamish.

> Hey, Hannah. Fancy meeting up later? I've got tickets for a gig at the Union. Let me know if you can swing it. Hope Jack is behaving himself!

They'd been talking to each other since the dinner at Cally and Tom's. It felt good to have a friend her own age. The fact that he had known Connor was the icing on the cake. Maybe one day she'd be able to talk about the stuff she had been pushing down for so long. She desperately wanted to go and do something fun for a change. She would need to find a babysitter. Maybe she could ask Jean? She would understand. She fired off a text to Jean and resigned herself to a long wait. Jean was someone who was the complete opposite of glued to her phone. Probably wished she had her own dedicated phone box from the olden days.

She started at the end of the row of suites as she usually did. She'd seen no sign of Nikolai this morning but she was still careful to knock before going in. She was still really nervous about the secret passage. The police had removed Igor Sokolov's body but as far as she knew there had been no workmen in yet to properly block it off aside from a partition in the cellar to stop people leaving the house that way. She went up to the spyhole and felt with her fingers. From this side it was impossible to tell if it was open or closed. It was barely detectable.

Hoping for the best, she turned to the wardrobe and quickly ran her fingers through all the jacket pockets. He wasn't the tidiest person. Probably because he had the likes of her picking up after him the whole time. It pained her to put all the used tickets, gum wrappers and tissues back in but she had no choice. Conscious of time passing, her body prickled with alarm as she shot a nervous glance back at the wall. Finally, she tried his blazer and thought she had struck out once again until she took a second look at the theatre ticket stub. He'd been at the ballet the night that Igor Sokolov was abducted. How come nobody had seen him? She took a pic with her phone before putting it back. Grace had explained to her about the chain of evidence and she had decided she never wanted to be the weak link that broke the chain. The sensation that she was being watched started to eat away at her, causing her hands to shake and her stomach to churn. She knew it was most likely her imagination playing tricks on her but the sensation continued to build until she was fighting the impulse to run out of the room.

Having exhausted the wardrobe, she dropped to her knees and inspected under the bed. There was a brown leather suitcase under there that wasn't heavy but it rattled tantalisingly when she shook it. She tried to open it, but it was locked. Groaning in frustration, she shoved it back and looked for the key. It was nowhere to be found.

She couldn't waste any more time in here. Spraying some furniture polish in the air, she did a quick vacuum then dashed in to do a cursory refresh of the ensuite. His dressing gown was on the back of the door. She stuck her fingers in the pockets and pulled out what looked like the keys to the suitcase. Bingo! She was on her way over to dig it out from under the bed when she received a text from Jean. Excited, she opened it at once.

Phone me now. It's about Jack.

Hannah pocketed the keys and flew out of the door.

FIFTY-SIX

Grace noticed Hannah's car wasn't in the car park when she returned from the Hamiltons.' Glancing at her watch, she figured she must have left early to pick up Jack. She let herself in the staff entrance. The castle, which had been full of hustle and bustle when she first came here, now had a faintly dilapidated air. They had lost staff members but hadn't got round to replacing them. There were no signs of habitation. No strains of ballet music softened the atmosphere of neglect. She arrived in the handsome octagonal hall and paused to listen. Only the sonorous tick-tock of the ornate grandfather clock punctuated the air. The door to the library was ajar. Grace saw Sacha Komarov sitting in his customary seat by the fireplace, lost in contemplation. She knocked on the door and his head shot up. Seeing her, he motioned with his hand that she should sit opposite him. There was a tumbler of vodka beside him. It looked like it wasn't his first. On her way over, she presented the box containing the replica egg to him. He opened it and sighed wearily as though its reappearance brought him no joy.

'Where did you find it?'

'On display in Harris Hamilton's private gallery.'

'What?' he expostulated, jerking to life. 'That scoundrel! I'll have him for this.'

Grace held up her hand to shut him down. 'He didn't steal it. And his wife had absolutely no idea about any of this.'

'What do you mean, he didn't steal it?'

'He was approached by email. The sender said they wanted £100,000 for it as they were getting ready to cut and run. He had it authenticated and discovered it was a fake. He feels like a gullible idiot.'

'That's because he is one,' snorted Komorov, his lips twitching into a reluctant smile. 'Well, I must say that you have exceeded my expectations, Grace. You must send me your account for settlement.'

'I still intend to identify the actual thief but now that the replica has been recovered, I will happily send you an interim account. Katya told me that you are now aware of the issues she's been having with a stalker and that she's instructed me to investigate?'

'I doubt that will be necessary now,' he said, a flicker of annoyance on his face. 'I am perfectly capable of protecting my wife.'

'That might well be the case in the normal course of events but three people have already been murdered. There's no way of knowing if the stalker and the murderer are one and the same.'

'I hadn't thought of that,' he muttered. 'The stalker seems to predate the murders, so I assumed it was a different person. Simply some deranged fan with a link to a member of staff.'

'That may well turn out to be the case, but assumptions can be dangerous.' Grace sat back in her chair and studied her client. He seemed less perturbed than he should be about the bizarre deaths under his roof and the fact that a deranged psychopath was still potentially roaming unchecked throughout the castle. The silence grew heavier as neither of them spoke for several minutes.

'You have to understand, I'm no stranger to death,' he eventually said with a sigh. 'It's stalked me many times over the years. Life in Russia was hard. When my father abandoned us, my mother and I both had to live lives on the hard edges of society. We had to scrabble around for food to put on the table. Many times we had to make choices we were not proud of. We tried to keep things as normal as possible for Nikolai. We hoped he would represent the best of us and not the most vile and degrading aspects of our fight for survival. He was our little prince, a symbol of hope.' He gave a bitter laugh. 'We needn't have bothered. He's a prince all right. As spoiled and entitled and uninspired as the best of them. Perhaps the killer should have struck him down and done us all a favour.'

'I'm sure you don't mean that,' said Grace, shocked, though it looked very much like he had meant every word of it. Her eyes drifted uneasily to the spyhole.

Sacha caught her and threw back his head and laughed. 'You think he is listening? Let him! Whoever it is can creep about inside the walls if they are not man enough to speak to me directly.'

'I really don't think you should be trying to provoke him,' said Grace, keeping her voice low and urgent. 'What have the police been saying about the investigations?'

'Pah, what do they care? Since the invasion of Ukraine by Putin they probably think that the only good Russian is a dead Russian.'

'That's absolutely not true,' said Grace firmly. 'I know Brodie McKenna, remember, and he is a dedicated investigator. Your nationality is completely irrelevant to him unless it's pertinent to the investigation.'

'He is meant to be coming here shortly to give me an update

on how they have all been sitting twiddling the thumbs, like so.'
He demonstrated.

This wasn't good, thought Grace. He was already three sheets to the wind and Brodie would be far from impressed. She took her leave and headed for the car park. Looking down the drive, she saw Brodie's car heading towards her. He came to a halt in a spurt of gravel beside her car. Flinging open his car door, he walked towards her with an unmistakeable sense of urgency. Something was clearly very wrong.

'Brodie, what is it?' she demanded, meeting him halfway.

'Grace, hurry, it's Jack. Someone put a threatening note in his bag at nursery. I had just got here when Jean texted me.'

'Is Jack all right?' she managed, her heart in her mouth.

'Yes, he's fine but we have to get ahead of this. I'm heading back to the agency now. Hannah's on her way back too.'

'I'll meet you there,' said Grace and without further ado she ran to her car, threw it into gear and set off, her knuckles white as she gripped the steering wheel.

FIFTY-SEVEN

Hannah ran into the agency at full pelt. Jean made a stop sign with her hand and put a finger to her lips. Standing at the door to Grace's room, where Jack hung out after school, she looked back over her shoulder then moved forward towards Hannah.

'He's settled on the couch watching CBeebies on the iPad.'

'What happened?' asked Hannah, sitting down abruptly as her legs threatened to go from under her. 'When I got your text...'

'I went to pick him up from nursery, as we'd agreed. The nursery teacher took me aside to say that she'd found this disturbing drawing in his backpack when she was putting back his lunch box.' Jean pulled a piece of paper out of her desk drawer.

Hannah grabbed it from her and gasped in horror. It was a crude drawing of the game hangman with a child with dark hair swinging from the noose wearing the clothes Jack had gone to nursery in. Beside the drawing was a note.

CLUE: What happens to someone poking their nose in?
ANSWER: D - - D

'Dead?' whispered Hannah, tears spurting to her eyes. She had never felt fear like this in her life. 'He's only a little boy. Why would someone want to hurt him?'

'It's obviously intended to be a threat,' said Jean. 'I think that the stalker-slash-killer feels you and Grace are getting too close to unmasking him.'

'How did it get into his backpack in the first place?' asked Hannah. 'One of the reasons I chose that nursery is that they're very security conscious. They don't just let anyone come in and wander around.'

'According to the nursery, they had a plumber in to check the pipes in the toilets. It had been arranged by email in advance and the man had a council lanyard though I suspect they didn't check it too thoroughly. He was never in the room with the children, just in the toilets off the cloakroom.'

'Where the coats and bags are kept on pegs with their name on them,' supplied Hannah with a sigh.

'Jack seems fine. He wasn't best chuffed to find out you weren't here, but then he went off looking for his snack and drink like nothing untoward had happened.'

'Did you call the police?' asked Hannah.

'I called Brodie. He's on his way here with Grace. He figures it's a warning this time but that we might not be so lucky if there's a next time.'

Hannah wiped her eyes, pasted a smile on her face and went through to her son.

'Mummy!' he yelled. 'You've been ages!'

She enfolded his warm little body in hers. If anything had happened to him... she couldn't even bring herself to go there.

Grace and Brodie arrived minutes apart. Once they'd made a fuss of Jack, Hannah took them both aside and showed them the warning from his schoolbag.

'This guy is going to wish he hadn't been born,' growled Brodie.

'If anything had happened to Jack...' Grace covered her face with her hand as she fought for control.

'Brodie, can you test it for prints and whatever else you can think of?' asked Hannah.

'Don't you worry, Hannah, I won't rest until they lock up whoever did this and throw away the key. I'm heading to the station now. The nursery staff are being picked up to give statements.'

Grace nodded but still looked stricken. She needed to snap out of it for Jack's sake, thought Hannah. 'What should I do tomorrow?' she asked. 'Also, I don't want to go home to my mum's house with Jack in case I put the other kids at risk.'

'Stay at mine tonight,' Jean said firmly. 'I can work from home tomorrow. Brodie and Grace need to keep figuring this out and I think you and Jack should have someone with you all the time.'

'Are you sure, Jean?' said Hannah, touched that Jean would put herself out to this extent. There was a single loud woof from Harvey, who had been sleeping under Jean's desk.

'Take Harvey,' said Grace. 'I'll drop off a bag of clothes and toys later. I can get stuff at that twenty-four-hour supermarket in Musselburgh. I agree you should avoid your house for now.'

'I'll have a couple of plain clothes officers posted to watch your house in an unmarked car, Jean. I'll also make sure that a patrol car goes past every so often as well. Here's my team's direct dial number, just in case.' Brodie passed it over. Jean looked worried but determined. Hannah got a tired Jack ready to leave and Jean shoved all her work stuff into a large leather holdall.

'Ready for our sleepover, Jack?' Jean said in a bright voice.

'Is Mummy coming?'

'Are you kidding?' Hannah laughed. 'Can't let you have all the fun! Even Harvey is coming!'

'Yes!' shouted Jack, perking up at the thought of a night with his favourite dog.

Hannah glanced around nervously as they left the safety of the office. The person who did this had had the audacity to get to her son in his nursery, so she felt that nowhere was safe. She held on to Jack tightly and Jean held his other hand. She just had to trust that Brodie and Grace knew what they were doing and were able to bring matters to a swift conclusion. As they drove away in Jean's car, she felt that she was entering unknown territory. She had no idea when she would even be back at work. Nothing was more important than keeping her precious son safe. Suddenly, she remembered the keys in her pocket.

'Jean, stop the car, I need to give something to Grace!'

Jean pulled in to the side of the road and Hannah left the car and ran up to her boss, who was standing talking to Brodie now by their cars.

'What is it, Hannah?' she asked.

'I just remembered,' Hannah said, handing over the small keys. 'There's a locked case under Nikolai's bed. I found these keys in his dressing gown pocket which might open it. Also, there's a ticket stub in his blazer that proves he was at the theatre the night Igor went missing. I thought I'd best tell you as with everything going on...'

'Thanks, Hannah. Great work! Now, put the cases out of your mind and concentrate on Jack until we're satisfied he's no longer in any danger. Brodie and I have got this, I promise you.'

FIFTY-EIGHT

Grace turned to Brodie once the car was out of sight, her face a mask of anguish.

'This is all my fault! If I hadn't taken on these damn cases none of this would have happened. If anything happens to Jack, that's me done, Brodie. I mean it.'

'Grace, come here,' he said, enfolding her in a hug. 'Just take a breath. This is not on you. It's on the sadistic nutter we're trying to catch. Jack is fine, and we're all going to make sure that he stays that way. We're going to catch this scumbag and put him away for so long that Jack will have a grandson of his own before he gets out.'

'You really think so?' she mumbled into his jacket.

'I know so.' He kissed the top of her head and released her. Grace suddenly had a desire to cling to him like a barnacle. She knew why she was falling apart. Jack being abducted had catapulted her back into the same emotional territory as when she had lost Connor. She had to get a grip. Hannah and Jack needed her to bring her A game.

'Sorry,' she managed. 'It was the shock. I'm fine now, honestly.'

Grace wanted to go into the police station with Brodie but she no longer had the right.

'How did they even find out about Jack and what nursery he attends?' wondered Grace.

'They must have twigged that Hannah was there in an investigative capacity and followed her,' replied Brodie.

'The only person that I told was Sacha Komorov,' said Grace. 'Hannah and I were always careful to keep our distance from each other when at the castle. We arrived and left separately.'

'You do know that Sacha Komorov is still a suspect in relation to the murders, Grace?'

'Yes, of course,' she replied, striving to keep her tone neutral. She couldn't admit that she had her own doubts about Sacha. Not yet, anyway. That stunt he'd pulled with the Fabergé egg showed he was an arch manipulator. It had left her feeling queasy, particularly given the whole carry-on with the doll's house. Surely Komorov couldn't be behind the murders, too? A horrible thought occurred to her.

'What are you going to do now?' asked Brodie. 'You're not going to do anything crazy, are you?'

'Of course not,' she reassured him. 'I'm just going to get together some stuff to take over to Jean's house for them, that's all.'

Grace waved him off then got into her car. She hated having to lie to Brodie but there were some things he was better off not knowing. Twenty-five minutes later, she drove into the driveway of the castle but instead of proceeding down the long drive she turned hard left onto a logging track used by timber lorries. After bumping up the track for a few seconds, she found the perfect spot behind some logs which were stacked ready for transport to the sawmill. She stuffed her phone and torch into her pockets having decided to approach the house through the woods so she could enter the walled garden and use the staff entrance at the side of the castle without being spotted. Her route would take her past Viktor Levitsky's house but with a bit of luck he would be occupied elsewhere. The sun was setting behind the castle, streaking the sky with blood-dipped fingers. An owl hooted overhead, causing her to jump. Her senses on heightened alert, she crept along the overgrown path, hugging the treeline in case she needed to take cover. A slight breeze whispered among the branches. She froze as a young deer pranced across the path with its mother. She must have been downwind of them as they didn't notice her. Feeling a little cheered, she carried on until she noticed the lights of Viktor's cottage. Against her better judgement she crept closer, moving from tree to tree. An unholy scream rent the air. Some poor creature caught by a predator. She felt a bit like prey herself right now, sure that if she was discovered creeping about things would not go well for her. The moon rose in the sky, a welcome beacon of hope.

Viktor's television was on. She could see the flickering images but there was no sign of him. There was no doubt in her mind that he was capable of brutality. With his background in the FSB, he was never going to be a Boy Scout but was he damaged enough to be holding them all in thrall with his terrifying games?

Suddenly, the door was flung wide and an oblong of light spilled out onto the encroaching darkness. Grace froze as the silhouette of Viktor Levitsky filled the door frame. Then, she saw the red tip of a cigarette and relaxed again. He was just out for a smoke. By the time he had finished she was gritting her teeth to stop them chattering with the cold and it was fully dark. *Whoa.* What was he doing? Grace flattened herself against the bark of the tree she was hiding behind as the arc of a powerful torch swept the woods, passing right over the tree she was hidden behind. Temporarily blinded, she heard the cottage door shut and peered out anxiously. Had he gone in or had he shut the door and crept up on her while she had been blinded by the torch? Either way, she was getting out of here.

Hurriedly, she walked back towards the main path, her nerves screaming as she was pulled to the ground by a predatory briar. *So much for keeping quiet*, she thought as she rubbed the gash on her ankle. Limping slightly and hearing no signs of pursuit, she set out for the castle again, sighing with relief once she reached the manicured paths of the walled garden. Hugging the wall, she was able to pick up her pace and just a few minutes later she was letting herself into the staff door by pressing this week's code into the keypad.

The place was deserted. Her excuses for being there so late were all prepared but she didn't need them. The lights were on in the staff quarters and the kitchen but there was nobody there. Perhaps they had all retired to their quarters for the night. Quickly she made her way down to the cellar. Her plan was to use the secret passageway to creep round the house and see if any of its inhabitants were up to no good. Her end point was the nursery. She could barely bring herself to admit it, but she had developed an obsession with the doll's house and was desperate to inspect it to see if any harm was prophesised for little Jack.

'You might as well be addicted to fortune tellers,' she muttered in the silence, cross with herself but compelled nevertheless. She paused outside the secret door in the cellar, screwing up her face as she remembered the previous horror that she had encountered on the other side of that door. Even though she knew that all traces of Igor Sokolov had by now been removed, she still shuddered as the door swung back, revealing a cavernous void. Instead of continuing on out of the castle and into the woods the passageway now stopped to the right of the door because of a firmly attached plywood wall blocking the way. Feeling a visceral fear that was only topped by the fear for Jack's safety, she stepped into the black hole and, switching on her torch, she swung the door closed behind her. Carefully pointing her torch to the floor, she advanced cautiously to the left, worried in case the light might shine through any spyholes that were open, alerting others to her presence. She forced herself to go more slowly than she had the last time she had passed through because she wanted to examine the areas around each spyhole in detail in case there were any clues as to the identity of those that had passed through here.

As she stumbled up the stairs from the cellar and reached the next floor, she heard the strains of ballet music playing quietly. Surely, Katya wasn't still dancing at this time of night? She could see two points of light penetrating the gloom ahead and immediately turned off her torch. Finding her way to the peepholes by inching her way along the wall by touch, she saw that Katya was indeed dancing. There were no visible signs of her pregnancy yet in her practice tutu but her hands seemed drawn to return there as if they didn't want to stray too far away from her precious cargo. Grace quietly closed the peepholes and then turned her torch on to examine this space where Katya's stalker must have spent hours watching her as his thoughts turned slowly from love to hate. There was a wooden stool set against the wall and a half-empty bottle of vodka. Scanning the area under the stool, she discovered a cigarette butt. Surely, this must have landed there since Brodie and the forensic team had finished their work here. She couldn't imagine them having missed it. Feeling in her pocket for an evidence bag, she bagged it just in case. She took a quick photo first so they could see how it had been positioned. As she did so, she noticed that there was no reception. Hardly surprising really with the walls being so thick. The sweat was pouring off her. It was so hot and stuffy back here, like being buried alive.

Pointing her torch down to light the way, she moved along to the next set of roughly hewn stairs. Turning it off, she felt her way by grabbing on to the rough wall, scratching her hands in the process as she clawed her way upwards to the next floor.

The darkness pressed in on her as she listened intently. Nothing. She glanced at her watch – it was coming up to eight o'clock. Her heart in her mouth, she switched on her torch once more. Hurriedly she rushed along to the next room with peepholes, which was the library. Once she had located the holes, she peered through into the room; at this time of night, it was lit only by a few lamps and the dull glow of the fire. It was empty. Wait, no, it wasn't. Nikolai lurched into view holding a tumbler half filled with what was no doubt one of his brother's rarer malts. He was clearly three sheets to the wind, his face flushed and bad tempered. He threw himself down in Sacha's chair, bumping into a side table and knocking an ornament to the floor. Knowing Sacha, it was probably worth more than the whole contents of her flat. Cursing, he leant over and gathering up the shattered remains, lobbed it into the fireplace with a satisfied smirk. *Charming*, thought Grace.

She was starting to wish she hadn't bothered coming to the castle. She'd learned nothing new and possibly put herself in jeopardy for nothing. She had to get out of here. Hurrying on, she found the last set of steps and fell over in her haste to get up them. She was so over this secret passage lark. Dimming her torch, she stopped at Nikolai's room. She could probably risk a quick look to see if she could get the suitcase open as she'd just seen him downstairs. It would probably contain nothing important, but she needed to cross it off her list. She also wanted to get a look at his personal papers to see if she could trace any suspicious items purchased and shown on bank or credit card statements that might implicate him in relation to the stalker, murderer or both. The same applied to Sacha Komorov, Oliver Compton-Ross and Viktor Levitsky. This case had now reached out to entangle her beloved grandchild. She must do whatever it took to bring matters unequivocally to an end.

Sliding out of the door, she made a beeline for under the bed then sighed in frustration. The case was no longer there.

Jumping to her feet, she made for the desk against the wall. All the drawers were locked. Was that entirely normal? she wondered. This was his own designated space. Mind you, staff were in and out all the time, so it perhaps wasn't that surprising. She tried the keys Hannah had given her just in case but no joy. Suddenly, she heard voices outside the door. The handle started to turn. She couldn't get back to the passageway door in time. Nor could she make it to the ensuite, which had nowhere to hide in any event. She raced over to the bed and flung herself underneath it, her heart pounding. If she was caught the agency would be fired without a doubt.

She saw a pair of slender ankles and ballet ribbons as their owner sat on the chaise longue at the end of the bed.

'Drink?' said Nikolai, his voice still a bit slurred but now clearly on a charm offensive.

'You know I can't,' Katya's voice replied. 'I'll take a sparkling water if you've got it.' Grace heard the fizz of the bottle opening and the clink of ice into glasses. She was parched herself. Her mouth was so dry she was terrified she might cough.

'Sacha wouldn't like me being here, you know that,' said Katya, her voice tinged with fear. 'I have nothing to say to you.'

'That wasn't what you said before Igor Sokolov came on the scene. Back then you couldn't get enough of me. You were all about leaving Sacha and coming away with me.'

'I know. I'm sorry. Have you never made a mistake, Nikolai? I have apologised. I don't know what else I can do. You and I? We were never meant to be.'

Grace couldn't believe what she was hearing. Katya had clearly been in a relationship with Nikolai and hadn't told her. What else was she keeping from her?

'That baby you're carrying,' he said, his tone turning nasty. 'Could it be mine?'

Katya sighed and shifted her weight, causing the bed to creak.

'I told you. The baby is Sacha's. He knows all about Igor and he doesn't care. He wants us to move forward together.'

'You know, I used to think you were something special,' sneered Nikolai. 'I don't know how I could have been so mistaken.'

'I used to think you were a gentleman,' Katya retaliated, getting to her feet. 'I don't know how I could have been so mistaken.'

Uh oh, this is turning nasty, thought a horrified Grace under the bed. She desperately hoped that she wouldn't have to intervene.

'Sacha loves me. He has always loved me. You don't want a real woman. You want perfection. Well, I have news for you. You're far from perfect. You're arrogant and spoiled and always running to your brother with your begging bowl like a child. Sacha is more man than you will ever be.'

The feet stormed towards the door but suddenly stumbled.

'Let go of me!' Katya yelled. She stabbed her heel backwards into Nikolai's knee and he howled in pain.

Ouch, thought Grace, wincing under the bed. *That must have hurt.*

The door slammed. There then followed a few minutes of what she assumed was cursing in Russian. Grace was furious with herself for getting trapped under the bed. What if he didn't leave the room for the rest of the night? She bit her lip. Wait a minute, the bathroom door had closed. The shower started up. Dare she? It was better than the alternative. She slid out from under the bed and rushed towards the wall. Seconds later she was hidden once more, her heart beating like a drum in the confined space.

She decided to carry on along to the nursery then return the way she had come. Although she knew it was risky, she had developed a morbid fascination with checking in there for further changes as it seemed to be the room where the killer seemed compelled to enact some of his darkest fantasies. She was almost there when she heard a door close. Horrified, she froze. The noise had come from the direction of the nursery. She flattened herself into one of the irregular curved recesses in the back wall that she had just passed, thankful that she wasn't wearing bulky clothing. She could hear the footsteps approaching and the sound of ragged breathing.

Willing her own breathing to slow, she turned her face to the side against the wall. If she pressed against the wall any harder she would have melted into it. The footsteps paused in front of her. She held her breath, sensing that whoever it was definitely knew that she was there in the velvet darkness. Not even daring to inhale, she closed her eyes lest even a glimmer of white reveal her. After what seemed like an eternity, the footsteps moved on, more swiftly now. She remained frozen in place for some minutes after they disappeared, too frightened to move. The fear of being killed then entombed behind that wall was not one that was going to leave her any time soon. Stealthily, she crept along from where they had come, which could only be the nursery. Opening the spyhole, she ascertained that no one was in the room before opening the door and stepping through.

This time she didn't hang about but went straight for the doll's house. Opening it, she gasped in horror, even though part of her had been expecting it. Whoever was behind these killings was a sadist. One of the rooms had children sitting round a table in a nursery setting. In one corner of the brightly coloured room was a noose with a little dark-haired boy swinging by the neck. It was clear to her that this was meant to portray her grandson, Jack. She had just received the direst of warnings.

FIFTY-NINE

After her close encounter, Grace hadn't been able to face going back into the secret passage and, instead, ran lightly down the main stairs and out through the staff entrance. Fortunately, no one had seen her. She drove back to her flat and picked up enough clothes and toys for Jack to last him a few days. She also picked out a few items from her own wardrobe for Hannah as they were about the same size even if their style differed enormously. Grace was a pragmatic dresser whereas Hannah favoured pops of colour and bright accessories. She didn't need dog food as Jean was so besotted with Harvey, she kept her own supply of food and tasty treats.

It was already 10 pm as she drove into Jean's driveway. Jean threw open the door as she arrived and Harvey dashed out to take her wrist and pull her inside.

Jean made her sit down for a coffee and a sandwich. 'Hannah and Jack are in bed upstairs. I put them in the double as poor Hannah couldn't bear to be parted from him. Jack, bless him, is oblivious. Also, Cally phoned and offered to take Jack and Hannah for a few days to keep them out of harm's way,' said Jean. 'She and Tom are both working from home at the moment and Hamish is home on study leave. They could keep a good eye on them.'

Grace's eyebrows shot up. 'How did Cally hear about it? I mean, I would have told her but...'

'Apparently, Hannah and Hamish have been texting each other since your family dinner. They were hoping to meet up tonight, but Hannah obviously cancelled.'

'Oh, I see...' said Grace, not quite sure how she felt about it. Anyway, it was none of her business. 'I suppose that would make sense.'

'Hannah wants a couple of days off to settle him in. She's desperate for this case to be over.'

'She's not the only one,' said Grace fervently. She brought Jean up to speed on her activities that evening.

'Grace, I can't believe you went and did all that at night without the client even knowing you were there. That was far too risky! What were you thinking?'

'I know,' she admitted. 'I shouldn't have done it but when whoever it is went after Jack, all reason went out the window.'

Jean patted her hand across the table. 'I've been thinking. This doll's house business... I can see how addictive the killer finds it, almost like it's his calling card to show how clever he is, but... I wonder if it might be the means by which to trip him up?'

Grace leaned forward. 'Go on.'

'Well, where is he getting his supplies from? There are only a few specialist doll's house shops in Edinburgh. Either he or she is shopping in person or they're ordering stuff online.'

'Good point, Jean. Sometimes it's the little details that trip a killer up, not the big moments. I'll be seeing Brodie later tonight so perhaps he can get a warrant to access everyone's online order history.'

'I can go to visit the shops in Edinburgh tomorrow,' said Jean. 'Can you send my phone some of the images you've taken of the doll's house and furniture? I can enlarge them and print them off to see if anyone recognises them. I'll also print off photos of all our potential suspects if we strike it lucky with the furniture, to see which of them purchased it.'

'If you're going to do that,' said Grace, 'it's probably best if you stick to a story that you've seen one you greatly admire and want to get something similar for your granddaughter. I won't send you any that are staged as we don't want to do anything to compromise the police investigation. The last thing we want is for it all to get out into the public domain. However, I do have some individual photos of the furniture pieces placed on a table.' She thought for a moment. 'What about the weird two-faced doll in the crib?'

'There's a doll's hospital in Edinburgh. I'll run it by them and see what they make of it,' Jean replied. 'I can say it's for fraternal twins with different coloured eyes or something.'

Grace got to her feet and took her leave. She was more tired than she had ever been in her life, but she couldn't stop now. She couldn't lose another member of her family. Harvey sleepily trailed out after her and jumped into the boot. Fortunately, Jean had already walked him before she arrived. Once in her car she phoned Brodie to check he was still at the station before heading in there.

'Grace, where have you been?' he greeted her. 'I thought I'd hear from you before now.'

She sighed. 'It's a long story. I'm just leaving Jean's house now. I've got some stuff to tell you. Should I still come in?'

'No, I'm heading out now. Shall I come over to yours?'

'Yes, I'll be there in a few minutes. I'm going to order Chinese. Are you hungry?'

'Famished. I forgot to eat today. One of the lads will drop me off. My car's still at home.'

'See you soon.' Grace terminated the call.

SIXTY

Grace had time for a quick shower. She jumped into her pyjamas and cosy dressing gown seconds before the food arrived, closely followed by Brodie.

'That smells good,' he groaned, petting a sleepy Harvey. 'My stomach thinks my throat's been cut.'

They ate at the kitchen table, too hungry for small talk then sat back in their chairs, replete.

'More wine?' asked Grace.

'Sure, why not?' Brodie said. 'This is the first time I've stopped all day.'

They carried their glasses through to the couch and flopped. Harvey jumped up between them and promptly went to sleep. After a fortifying glug, Brodie turned to her. 'Okay, Grace, spill. What have you really been up to tonight? I'm not stupid and I know you all too well. The unedited version, please.'

She brought him up to speed on her activities and he shook his head and scowled at her, getting off the couch to pace angrily up and down the living room. Harvey raised his head and looked at him, head tilted to one side as he tried to work out a reason for the sudden change in the atmosphere.

'Grace, you need to be more careful. If you're right and you were stuck in that passageway with the killer, he could have murdered you there and then. You could have been stuck behind that wall for ever.'

'I'm sure you'd have got around to digging me out,' she said, trying for a measure of levity.

'It's not remotely funny!' he shouted, his face reddening in anger. 'I want you *out* of that place. You found the missing fake egg. Can't you collect a fat fee and call it quits?'

'Hey, Brodie, take a chill pill,' said Grace, looking at him in alarm. 'This isn't like you.' Clearly, the stress was getting to him. 'I still have Katya's stalker to deal with, Brodie. She's pregnant and is relying on me. I can't just abandon her when the going gets tough. What would that say about me and the agency?'

'Grace, you have people who love you. Think of *them* once in a while.'

Ouch, but was he one of them? she wondered. 'Coffee?' she asked, hoping it would change the subject.

'Go on then,' he sighed, sitting back down. 'Jean's ideas about sourcing where the killer's raw materials come from are good. We'll apply for a warrant to obtain those payment records tomorrow.'

'Have the police had any joy with tracking down the fake plumber at the nursery? I take it Blair hasn't allowed your team to be involved?'

'No. He had a beard, glasses and was wearing a face mask and a baseball cap so they didn't get all that good a look at him.'

'CCTV?'

'Nothing doing. His face was obscured and he kept it angled well away. You can come in and see it in case it rings any bells but I'm not holding my breath.'

'Hannah and Jack are going to my sister's tomorrow for a couple of days just to be on the safe side. She's keeping Jack from nursery until this case is resolved.'

'Good, that gives me some peace of mind. How are your family? I miss Cally, Tom and the kids. Your mother, not so much.'

Grace laughed. 'I miss your folks, too. It's something you don't think about, the kind of loss you never factor in during a breakup. It hits you later, I suppose.'

'I wish we were still a family,' Brodie said in a low voice, looking away from her.

'We are,' she replied, gently, 'in every way that matters. Are you okay?' Normally, she wouldn't pry but having seen Julie's mask slip so spectacularly, she was concerned he might not be as happy with her as she had thought. He also seemed unusually tightly wound.

'Honestly? I've been better. Blair's been giving me a hard time. Starting to make jokes about when I'm going to make him a grandfather. We're not even engaged yet. I know Julie wants to take our relationship to the next level, but something is holding me back... Sorry, it's a bit weird discussing this with you but I've no one else I can talk to.'

Grace looked at him. She still loved him. Part of her wanted to tell him what she had discovered about Julie and warn him to run for the hills. He would need very little encouragement to turn back to her right now. However, deep down she knew that he had to make that decision himself, free of pressure from her or anyone else.

'That's tough, Brodie,' she said carefully. 'I would take the Super's nonsense with a pinch of salt. It's none of his business. If he got his own way, he would cut out the middleman and his grandchildren would just be clones of himself.'

Brodie laughed but even his laugh sounded forced and miserable.

'Julie, on the other hand,' she continued carefully. 'She's a few years younger than you, which is good if you're planning to start a family together. I guess the important questions are: Can you imagine life with her? Can you imagine life without her? Anyway, what do I know? All I know is that any woman would be lucky to have you. Just take your time and don't bow to pressure. These things can't be rushed. When you're sure, either way, you'll know it without a shadow of a doubt.'

'Thanks, Grace.' He squeezed her hand then let it go. 'Right, I'd best get off. Don't want to miss the last bus home.' She saw him down the stairs. As she opened the door to let him out, he enfolded her in a hug. At first, she stiffened, taken by surprise, but then she relaxed into it, her body feeling like it had never left. After a while he pulled away from her and they stared into each other's eyes. His gaze was intense. Grace slid her eyes away, fearful he would read what she had been at such pains to conceal from him.

'Night, Brodie,' she said and closed the door behind him, her thoughts in turmoil.

SIXTY-ONE

Jean's feet were killing her. She'd been tramping round Edinburgh all morning showing the photos Grace had sent her to a number of doll's house shops. She'd had no idea that half these places even existed but it was clearly a passion for adults rather than children. She only had one more shop on her list and, of course, it had to be at the top of one of Edinburgh's steeper streets. Huffing and puffing with exertion, she paused outside the shop window to catch her breath. The window display was exquisite, definitely the best she had seen so far. She could lose herself in the tiny bone china tea sets and little children and their toys, all in miniature. Wait a minute... She consulted the printed photos in her bag. Wasn't that tiny crib identical to the one in the picture? She compared them and they seemed exactly the same. Emboldened, she pushed open the lead-paned door and a bell tinkled to announce her presence.

A wizened old woman dressed in black from head to toe aside from a white lace collar rose from her seat behind the counter. 'Can I help you?' she asked in impeccable English which contained a hint of Eastern European accent. Maybe she was Russian, wondered Jean with mounting excitement.

'When you are ready?' said the old woman, making as if to return to her seat. She was quite bent and arthritic looking, as if moving was painful to her.

Jean smiled and approached. 'Good morning, I was admiring that beautiful crib that you have in the window. Is it for sale?'

'Yes, it is very special. It was made in Russia by a specialist craftsman. I let you see. Yuri!' she shouted, her voice sounding like rusty nails.

A glowering teenager with a black apron emerged from the back of the shop.

'Show madam the crib from the window.'

Silently, he unlocked the window, reached in and extracted it for her to look at.

'It is a replica of one that the Tsarina had for her children,' she said.

'Do you sell many of them?' asked Jean, examining it minutely.

'No, we only had this and one other. These are carved by hand, not mass produced.' The pride in her tone was obvious. 'It was custom job. One went to customer, and we had another made to sell in the shop.'

'It's beautiful,' said Jean. 'I've recently inherited a doll's house. I have a young granddaughter and want to furnish all the rooms until I can surprise her with it when she's old enough.' Jean wished in that moment that what she was saying was true.

'We have everything you need for that here. We do wallpaper, carpets, wooden flooring and, of course, all the furniture you could possibly need.'

Jean's eyes were caught by some teeny tiny ornaments in a tiny walnut cabinet. 'My goodness, is that a Fabergé egg?' she asked, peering at it in wonder.

'Yes, those too come from Russia. They are very popular with certain types of client.'

Murderous stalker ones? wondered Jean. 'Do you ever do custom house designs?' she asked. 'I thought my granddaughter might enjoy having the doll's house with similar decoration to my own in terms of wallpaper, for example. That way, she could remember the fun times we share when she's not with me.'

'We do this for some of our... wealthier clients, but not for everyone. It is very expensive. Everything is custom made. We have an extensive network of suppliers to enable such wishes to be fulfilled.'

'I see,' said Jean. 'You've given me an awful lot to think about. May I take a photo of the beautiful crib? How much is it?'

'£150. I am not supposed to let you take photo, but one will not harm.'

Her grandson fired off a fiery torrent in Russian and stormed off into the back. Jean hastily took her photo and left as an attractive woman burst out from the back of the shop and ushered the old woman away.

Jean left hurriedly before she came back and challenged her. There was no doubt in her mind that this shop was the supplier where the murderer had obtained his pieces of theatre from. She crossed the road and took refuge in a local café in case someone from the shop came looking for her. Hopefully, they had believed her story and not become too suspicious. She had no way of knowing. Hurriedly, she emailed Grace asking her to get Brodie's investigative team out here pronto. This could be it. The break in the case they had all been waiting for.

SIXTY-TWO

Grace was sitting in Brodie's office looking at the CCTV footage taken at Jack's nursery when the text came through from Jean. They'd struck out as expected.

She jumped to her feet. 'Brodie, it's Jean. She's discovered the supplier of items from the doll's house. They're even Russian, would you believe? She found an exact match for the crib, and it was a custom job with only two made. How quick can you get a warrant?'

'I can get it before a sheriff in forty minutes. You're sure?' he said, getting up from behind his desk.

'Positive. Here's the photo Jean took at the shop and here's the photo I took at the house. I suspect our perp has an account with them so can order very specific stuff and his request will be met as soon as they can fulfil it.'

Brodie studied the two images. 'Good enough. I'll go arrange that now. I'll also get a team mustered ready to head out to the castle.'

Grace thanked him and hastily left after forwarding Jean's text, which contained the name and address of the premises as well. It had been a long shot that she hadn't expected to bear fruit but now she thought about it, it made perfect sense. She wondered how often the murderer visited the shop or if everything was done online through anonymous accounts. Perhaps he went in person because, otherwise, he would have a suspicious number of small parcels delivered to the castle that he wouldn't want anyone else to open.

She got out her phone and texted Jean as she was walking along the road to her car.

> Brodie coming with a team and search warrant within the hour. I know it's a long shot but can you discreetly watch the shop meantime? DO NOT PUT YOURSELF AT RISK!!

That done, something else occurred to her. Was there any commonality between the items the stalker had left for Katya to find in her room and the various items that had turned up in the doll's house in the nursery? Could the murderer and the stalker be one and the same or were they two different people? Some of the items had been very small, like the ballerina inside the Fabergé egg. Could they also have been sourced from the same shop? She needed to find the locked brown case that Hannah had seen under Nikolai's bed.

Driving out to Traprain Castle, the beautiful scenery failed to calm her and she was frustrated at being repeatedly trapped behind tractors and trailers. Angrily, she wished there was a motorway all the way there instead of the continuous bends in the road that slowed her almost to a standstill at times. A headache started to throb in time with her pulse. Eventually she got there. Swiftly she entered and tracked down Katya in the drawing room. She was lying on the huge couch reading with her hand curled protectively around her stomach.

Grace tapped lightly on the open door so as not to startle

her and, at Katya's invitation, joined her on the couch. 'Katya, I need to speak to you,' Grace said, her voice low. 'The police are on their way over with a search warrant.'

'Has there been a breakthrough? Do they know who it is yet?' Katya asked, her expression fearful.

'They're following a lead. That's all I'm at liberty to say,' said Grace. 'In the meantime, is there anything that the stalker might have left for you that you haven't already authorised me to give to the police? Can we go to your room and check?'

'Of course,' said Katya, leading the way across the room. Once they'd climbed the stairs and were ensconced in Katya's room, Grace opened the secret passage and checked the peephole remained closed. Turning to Katya, she saw the look of terror in her face as she stared into the gaping dark hole. Hurriedly she closed the door and stepped back through again.

'Relax, it's fine.' She smiled. Grace perched on a chair while Katya opened and closed various drawers and poked about in her huge antique wardrobe.

'There's nothing left,' she said. 'DS McKenna must have it all.'

'Are you sure?'

'There might be one thing.' Katya moved across to her extensive collection of Fabergé eggs and her face lit up. 'Here,' she said, picking one out from a shelf. 'I forgot about this one.' She handed it to Grace, who opened it carefully. Fortunately, it still contained the tiny ballerina with the smashed leg. She placed it in an evidence bag and handed it back to her.

'Keep that somewhere safe until the police arrive then give it to them,' she said. 'Are you back sleeping in this room or still sharing with Sacha?'

'I use my own room during the day and for dressing sometimes but I feel safer when we are together. I know he can protect me.'

'The stalker doesn't seem to have been active lately,' said Grace. 'Why do you think that is?'

Katya shrugged. 'I do not know. Maybe whoever it was has been frightened off by everything that has been happening here.'

'Or they have accepted that they are unable to come between you and Sacha now,' said Grace. 'Are you content in your decision? To stay with Sacha, I mean?'

'There is no passion, but I now believe that there are different kinds of love. I will settle for contentment and make the best of things for the little one's sake.' She patted her still flat stomach with a tender smile.

It was now or never, Grace thought. 'Does Sacha know that you had an affair with Nikolai?' she asked, staring her client down.

Katya froze, her eyes darting about, refusing to meet her gaze. 'How did you find out?' she whispered.

'That doesn't matter. I'm not here to judge. My only concern is to identify your stalker and keep you safe. Does Sacha know?'

'No, he does not. Please,' she begged. 'It's over now. Don't tell Sacha, he would never forgive me and probably kill Nikolai. Sacha was so serious and stern. His brother was fun. He made me laugh. He was the light to Sacha's shade.'

'Until your accident,' said Grace. 'Then he walked away and left his brother to pick up the pieces.'

'I cannot blame him. We were not serious suitors back then.' She shrugged.

'How did Nikolai take it when you threw him over for Igor?'

'He was not best pleased. He threatened to tell Sacha. I told him to go right ahead but that I would tell Sacha of our affair also. After that he backed down. He is still a boy, not a man,' she said, her voice dripping with scorn. 'At least Sacha is honest and honourable. There is much to admire.'

Grace wasn't so sure about that. The doorbell rang. That would be the police. She left Katya and ran downstairs in search of Sacha. It was all becoming clearer to her.

SIXTY-THREE

Jean sat at a table for two in the window of a very nice café directly across the road from the doll's house shop. She was sipping a latte and eating a piece of carrot cake, her eyes fixed on the door to the shop with such intensity that she forgot to blink, causing her vision to blur. She hoped that the police were going to arrive soon as she hadn't the faintest idea what she was meant to do if someone turned up from the castle. Hit them with her handbag? Mind you, it did have a rather large library book in it.

She looked at the photos that Grace had sent her again. Sacha and Nikolai were both tall and dark as was Viktor Levitsky. Oliver was blond and so was Harris Hamilton and both of them were smaller than the three Russians. Mind you, thought Jean, it would be fairly unusual to see a man on his own at the shop anyway. Most little girls would go with their mothers or another female. Anxiously, she glanced at her watch – it had hardly moved since the last time she looked at it. Normally, she loved carrot cake but her mouth was so dry with nerves that she was struggling to get it down. She pushed her plate to one side and continued to sip her coffee.

Suddenly, her spine jerked as though someone had jabbed her with a cattle prod. A man had just gone into the shop! She had only seen him from behind so hadn't been able to identify which of the three dark-haired men it might be. What on earth should she do? She couldn't go back in or that would look really suspicious. It might make him leave without buying anything incriminating. No, she had to wait it out. Her tummy rumbled. After what felt like an age the man reappeared. He was carrying two carrier bags that he had not had with him when he went in. Jean could only see his face side on. Frustratingly, she still couldn't tell which of the three dark-haired men it was. She surreptitiously took a photo with her phone whilst pretending to study the menu. Still no sign of the police. She'd have to follow him. It was imperative that they identified him. At least, as long as she kept her cool, he shouldn't suspect her. One of the rare advantages of attaining the age of invisibility.

Hurriedly, she fired off a quick text to Grace with the exact times he entered and left the shop. She also sent a copy of the photo she had taken. Hurriedly, she left the café and set off in pursuit. He was already far ahead of her but she didn't want to get too close, just in case. Her own bag was weighing her down but she ignored her tired shoulder muscles and hurried after him. It terrified her to think that she was most likely chasing down a cold-blooded killer. They were still in the New Town. He'd passed several bus stops and they were a long way from Waverley Station so he probably had a car stashed somewhere. If she could just keep eyes on him until the police caught up with them then they'd catch him red handed with all his creepy supplies. Grace would hopefully be tracking her via her phone and relaying her whereabouts to Brodie.

Suddenly, she stopped dead in her tracks. Where had he gone? He couldn't have vanished into thin air. She resumed walking, her heart pounding with fear. Had he clocked her following him? She saw a sign on her left for a multi-storey car park. Maybe he'd cut up there. She hesitated at the deserted side street, but it made more sense than any of the other options in front of her. Swapping her heavy bag to her other shoulder, she set off purposefully.

A hand snaked out and grabbed her, spinning her round with her back to the wall. It was him! Terrified, her eyes swung from left to right but the narrow alley he had pulled her into was deserted. He held a switchblade to her throat and looked like he knew how to use it.

Jean decided her only option was to play dumb. 'What do you want from me?' she quavered. 'Is it my phone? My purse? Take the lot, just don't hurt me, please, I'm begging you!'

'Don't play the innocent with me, lady,' he snapped, his pale blue eyes cold and empty. 'I know when I'm being followed. What I want to know is why?'

Jean knew that she had to keep him from disposing of the incriminating bags at his feet before the police got there. How best to achieve that?

'Talk! I do not have all day.' He pressed the tip of the knife into her skin.

'Ow! There's no need for that,' she protested. 'I'm a film and media journalist. I thought you were Rufus Sewell.' She plumped for the star that most resembled him. 'I was just having a coffee in that café opposite the lovely shop that does furniture for doll's houses when I saw you come out. There's Rufus Sewell, I said to myself. Obviously, if you *had* been him and I'd got an interview, that would have been quite the coup. Now let me go! This is ridiculous. If you hadn't pounced on me, I would soon have realised anyway and that would have been that! At least Rufus Sewell is meant to be a gentleman.' She huffed, hoping he would take in her middle-aged attire and assess her as presenting no threat. 'If you want to cause a scene by murdering me here in broad daylight and have a manhunt track you down then go right ahead,' she snapped, staring at him defiantly.

At that moment she heard the screech of police sirens approaching. She could see the indecision on his face. Taking advantage of his momentary lapse in concentration, she managed to hoist the pepper spray she had grabbed hold of in her pocket and spray it in his face, taking care to close her own eyes first.

With a howl of rage, he pushed her away from him and clutched at his eyes. Jean stumbled, almost fell, but ran to the corner of the street. Two police cars had pulled into the kerb beside the store. Brodie was on the pavement staring round him, looking for her.

'Over here,' Jean yelled, waving her arms. 'It's Sacha Komorov. He's getting away!' Her eyes were burning and she could hardly see due to her own proximity when she'd fired the spray. Brodie and a couple of young detectives sprinted down the road following in the direction she pointed them in. Grace pulled up in her car and parked by her side, despite the double yellow lines.

'Don't rub them,' Grace cautioned. 'It'll make it worse.' She passed a bottle of water and some tissues out of the window to Jean. 'Are you all right?' She noticed the blood. 'What happened there?'

'Oh, it's nothing.' Jean shrugged. 'He just held a knife to my throat for a bit. Are you going to go after them?' she asked as Brodie and the other officers disappeared round the corner. She could tell that Grace longed to do so but instead she tucked her arm through Jean's and walked her back to the café along the road.

'I think a cup of tea is in order,' Grace pronounced. 'I'll message Brodie to come and find us here. He'll no doubt want you to go to the station and give a statement so we might as well wait for him.'

Jean nodded, struggling not to break down as the adrenaline left her body. She started to tremble uncontrollably. 'I thought he was going to kill me,' she said in a low voice once their tea had arrived, and they were seated at the same table in the window that Jean had occupied earlier.

'But he didn't,' Grace replied. 'Thanks to you the police have a real chance at catching a serial murderer. Hopefully, his car is stuck in that car park. He'll not get far on foot. You're sure it was Sacha?'

'Yes, he had dark hair with a streak of silver and pale blue eyes. I couldn't tell when he first came out the shop as I could only see him in profile. You didn't think it was going to be him?' asked Jean.

'No, I really didn't,' Grace admitted. 'He's far from being an angel. I reckon he's got some seriously unsavoury stuff behind him but a murderer? I didn't have him pegged for that. The murders on their own could simply have been down to expediency. But the doll's house ritual takes things to a whole new level.'

'He seems to have become increasingly unhinged,' said Jean.

'Yes, look at the risk he's still willing to take to get further supplies.'

'I hope that doesn't mean he's planning more deaths,' said Jean with a shudder.

Grace bit her lip but said nothing.

SIXTY-FOUR

Brodie came back into view and they rushed outside to meet him.

'We lost him,' he said, shaking his head in frustration. 'He didn't even dump the bags of stuff when he was fleeing.'

Jean's face sagged with worry. Grace squeezed her arm. 'What did the people in the shop say? Could they identify him?'

'Yes, they were reluctant at first. He's one of their best customers but when they heard what he's been up to, they caved. The mother, her daughter and grandson are down at the station giving statements now.'

Grace nodded. She had noticed an elderly woman and two others being escorted out of the shop and into a police car by a young policeman whilst they had been having their tea. The 'Closed' sign was now hanging inside the door.

'I take it you need me to come to the station, too?' said Jean.

'Yes, that would be good. You can come in my car,' said Brodie. 'Grace, there's nothing more you can add?'

'Not right now,' said Grace. 'I didn't see anything.' A traffic warden appeared heading straight for her car. 'Oops, that's my cue to get out of here,' she said, sprinting for the driver's door before she got a ticket.

Grace pulled into the car park and stared at Traprain Castle. Its windows stared back at her, closed and inscrutable. Although she'd got here ahead of the police, Grace had no doubt that they wouldn't be long behind her. She hadn't wanted to interfere with Jean's perception of events, but something felt off to her. Sacha Komorov had his faults in spades but she still didn't feel he had it in him to murder in cold blood. In the heat of passion, perhaps, but to develop all these rituals in connection with the nursery and doll house, she just couldn't see it. Also, to murder his half sister Irina when he had kept her safe for so long? It made no sense. She had to speak to him before the police did. Once they arrived and arrested him, her access to him would be completely cut off. She knew that Brodie would have a blue fit if he knew what she was up to, but she felt that she had no choice. It was now or never.

She entered in her usual fashion and made her way to the library. If he was truly guilty and anticipating imminent arrest, she did not expect to find him there. She tapped lightly and stuck her head round the door.

'Grace, won't you come in?' He was seated by the fire reading the daily paper, sipping coffee. There's plenty left in the pot,' he said, pouring a cup for her. There was no sense of urgency about him at all. Something was very wrong in this scenario. Grace could feel it in her bones. She decided to take a gamble and hoped that she wasn't wrong.

'Sacha, the police are on their way here to arrest you.'

'For what?' His body stiffened.

'They think that you committed all the murders and are behind all the crazy doll's house stuff!' she blurted out.

'Doll's house stuff? What are you talking about?' he asked,

his expression confused. *He doesn't know*, she realised. She certainly hadn't told him as it was outside the scope of her investigation. It appeared that Brodie and his team hadn't mentioned it either. Perhaps they hadn't wanted to alert him to the significance of it as signposting the killer's intentions when he was still a potential suspect himself.

'Look, I don't have time to explain. Someone has been trying to frame you for these crimes. You've been identified incorrectly as the perpetrator, but the real murderer has been planning this for some time and we are horribly behind the curve. Do you trust me?'

He gave her a long look then nodded. 'Yes.'

'You need to phone your lawyer right now and get him to meet you at St Leonard's Police Station. If he's not an expert in Scottish Criminal Law, he needs to find someone for you who is. Until he gets there you must make no comment other than to confirm your name and address. Do you understand?'

He hurriedly phoned his lawyer, spoke tersely into the phone, then hung up after ensuring his lawyer was available. The doorbell rang. Someone started banging on it.

'Don't let them know that I've been here,' Grace said as she turned to flee. 'I'll hide until they're gone. You'd best let them in or they might break the door down.'

'I'd like to see them try,' he said, nonetheless getting to his feet and walking into the hallway.

As she reached the top of the stairs and sped out of sight, she heard Brodie's voice in the hall below reading Sacha his rights. He put up no resistance and left with them quietly. The castle fell silent once more. Katya's door swung open and she opened her mouth to speak but Grace silenced her with a finger to her lips. She followed Katya back inside her room and motioned her into the bathroom, away from prying eyes.

'They've just arrested Sacha for the murders,' she said.

Katya's hands flew up to her face in shock. 'I don't think that he did it. Someone is trying to make it look as though he did.'

'But who?' Katya asked, shocked.

'I'm not completely sure yet. The police will be arriving shortly with a search warrant. I need to conduct my own search before then. Tell me, have you seen either Viktor or Nikolai today?'

'Viktor, I haven't seen, but Nikolai was here a few minutes ago. He tapped on my door to ask if I'd seen Oliver. Something about an auction they had coming up that he might be interested in.'

Or trying to establish an alibi, Grace thought. 'Did you notice anything strange about him? What about his hair, for example?'

'It was wet, if that's what you mean. He must have had a shower.'

'What about his eyes? What colour were they?' demanded Grace. Katya looked at her as though she'd taken leave of her senses.

'Brown, same as they always are.'

'I need you to help me. Can you find a way to get Nikolai out of his room and down to the library? Tell him the police have been to arrest Sacha for the murders and act like you believe he is guilty. Ask him to come down to the library with you as you don't want to be alone. Say you've ordered refreshments. Act scared.'

'I *am* scared,' Katya said, shooting her a look. 'All right. I'll do it.' She turned to the mirror and applied a thick layer of red lipstick then spritzed herself with a perfume way out of Grace's price range. 'I am ready,' she said with her shoulders straightened and her chin lifted.

Grace left the door open by a mere crack so she could hear what was going on along the corridor.

'Please, Nikolai. I need someone to talk to. They're accusing

Sacha of having done all these terrible things. I need you! I have no one else to turn to. I'm going crazy in my room alone. Come to the library with me. We can have tea and make a plan. I don't know what to do. I need your help.'

'Then you shall have it.' Nikolai's voice sent a shiver of fear through Grace. She couldn't let him frame an innocent man and get away with murder.

SIXTY-FIVE

Grace watched them walk down the main staircase and turn into the library before she closed Katya's door behind her and hurried along the corridor to Nikolai's suite. Hurriedly, she entered and shut the door behind her. She flew over to the bed and looked underneath. The suitcase that Hannah had told her about still wasn't there. She'd wager that it was now stashed under Sacha's bed to implicate him. Hurriedly, she searched his room looking for materials for the doll house. He'd had two big bags of stuff with him when he'd fled, according to Jean.

The two brothers looked alike in most matters but style. They dressed very differently. Sacha dressed older than his years and favoured waistcoats and more formal attire, whereas Nikolai was into designer brands and dressed more casually in jeans and a leather jacket when not working. Also, Sacha had a pronounced streak of silver in his hair but Nikolai had no grey in his whatsoever. However, the biggest convincer for Jean had probably been the colour of his eyes. Sacha had piercing blue eyes but Nikolai's eyes were brown. If her theory was correct, Nikolai must have used coloured contact lenses to make people confuse him with his brother. If only she could find them! She couldn't let her client go down for crimes that he didn't commit. He was no angel, that much was clear, but his brother was cut from a darker, more evil cloth. His appetite had been whetted for killing now and someone had to put a stop to him. It looked like that someone had to be her. She searched high and low, but nothing sprang out at her. There was no hair dye in the bathroom, no contact lens cleaner, no doll's house stuff. Exasperated, she flung her hands in the air. The whole time Nikolai had been one step ahead of them. Her phone pinged.

He's coming.

Hurriedly, she ran to the door. She opened it an inch and saw to her horror a pair of feet almost at the top of the stairs. She couldn't exit this way, or he'd see her. She had no time to make it across to the secret passage, Grace flung herself under the bed at the last minute, wriggling to the far side so that he was less likely to see her. The door opened and closed. Opera music started up. Great! Not only did she not love opera, but the noise made it harder for her to work out what he was up to. Was that intentional? Did he know that she was in here? Had Katya cracked and told him?

His enraged face suddenly appeared at ground level on the opposite side of the bed, looking right at her.

She choked back a scream. 'Nikolai, the police know all about you. Don't make a bad situation worse.'

He laughed and the sound sent shivers up her spine. 'That would be why they arrested my brother then,' he said, voice laden with sarcasm.

'Sacha's just gone to the station to help them with their enquiries,' she said. 'They know he didn't commit the murders.' She dialled Brodie's number, hoping he would pick up. He didn't. Seeing what she was doing, Nikolai let out a roar of rage and grabbed hold of her leg. She kicked out at him with the other leg and held on to the struts of the bed with both hands. The pressure on her leg eased although he was still holding on to it. Peering round at him, she saw he had a serious-looking switchblade in his hand. He raised it above his head.

'Stop!' she shouted. 'I'll come out.'

He let go of her leg and she exited the bed on the opposite side of him so that the bed stood between them. Her phone rang from under the bed. It had fallen out of her pocket in the struggle. Grace's heart sank. Now she had no means of calling for help.

Nikolai came at her with the knife. She managed to block the first few thrusts but then he got under her arm to pierce her side. Grace cried out in pain, and he pushed her down onto a chair as she stumbled in an attempt to get away from him. It didn't take him long after that to secure her to the chair with duct tape. She fought against the wave of blackness threatening to engulf her. If she passed out it was game over for her.

'Why did you kill Irina?' Grace asked. 'Did you find out that she was your half sister? Is that it? Were you worried she might replace you in Sacha's affections? That she might drip poison into his ear about you?'

'That wasn't it,' Nikolai growled, pacing up and down like a caged animal. 'I knew it would wound my brother beyond repair. That was reason enough.'

Grace knew that the fact he was talking didn't bode well for her. He meant to kill her, of that she was sure. Her only hope was that Katya would manage to alert someone to save her, assuming she wasn't completely paralysed by fear.

'Why do you hate him so much?' she asked. 'He's paid for your education and welcomed you into his home. Why are you so driven to do these terrible things? What had Polly ever done to you? She was just a kid.'

A flicker of regret passed across his face. 'Polly was in the wrong place at the wrong time and couldn't be trusted to keep her pretty mouth shut. I was coming out of the passage into Katya's room and Polly appeared from the ensuite. She screamed and I had to shut her up. It lacked my usual finesse, I have to admit.'

'And Igor? Why kill him?'

'Because Katya would have gone with him. I saw them together in her room. They were planning to run away together and have him claim asylum. She was meant to be mine. I intended to snatch her from under my brother's nose. Igor got in the way,' he snarled.

'And now? You think she will love you now?'

'She would have done had you not poked your nose in,' he said, waving the knife at her, its serrated edge still stained with her blood.

'You're sick, Nikolai,' Grace said, trying to keep the despair from her voice. 'These rituals with the doll's house, don't you see? It's a compulsion. You've lost control!'

'Says the woman tied to the chair, bleeding to death,' he laughed, the sound jarring. 'You are going to be the final room in my house.'

With that, he ran into the bathroom. Grace could hear the bath taps being turned on. Her phone was pinging with texts she was unable to answer. All she could see ahead of her was a watery grave before she was entombed to rot behind the castle walls.

SIXTY-SIX

Hannah walked through into the lounge where Hamish was sitting studying. Cally and Tom had taken Jack out to the park with Emily and Archer so they were the only ones left in the house.

'Something's not right,' she said with a worried frown.

'How so?' Hamish asked, pushing back his chair.

'Well, I've tried to contact both Jean and Grace to see what's going on but they're not answering their phones.'

'Maybe they're just busy,' said Hamish.

'I don't think that's it. Grace insisted we each have apps that can trace our phones. Jean's phone is at the police station and Grace's is at Traprain Castle. It hasn't moved for ages. Something is wrong. I can feel it! I need to go out there.'

'Hannah, you're meant to be staying here with Jack until he's no longer at risk,' he said, shaking his head.

'He's not even here, he's with Cally and Tom,' she pleaded. 'Look, I'm sorry, but I'm going. My mind's made up.'

'I'll come too then,' he said, leaping to his feet.

'You can't!' she stuttered. 'How unprofessional would that be? Rocking up with some randomer in tow.'

'Charming,' he said, rolling his eyes.

'You know what I mean.' Hannah glared. 'I need to do this on my own.'

'You win,' he said, holding up his hands in mock surrender, 'but phone if you need me.'

'Everyone's numbers are on the fridge,' she said. 'If you haven't heard from me in, say, three hours, call them all until you get someone.'

'Okay, be careful out there,' he said, pulling her into a warm hug. She allowed herself to relax against his chest for a few moments before pulling away.

'Right, hit those books, mister,' she said with mock severity and dashed out of the door.

Pulling into the car park at Traprain, the first thing that struck her was how quiet it seemed. Normally, there would be other vehicles coming and going, the sound of a hedge being trimmed or grass cut. She spotted Grace's car looking rather lonely and pulled up beside it. She looked at her app and saw that her phone hadn't moved from the last time that she had inspected it. Exiting her car, Hannah ran to the staff entrance. Once inside, she paused to listen. All was quiet. She stuck her head around the door to the large kitchen, but the cook must have gone home. Racing up the stairs to the ground floor, she peered round the door to the library. Empty. Walking along to the drawing room, she came upon Katya, who was sitting in a corner of the couch crying quietly.

'Katya, what is it? Where is everyone? Have you seen Grace?'

Katya stiffened and wiped her eyes. 'What do you want with Grace?'

Hannah took a decision. 'I work for her. I'm worried she's in trouble.'

Katya crumbled again. 'You are right. She was searching Nikolai's room while I distracted him downstairs. Then he left me. I texted her that he was coming but I have heard nothing else. I'm trapped here. I don't drive. I was frightened to go and look. I have to protect my baby. Sacha has been arrested. They say he has done terrible things. Grace says they are wrong.'

'Okay,' said Hannah, taking charge. 'Here are my car keys. Go to the small red car in the car park and get into the back seat. Lock the doors and lie down on the back seat, covering yourself with a blanket. He shouldn't look for you there. Once you are safe call the police on your phone by dialling 999. Got it?'

Katya nodded and took the keys before running to the front door. Hannah padded quietly up the stairs and paused outside Nikolai's suite. She could hear him shouting at someone, his voice filled with menace. She glanced down at the app on her phone. She was nearly on top of the signal so both Grace and her phone must be in there. She needed to know if she was all right but dared not alert Nikolai to her presence in case he lost control and hurt Grace. How could she see what was going on in there?

Suddenly, she had it. She ran and opened the door into Sacha Komorov's room and closed it quietly behind her. Although she had never been in the secret passage herself, Grace had showed her how to open the doors in and out and how to feel for the wooden slides of the peepholes. She could use the torch on her mobile phone to see. Grace had also warned her to be careful to point it downwards. After a few seconds fumbling on the back wall, the door slid open and Hannah, cranking up her courage, stepped inside. The door shut and Hannah was left in total darkness. It felt like she was entombed and she strove to master her panic. Grace needed her. She had to deliver here. Failure was not an option. She swiped up and got her torch on, feeling a bit better but not much. It was horribly creepy back here and if there were spiders they were probably bucket-sized. She practised with the slider then moved to the left, switching off her torch and feeling her way gently.

She had just located the slider for Nikolai's room when she was seized from behind in a vice-like grip that knocked the air from her lungs. As she drew in a breath to scream, a hand pressed hard against her mouth. Terrified, she wondered who it could be.

SIXTY-SEVEN

A hot voice tickled Hannah's ear. 'Do not scream. I'm on your side. Nikolai has Grace and he likely will kill her if we don't stop him.' Hannah nodded, tears spurting from her eyes and over the man's hand. Slowly, he released his grip and striving to keep herself together she turned towards him.

'Who are you?' she whispered in the dark.

'No talking here. We go to nursery.' He led the way and Hannah stumbled after him, hoping she wasn't walking into a trap. It was only when she stumbled into the nursery after him that she recognised Viktor, the head of security. Hannah looked at him warily as she remembered that Grace had clashed with him previously.

'Relax, little girl,' he said, looking down his nose at her. 'I have no wish to harm you.'

Hannah drew herself up to her full height. 'I'm a grown woman, not a girl, and also a professional investigator.'

He rolled his eyes. 'The women in this country talk too much.'

'Yeah? Better get used to it,' she snapped. 'Nikolai is holding my boss against her will. I was just about to rescue her when you got in the way.' To her annoyance he merely laughed. She turned on her heel abruptly to go back the way she had come but he barred her way.

'I will help you. Nikolai is a very bad man. He is not right in the head.'

Hannah gestured at the doll's house. 'Are you aware of all this creepy shit? The police think it's Sacha. He's down at the police station right now. Katya is terrified. I've got her away from the house.'

He nodded. 'I knew about the doll's house. I was not sure which brother had done it so I have been watching them both.'

'So how do you want to tackle this?' she said, trying to sound more confident than she felt. 'I don't suppose you have a gun or anything?'

'Of course,' he said and produced one from behind his back. Hannah gulped.

'Good to know,' she managed. He handed her a knife.

'Take this, you might need it.'

Hannah did as instructed, though, knowing her, the only thing she'd manage to cut with it would be herself.

'I will go in from the bedroom door at precisely 16.15 hours. I will either enter and start shouting or, if the door is locked, I will shoot the lock off and kick it open. As soon as you hear me, quietly open the passage door and free Grace if you can. Hopefully, Nikolai will be distracted by my dramatic entrance and not notice you creeping in. I will hopefully subdue Nikolai and keep him that way until the police can get here. I've phoned them already. Are you clear on the plan?'

'Yes,' said Hannah faintly.

'If something goes wrong, I want you to run away as fast as you can. Grace would not want anything to happen to you. Are we clear?'

'Clear.' Hannah nodded, though she had no intention of running away unless Grace was running with her.

She went back into the passage and closed the door behind her, moving as quickly as she could back to Nikolai's room. Things had gone quiet. She was terrified about what that might mean and swiftly opened the peephole to peer into the room. She could see Grace sitting on a chair. Her mouth was duct taped and so were her wrists and ankles. She was very pale and her chin was lowered to her chest. Hannah's eyes widened in horror as she noticed the drip of blood from her side to the floor. She had to get her out of there and to a hospital. She strained her eyes but she couldn't see or hear Nikolai. Maybe he was in the bathroom. Wait a minute, what was that sound? Was he running a bath? At a time like this? Then the realisation flooded her brain. He was going to drown Grace.

Hannah broke out in a sweat. Dragging her eyes away from Grace, she focused instead on the door handle. She saw it turn, then nothing. At that moment, Nikolai entered the room from the ensuite bathroom. He tilted the chair and started pulling it backwards, Grace's head lolling to one side. Grace couldn't tell if she was putting it on or she was actually unconscious.

'You'll wish you'd never poked your nose into my business, Grace McKenna,' Nikolai said savagely. 'I had a brilliant plan and you've ruined it. I could have had it all but you just had to mess things up for me. Well, actions have consequences and you're about to pay the price for yours.'

SIXTY-EIGHT

Hannah saw Grace jolt awake and start to struggle against her restraints but there wasn't much she could do. What was Viktor waiting for? It was 16.19. Had something else happened? If he didn't hurry up then she was going to have to deal with the situation on her own. Jack's face flashed into her mind. She pushed it away. She couldn't let fear get the better of her. As Nikolai reached the bathroom he disappeared as he continued to drag Grace across the threshold. Hannah slid open the door. She couldn't risk waiting any longer. It didn't take long to drown someone. Stealthily, she made her way over to the bathroom door with Viktor's knife held out in front of her. She didn't want to use it, but she knew she absolutely would if it was needed to save her boss. There was a massive splashing sound as the water sloshed over the side of the bath and onto the floor. Grace was clearly trying to shout but the sound she made was muffled by the tape. Hannah stood by the bathroom door, readying herself to leap out.

All of a sudden there was a massive bang that scared her half to death. Hannah dropped to the floor reflexively with her hands over her head. She felt a stinging sensation in her right shoulder which had caused her to drop the knife. Had she been shot? No, it was just a graze. Her ears were ringing. She looked towards the door and saw Viktor standing in the open doorway like some action hero from a film. He had shot the lock off the door. Their eyes met. It was now or never. She picked up the knife and charged into the bathroom before Nikolai thought to lock the door on them. Grace was already in the water with Nikolai holding her head down. She was wriggling with all her might but handicapped by not being able to move her arms and legs. Hannah yelled in rage and started lunging at him with the knife, getting in one or two jabs, not enough to disable him but enough to provoke his temper.

'Viktor, help me,' she yelled. Calm and implacable, his large frame filled the doorway. He took in the situation and pointed the gun at Nikolai. Grace's eyes were frantic. She was trying to tell her something, jerking her head back and urgently looking behind her. It was only then that Hannah saw the gun on the vanity unit. Before she could react, Nikolai grabbed it and pointed it at Viktor. Hannah ran to the bottom of the bath and cut the restraints off Grace's ankles while he was distracted by Viktor and then pulled Grace towards her by her feet. She cut the tape binding her wrists and ripped off the tape from her mouth. Grace tried to get to her feet but fell back down, causing even more water to slosh over the sides. Hannah half pulled, half dragged her boss out and they both slid past Viktor to safety.

Grace gave her a brief hug then let her go.

'I'll take that,' she said, holding out her hand for the knife. Hannah gladly handed it over.

'You've been stabbed,' she said to her boss, pointing to her side.

Grace shrugged. 'Just a flesh wound.' They turned to listen to what was going on in the room they had just left. The door was hanging to one side where Viktor had burst the hinge.

'Give it up!' shouted Viktor. 'You are sick in the head. Put the gun down or I shoot.'

Nikolai laughed. 'You're nothing but my brother's lackey. You're the thing on which he wipes his feet. I should put you out of your misery like the dog that you are.'

'Sacha is hard man, but you are spoiled child with your deadly games. You bring dishonour wherever you go.'

'You stole the Imperial Egg!' shouted Nikolai. 'I kept my mouth shut about that. You owe me.'

'You received £100,000 for your silence. It was payment enough.'

Both guns fired simultaneously as Hannah and Grace raced for the stairs along the landing. Nikolai staggered out after them when they were halfway down the stairs. He was covered in blood but still pointing the gun at them with a wavering hand. There was nowhere to hide. *This is it*, thought Hannah, bracing herself. Grace knocked her flying, covering her body with her own. There was the sound of a shot being discharged and Hannah flinched, screwing her eyes up tightly, feeling the weight of Grace's body over her. Tears spurted. He must have shot Grace. Wait a minute, she was moving! The weight across her suddenly lifted and Hannah was ecstatic to realise that Grace was unhurt. As she scrambled to her feet, she saw Nikolai slumped over the top of the steps. Viktor stood behind him. He had clearly been shot himself. Hannah and Grace looked at him. He nodded and walked away from them and back into Nikolai's room.

'He's going into the secret passage,' said Grace, her voice sounding faint. 'He's going to escape.' With that, she crumpled to the floor unconscious with Hannah just managing to stop her rolling down the rest of the stairs.

'Grace!' she yelled, distraught. 'Wake up!'

The doorbell rang. Hannah left her boss lying there and ran to the door. It was Brodie and his team.

'Hannah, what's going on?' he asked, taking in her blood-spattered, tearstained face.

'It's Grace,' she managed, pointing behind her to the stairs.

Brodie charged past her shouting Grace's name. One of the officers he was with phoned for an ambulance then followed his boss in. Brodie crouched over Grace, tears in his eyes, cradling her inert body.

'Grace, dammit, wake up! Wake up!'

Hannah saw the tenderness with which he held her. She'd often suspected Brodie was still secretly in love with Grace and now she knew for sure. Wordlessly, she crept up behind him and squeezed his shoulder. He wiped his eyes roughly and reached for her hand.

'How are you holding up, Hannah?'

'Been better,' she said, struggling to keep it together. 'Will she be all right?'

'She's still breathing but she's lost a lot of blood, I reckon. Mind you, she's a fighter. Too bloody obstinate to die on us, I'm sure,' he said, his lips twisting in a grimace.

'Boss, the ambulance is coming,' shouted a police officer. Two paramedics rushed in and managed to stabilise Grace before loading her onto a stretcher.

'I'm going with her,' said Brodie, in a tone that brooked no argument. He flashed his warrant card and they let him board the ambulance.

'Look after her,' Hannah said. She watched the ambulance set off then trudged back into the castle.

PC Rhona Black walked over to join her at the foot of the stairs. Her sympathetic grey eyes took in the fact that Hannah wasn't far off completely shutting down.

'Hannah, I know you've been through a terrible ordeal but can you show us the bedroom for the deceased and then tell us exactly what happened?' she asked.

Hannah nodded, her stomach heaving at the thought of

having to walk past Nikolai's dead body sprawled still at the top of the stairs. PC Black linked her arm through Hannah's and she was grateful for her support as the strength seemed to have left her legs.

'Look away,' advised PC Black as they passed Nikolai's sprawled, bloodstained body. PC Reid also followed them up the stairs. A small sob escaped Hannah. It was all getting too much. Her breath started to hitch in her chest and she felt a wave of dizziness.

'Easy does it,' soothed PC Black. 'Focus on the pictures in the hallway, that's it, you're doing great, Hannah.

'I'm so sorry for putting you through that,' PC Black said as they reached the bedroom door. 'We have to leave the body in situ until the forensic team has processed the scene to their satisfaction.'

Hannah showed the officers Nikolai's room and walked them through everything that had happened. She had told them that Viktor had shot Nikolai in self-defence. It was the least she could do for him. After all, it was true. If he hadn't helped her, Grace would have died for sure. She also suddenly remembered to tell them about Katya, still hiding in her car. PC Reid instructed an officer downstairs to go and get her out of the car.

The door to the secret passage still gaped open like a ravenous mouth ready to swallow her up into darkness again. Hannah tore her gaze away from it.

The two officers stared at it in horror.

'You couldn't pay me enough to go in there,' muttered PC Reid to her colleague.

Once they had understood the sequence of events, Hannah was escorted back down the stairs, passing the white-suited forensic examiners with their blue shoe covers unpacking their kit to the side of the front door. As she walked through the heavy studded door and down the steps, Hannah vowed never to set foot in the place again no matter what. She was done.

PC Black offered to drive her home as she was in no fit state to drive. Mindful of Jack, she'd nipped into one of the bathrooms and managed to clean herself up a bit so that he wouldn't be frightened. Before she left the car, the kind police officer passed over her card. `

'Here are my contact details, Hannah. If you need anything or have any questions, anything at all, don't hesitate to get in touch.'

'Thank you,' Hannah said with a wan smile. Her family were wrong. Sometimes the police could be pretty great.

As she pulled up to the house, Hamish ran out to her and enfolded her in a hug. She shed a few tears into his woollen jumper then pulled away.

'Grace...' she began.

He nodded. 'Brodie called from the hospital. She's going to be okay.'

Cally rushed out of the house. 'Hamish, don't keep Hannah standing out there all day!' She grabbed Hannah's hand and towed her into the house. Jack was watching cartoons with Jean and his little face lit up when he saw her. It felt like coming home.

SIXTY-NINE

Grace sat on the side of her bed. She was dressed and packed and all she needed now was for Jean to collect her. She was a bit stiff and sore but nothing she couldn't handle. They'd only needed to keep her in for a couple of nights, thankfully. She glanced at her watch again. It was most unlike Jean to be late.

Brodie walked in. Her jaw dropped and her heart skipped a beat. 'What are you doing here? Jean's just coming to pick me up.'

'Nice to see you, too. I've spoken to Jean. We decided that you'd be itching to get an update on the case so... two birds, one stone.'

'You know me too well,' she said. 'I take it Viktor got away?'

'Yes. Apparently, he's been seen in Russia. We've still no idea how he got out of the country. It's thought that he may have been working with the FSB all along. Probably had him as a sleeper to watch over Komorov then activated him when they heard about the acquisition of the Imperial Egg,' said Brodie.

'So, he probably lured Irina in to help him by getting involved with her and then playing on her deep loyalty to the country she left behind. She could have deemed it patriotic to return the Imperial Egg to Moscow where it belonged? Sadly, we'll probably never know,' said Grace. Something else occurred to her. 'Did you check if the ballerina in the plastic bag I gave you came from the doll's house shop?'

'Yes, they said it wasn't one of theirs. They're two a penny on Amazon, apparently.'

'That's what I thought,' Grace said. Jumping down, she winced as she grabbed the bag with her things in it.

'Oh no, you don't,' said Brodie, grabbing it off her and sending her a cross look. 'You've got to take it easy for a while.'

Grace sighed but didn't protest. She was someone to whom taking it easy did not come naturally. They went down in the lift and out to Brodie's car by which time she was glad to be sitting down again.

'Can you drop me off at the castle so I can pick up my car?' Grace asked.

'Sure you're fit to drive?'

'Of course!' she replied. 'Now spill, Brodie. What else has been going on? Jean and Hannah came to see me last night but refused to talk about work. Can you imagine?' She shook her head in disgust.

Brodie's lips twitched in a smile. 'You really are incorrigible, Grace. Okay, since I know that resistance is futile, here's where we're at. Eventually, we found Nikolai's stash of stuff in the worn brown suitcase Hannah had mentioned.'

'Where was it?'

'Under Sacha's bed. He'd planted it there. I think his grand plan was to incriminate his brother and usurp him in every area of his life.'

'Almost as if Sacha had never existed. That's taking sibling rivalry to a whole new level. Did you find a pair of blue contact lenses in the case?'

'Yes, along with a silver spray dye. Jean identified the wrong brother. He'd thought of everything. He'd even set up an account at the doll's house shop in Sacha's name and not his own. He paid in cash for every purchase. However, it was his fingerprints all over the contents of the case. There wasn't a single one of Sacha's.'

'I take it you've released Sacha?'

'Yes, but he spent a night in custody until we got everything straightened out.'

'How's Hannah?'

'Still pretty shaken up, as you can imagine.'

'I'm going to insist she takes two weeks off to recover,' said Grace. She fell silent; the effort of talking had taken it out of her.

'I thought I'd lost you that time,' said Brodie, his voice catching in his throat. 'Don't ever do that to me again, Grace.'

Grace turned to look at him and the quick sideways glance he gave her told her all she needed to know about his feelings for her.

'Don't worry, Brodie, I'm fairly indestructible,' she said, patting his knee.

'You only think you are,' he sighed. 'I'm going to speak to Julie tomorrow night. She's been away for a few days. It's time we had a serious conversation.'

Grace said nothing. She didn't want to influence him in any way. However, the thought that he might come back to her made her heart beat faster.

SEVENTY

Grace had arranged to meet Katya for a coffee in Cockburn Street, near to Waverley Station. She had been staying at a women's refuge at a secret location until she got herself sorted out. As she joined her at a table in the window, she was pleased and surprised to see that Katya looked well and that some of her natural vivacity was showing once more in her face. As Katya stood up to give her a hug, she noticed that her stomach was now gently rounded.

'When's the little one due?' she asked, as they both sat down.

'At the beginning of June.' Katya smiled, patting her stomach. 'It still doesn't feel real but it makes me happy to know that part of Igor lives on. I've ordered tea for us both.'

'How have things been at the refuge?' asked Grace.

'The support workers have been helpful. It can be chaotic but everyone tries to pitch in. I am glad that you're out of the hospital. I was worried,' she said. 'That girl, Hannah, is exceptional. Had she not taken control, I don't know what would have happened to me. You are lucky to have her by your side.'

'No argument there,' said Grace.

Grace waited until the tea had been poured then leaned forward. 'Katya, I know that you've already been through so much but I have some disturbing news. I know who your stalker is. It may come as a bit of a shock.'

Katya stiffened. 'I don't know if I want to know. Everything has stopped now. It must have been Nikolai.' She shrugged, looking away.

'You don't really believe that, do you?' Grace said gently.

'No,' Katya sighed. 'I do not.'

'It was Sacha,' Grace said, unsure of how she would react.

Katya nodded. 'Igor told me something before he died. He said that Viktor had threatened to kill his family if he did not drop me in that way. He was deeply ashamed. He hoped the injury would be minor but instead it ended my career. I was angry but I forgave him. He had no real choice. The other things, the things that scared me, were because Sacha felt he was losing me. I had turned to him before. He thought I might do so again.'

'He arranged for you to be injured. He deliberately terrified you. The police know all about it now. What he did to you was not okay.'

'I am not entirely without blame. I betrayed his trust, not once but twice. My affair with Igor brought Sacha particular pain. He has lost me now for good. That is punishment enough. I am nobody's victim,' she said fiercely.

'So, what's next for you?' asked Grace.

'I'm going to move away for a fresh start,' Katya said. 'I'll reach out to some of the major ballet schools. I am sure that there will be an opening somewhere for me with my history. I may not be able to withstand the rigours of being a professional dancer but I like the idea of nurturing the next generation of dancers. One day in the future I hope to be able to start my own dance school.'

'You've no desire to return to Russia?' Grace asked.

'None. Russia has lost its way. The regime would try and use me for propaganda purposes. I'm nobody's puppet,' she said, fire snapping in her eyes.

Afterwards, Grace walked away feeling content that her feisty client was going to not only survive but prosper in her new life.

SEVENTY-ONE

Grace walked into the agency the next morning. The air felt stale like it hadn't moved in a while. She opened a window and the crisp sea air rushed in. It felt that she had been away for a very long time though in reality it had only been a few days. A shadow fell across the doorway, startling her. She opened it wide and was astonished to see Sacha standing there. Struck dumb, she just stared at him. What could he possibly want or expect from her now?

'You have told her?' he said, his face etched in suffering.

Grace threw the door wide and he walked in. His usual arrogance was gone and he looked diminished in stature. 'Yes, she knows it was you,' said Grace, gesturing for him to sit opposite her at Jean's desk. She had no desire to invite him through into her own office. 'Igor told her that Viktor threatened his family if he didn't drop her during that lift.'

'I was a fool with no idea of the possible consequences. I thought perhaps a twisted ankle that might keep her off for two or three months. When she faded from the public gaze, I thought I could persuade her to marry me.'

'Well, congratulations,' Grace said, her voice laced with sarcasm. 'Your plan worked.'

'The guilt ate away at me for years. That is why I built the studio for her. To give back some of which had been taken.'

'That might have been a little more convincing if you hadn't also seen fit to terrify her out of her wits by pretending she had a stalker,' snapped Grace.

'I was desperate,' he said quietly. 'I could feel her pulling away from me. First with Nikolai, my own brother, and then later with Igor. I had been through so much in life. Losing her would have destroyed me. I had lost everyone else.'

'Have the police charged you yet?' asked Grace.

'No. Given the whole circumstances the procurator fiscal decided to divert me to therapy. The charges will lie dormant on the file and provided I attend counselling for as long as the therapist deems appropriate and do not offend again within the next year, they won't be reactivated. I also agreed to pay generous compensation to Katya for the pain and suffering I caused her and the lifelong loss of earnings that I caused. I have already instructed a lawyer. It will be a substantial sum. It will be paid upfront once the amount is agreed through our lawyers to enable her to have a clean break. She never has to see me or hear from me ever again,' he said, passing a hand across his unshaven face. 'As part of my reparations, I will also settle her bill to you in full.'

'What you did was wrong on every possible level,' said Grace. 'However, I hope that you learn to be better and find some measure of peace in the future.'

'As do I,' he said, as he took his leave.

Grace wandered along the Esplanade. It felt like all the energy had drained from her body. She felt relieved that the case was over. It had taken too much out of all of them. She would have to pop round to Jean's soon to reclaim Harvey, who would no doubt expect the five-star service he had received with Jean to continue. It was a crisp autumn day and it felt like a long time since she'd had the headspace to even notice the world around her. It was already well into November. In just a few weeks it would be Christmas. Her heart leapt at the thought that she might be spending it with Brodie. A new beginning. She sat at a table outside the Espy, even though it was freezing cold, and ordered a hot chocolate instead of her usual caffeine fix. It was time she allowed her body to heal rather than trying to soup it up like a Ferrari all of the time. She still felt stiff and sore but her wound was healing well with no sign of infection so she was thankful for that.

Sitting back in the wooden chair looking out over Portobello Beach, she snuggled into her warm winter coat, closed her eyes and tilted her head back, feeling the gentle warmth of the autumn sun on her face. It felt good to relax for once and do nothing. She felt at peace.

After a while her thoughts turned to Brodie. She hoped he was going to break up with Julie tonight. After she'd realised how duplicitous Julie could be she'd known that they didn't belong together. Brodie deserved far better. The thought of belonging to him once more warmed her even more than the sun and she allowed herself a contented smile as she contemplated this new vision of her future.

It was after eight by the time the buzzer rang. Harvey barked his head off but Grace took the time to check her reflection before she buzzed him up. She'd worn a purple woollen dress that Brodie used to like and applied a little light makeup, feeling self-conscious about being seen to make too much effort until things between them were clearer. Her stomach was knotted with anxiety.

The doorbell to her flat rang and she walked over to open the door with Harvey beating her to it. As his dear face was revealed, she threw herself into his arms. So much for playing it cool.

'Did you tell her?' she whispered into his soft flannel shirt. Something was wrong, he was too stiff, he hadn't said anything. She pulled away and looked up into his eyes, seeing the pain in them.

'Brodie, what is it?' she asked, her voice breaking. The unexpected rejection skewered her more than any blade could have done.

'Grace, I'm so sorry. I intended to tell her but she had an announcement of her own. Grace, she's pregnant.'

A whole conversation passed between them unsaid as they looked at each other. His face was tight and strained as he struggled to keep his emotions in check.

Grace straightened and moved away from him, already feeling his absence. It was the cruellest of blows but she knew that Brodie would not be able to turn his back on his unborn child, especially after losing Connor.

'I see,' she managed, dredging up a smile. 'Congratulations.'

'I'm sorry, Grace. This changes things. I can't walk away... not now.'

He turned to go. Her smile wobbled but she nailed it back in place.

'Take care of yourself, Grace.'

'You too, Brodie.' As the door closed behind him, it seemed that all her hopes and dreams flowed out behind him. She would be fine, she told herself fiercely. *I've survived much worse.* Harvey looked up at her, sensing her distress. She sat on the sofa and turned on the TV, still in shock. Harvey placed his big head in her lap and made comforting noises in the back of his throat.

Tomorrow was another day. She would take a leaf out of

Katya's book and rebuild. Brodie and she would be able to go back to being friends again in time. Much as she loved him, it was time to close his door to her heart and hammer it shut. This time she wasn't going to retreat from the world to lick her wounds. She had the agency, her family and her wonderful dog. For now, it was enough. Maybe she'd even let Hannah set her up on one of those crazy dating apps eventually.

'Come on, Harvey,' she said, wiping away her tears. 'Let's get out of here and go have some fun.'

He didn't need to be asked twice and presented his lead to her with a flourish.

'I see a sausage in your future,' she said, giving him a pat as they headed out. She would grab something from the chip shop after their walk. Throwing her shoulders back, she lifted her chin and headed out the door, her faithful companion at her heels.

A LETTER FROM THE AUTHOR

Dear reader,

Huge thanks for reading *Murder at Castle Traprain*. I hope you were hooked on Grace McKenna's journey. If you want to join other readers in hearing all about my new releases and bonus content, you can sign up here:

www.stormpublishing.co/jackie-baldwin

If you enjoyed this book and could spare a few moments to leave a review, that would be hugely appreciated. Even a short review can make all the difference in encouraging a reader to discover my books for the first time. Thank you so much!

I was inspired to set this story in a castle after having the opportunity to explore Winton Castle in the run-up to my daughter's wedding. I am fascinated by Fabergé eggs. I loved the idea of the lost Imperial Eggs, which were commissioned by Tsar Alexander III for his wife. Each one, when opened, contains an exquisite secret. I have even started my own little collection!

Thanks again for being part of this amazing journey with me and I hope you'll stay in touch – I have so many more stories and ideas to entertain you with!

Jackie Baldwin

www.jackiebaldwin.co.uk

 facebook.com/JackieMBaldwin1
twitter.com/JackieMBaldwin1
instagram.com/jackie.baldwin.1088

ACKNOWLEDGMENTS

It takes a village to raise a child, the saying goes, and my experience with Storm Publishing has shown me that it takes a whole team to nurture a book, produce it and send it on its way into the world. I have been so thankful to have that team behind me. Huge thanks must go to my amazing editor, Kathryn Taussig, who helped me polish the diamond in the rough until it shone with her insightful (and challenging!) questions. Thanks also to Liz Hurst, copyeditor, Amanda Rutter, Melissa Boyce-Hurd, Anna McKerrow, Elke Desanghere and Alexandra Holmes for the part each has played in the process. A special thank you goes to the talented cover designer, Eileen Carey. It was love at first sight.

Thanks to my family for their unwavering support, particularly my husband, Guy, for his forbearance and keeping me sane when things become overwhelming. You are my rock!

And finally, last but not least, my sincere thanks to each and every reader for allowing me to share the voices in my head with you and hopefully loving my characters as much as I do. A writer without a reader would be a very lonely existence. Thank you for travelling this road with me.

Printed in Great Britain
by Amazon

41127559R00189